ONE DOG NIGHT

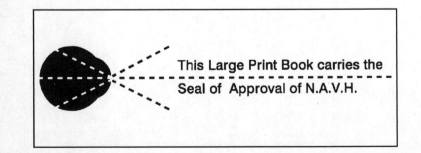

This Large Print Book carries the
Seal of Approval of N.A.V.H.

ONE DOG NIGHT

DAVID ROSENFELT

THORNDIKE PRESS
A part of Gale, Cengage Learning

Detroit • New York • San Francisco • New Haven, Conn • Waterville, Maine • London

GALE
CENGAGE Learning™

LIBRARY OF CONGRESS CATALOGING-IN-PUBLICATION DATA

Rosenfelt, David.
   One dog night / by David Rosenfelt.
      p. cm. — (Thorndike Press large print core)
   ISBN-13: 978-1-4104-4208-6 (hardcover)
   ISBN-10: 1-4104-4208-X (hardcover)
   1. Carpenter, Andy (Fictitious character)—Fiction. 2. Murder—
Investigation—Fiction. 3. New Jersey—Fiction. 4. Large type books.
   I. Title.
   PS3618.O838O55 2011b
   813'.6—dc22   2011031057

Published in 2011 by arrangement with St. Martin's Press, LLC.

Printed in the United States of America
1 2 3 4 5 6 7 15 14 13 12 11

This book is dedicated to Les Pockell. Without Les, Andy Carpenter would no longer exist. Trust me, that was the least of his many accomplishments.

When they came into the room, Noah Galloway looked at his watch.

It made no sense; he knew that as he was doing it. Noah had waited for them to arrive for six years, three months, and twenty-one days, and it was of no consequence what time of day it was when he finally saw them. Nor did he have any doubt who they were and why they were there. They might as well have been carrying a sign.

What mattered was that life as he knew it was over.

The audience giggled a little when he checked his watch; it's not the kind of thing you do during a speech. It makes it look like you're either bored, or anxious for it to end, or both. Noah remembered that the first President Bush got in political trouble when he did it during a debate with Clinton and Perot. But Noah was now in that kind of trouble times a thousand.

7

He was glad he was near the end of the speech, with only about a page and a half left. It was going to be hard to concentrate on the rest, but he'd muddle through. No sense cutting short the last speech he would ever give.

What remained of his ego also forced him to finish. While at that moment no one considered the speech in any way important, Noah knew that it would be replayed over and over on television, and would go viral within minutes. He didn't want to seem flustered, or panicked.

He would go down with what little was left of his dignity. He owed that much to Becky and Adam.

The four men had stopped, two on the left and two on the right, on each side of the stage. They were all dressed in dark grey suits, with apparently identical blue shirts and grey ties. They looked like a semiformal bowling team, waiting to receive their championship trophy.

"The battlefield extends farther than the streets of Detroit, the harbor in Miami, and the border with Mexico. It extends around the world; drugs are a global epidemic and all of us are facing the scourge together.

"Tomorrow, as most of you know, I will have the privilege of flying to Istanbul, where I will meet with representatives of fifty-one nations. I am not going there to dictate policy, to tell anyone it's 'our way or the highway.' I am going there to convey our President's message, and I am going there to listen."

Noah saw no reason to change the basic text of the speech; no one would care about the words anyway. He knew full well he was no longer going to Istanbul, and within minutes the world would know that his transgressions were a lot more serious than an inaccurate speech.

"Much in our modern world can be seen in both black and white; it seems as if everything comes with a 'plus' and 'minus' attached. Airplanes let us travel quickly across the planet, but the skies are much dirtier and louder for it. The Internet brings lightning-fast information, but that information is often abused and incorrect. Social networks let us connect with thousands of people, but the word 'friend' is devalued in the process.

"But the abuse of drugs offers no such choice, no inherent dichotomy. There is no upside to it, no rationalization we can make. It destroys and it debases all that it touches, with nothing positive left in its wake."

Noah paused and looked around the

auditorium. He was at the same time sorry and glad that Becky was not there, that she was taking Adam to the nursery-school parents' visiting day. It would be a horrible thing for her to witness; he could imagine the shock on her face, the outrage that would over time turn to devastation and, ultimately, acceptance.

But he knew that he would have to face her eventually, and that would be just as awful. He had let her down even before he knew her; let her down in a way that was horrible and unforgivable.

"So there are some who say we are in a war, and some who would not use that terminology. But it is certain that we are in a battle, a battle to reach our full potential as human beings. The good news is that the enemy is not hiding. He does not plant IEDs, or shoot from a covered position.

"This is an enemy we know, one which we can and will control, because the enemy is ourselves."

The applause was polite and restrained, which was to be expected. The platitudes he'd given them were nothing they hadn't heard for many years from many officials, and bitter experience had told everyone that actions would speak much louder than words. And over time those actions had not

10

spoken very loudly at all.

Noah understood that, just as he understood he would not be taking any more actions, ever again.

Noah smiled, turned, and left the stage. Out of the corners of his eyes he noticed the four men rise at the same time, and move to where they would approach him. He walked to the right to meet two of them in a place that would be out of the sightline of the audience.

"Mr. Galloway, Special Agent Joseph Scarlett, Federal Bureau of Investigation." As the man talked, he took out and showed his identification to Noah, providing visual confirmation of his words.

Noah didn't say anything, but was conscious of the other two men coming up behind him, to prevent him from trying to escape. Their presence wasn't necessary; Noah was not going to cause any trouble.

Agent Scarlett proceeded to tell him that he was under arrest, and he read him his rights. Noah was only half listening; he was in a bit of a daze, trying to process the fact that after all these years, his horrible secret was not a secret any longer.

Scarlett was finished speaking, and seemed surprised that Noah was not responding, not even asking why he was being arrested.

"Is there a statement you would like to make, sir?"

Noah paused a moment before saying, "No." Then, "Take me away."

"I don't understand tailgating," I say, as Laurie Collins rolls her eyes.

I'm finding that people roll their eyes a lot around me these days. Since Laurie and I live and spend a great deal of time together, it happens to be her eyes that do the bulk of the rolling.

We're on Route 3, heading toward Giants Stadium, stuck in game traffic even though the game will not actually start for four and a half hours.

"Here wc go," she says, frowning, as she addresses the empty backseat. "Ladies and gentlemen, presenting classic Andy Carpenter."

Since she thinks I'm going to launch into one of my negative rants, I decide to surprise her and gain the upper hand by not doing so. Instead, I'm going to drop the subject.

Except I can't.

"You mean you like tailgating?" I ask.

She nods. "I do, Andy. It's fun, the food is usually good, and I like the people."

I point across the highway and say, "See that place? That's a sports bar. It also has fun, good food, and likable people. You know what else it has? It has heat."

"Cold weather doesn't bother me."

"How could that be? It's supposed to bother you. It's bothered people for thousands of years. It's the reason they invented indoors."

Laurie decides not to continue the debate, and instead looks up ahead at the approaching exit and says, "We're looking for parking lot 'Blue 11.' "

"It will be all the way around on the opposite side of the stadium."

"Why do you say that?" she asks.

"Because the place I'm going is always on the opposite side. That's how they design these stadiums."

We pay for the parking, though when I ask where Blue 11 is, the person taking the money motions that we should talk to the attendant up ahead. We drive up to the attendant, whose sole function seems to be waving a small baton, directing people to keep driving forward. It's lucky they planted him here, otherwise people might decide to drive backward away from the stadium.

I roll down the window, letting in the frigid air again. "We're looking for Blue 11."

"Other side of the stadium, buddy."

I smile at Laurie. "I rest my case."

We drive around to Blue 11, a trip which takes slightly longer than it took Lewis and Clark to go wherever the hell it was that Lewis and Clark went. That's mainly because they didn't have thousands of cars to contend with, or idiots throwing footballs and trying to pretend they didn't lose their athletic ability during the Carter administration.

When we finally get there, we can't find a place to park, since tailgate parties take up about five parking spaces for each party. We find a spot in Blue 6, right next to a line of more than twenty portable toilet sheds, each one with a line of at least ten beer-filled tailgaters waiting to use it.

We walk over to Blue 11. That doesn't mean we've found our group; it merely means that we're in the right neighborhood.

"Andy . . . Laurie . . . over here!"

I look over and see Pete Stanton standing in front of a van, its back door open. There are trays of food in the back of the van, adjacent to three small barbecues and two coolers, no doubt filled with soda and beer. Surrounding all this sustenance are a

15

dozen men and four women, all bundled in parkas and assorted "Giants" outdoor weather gear. Everybody looks frozen, which is no great surprise, since it's twenty-two degrees and windy out here.

Pete is one of my best friends, a fact I currently regret, as that friendship is the reason I'm in the process of freezing my ass off. A while back I successfully defended the Giants starting running back, Kenny Schilling, when he was on trial for murder. Kenny has since been inviting me to stand on the sidelines during a game, an invitation that includes my bringing two guests.

I've been declining for years now, preferring the comfort of Charlie's sports bar, but I recently made the mistake of mentioning the possibility to Pete. He went nuts, and convinced me to accept Kenny's offer. Pete would, of course, join me, rather than sit in the nosebleed seat he usually occupies.

Laurie thought it would be fun, and chose to come with us. She is one of those life-half-full people. In fact, I think she's the only one I've ever met that I don't hate.

To show his gratitude, Pete made matters worse by inviting Laurie and me to join him and his buddies in their traditional tailgate ritual. Pete's a lieutenant in the Paterson Police Department, and his buddies are all

16

cops. Since I'm a defense attorney, I expect they would rather Pete had invited a Philadelphia Eagle.

Laurie, who occupies the dual role of love of my life and my private investigator, started her career in the Paterson Police Department, so she knows most of our fellow tailgaters. She spends at least five minutes hugging everybody there, with the notable exception of me.

It's the second time in three weeks that I've spent time with this group of people. I attended a funeral service with Laurie for two young officers, Kyle Holmes and Carla Harvin, who were killed in the line of duty. They responded to a domestic-violence 911 call, and walked into a barrage of gunfire.

The officers are believed to have been lured there for the purpose of killing them, and the murders are seen as executions. The killers fled the scene, and no one has been arrested.

One of the reasons I agreed to do this today is that Pete has been particularly down since the tragedy, perhaps because Kyle was someone he had taken under his wing since his arrival from the police academy. It clearly brings home the danger, in a manner that is impossible for any denial mechanism to cope with, of just what it is that these people face every day.

Of course, that doesn't mean I want Laurie to spend half the day hugging them, and it seems to take forever before she's finished with the ritual. She then comes over, not to hug me, but to point to an adjacent van, also open at the back and apparently part of our party.

"Look, Andy, a television."

There in the back of the van is a small TV, with rabbit ears for an antenna, and wavy lines where a clear picture is supposed to be. "Now that's more like it," I say. "Lucky we didn't go to that sports bar with fifty flat-screen TVs; that could have set off my plasma allergy."

"It's possible you may not be fully into the spirit of this," she says.

Pete comes over. "What's the matter?" he asks. "You look miserable."

"Apparently you can tell a book by its cover," Laurie says.

"I am not miserable," I protest. "Sitting at Charlie's, drinking beer and eating one of those thick burgers with crisp french fries . . . that would be miserable. Plus, it's so damn hot in there; it's gotta be seventy degrees. And you can have that indoor plumbing; I'd rather stand on line to piss into a plastic hole any day of the week."

18

Pete punches me lightly in the arm, then says. "Come on, man, this is part of the game."

"Really? Who's winning?"

I decide to give up and pretend to be enjoying myself, and before too long I actually am enjoying myself. It would be more fun if it weren't so cold that I can't feel my feet, but feet-feeling is overrated, and by the fourth beer I don't care much either way.

About an hour before the actual game is to start, I tell Pete and Laurie that we have to head into the stadium; there's a member of the Giants publicity department that is going to meet us and escort us down to the field.

Pete is only too anxious to get there, and as we depart he tells his friends, "If you losers are looking for me later, check out the fifty-yard line."

We start walking toward the stadium, but stop when we hear, "Hey, Pete, look at this."

It's one of Pete's fellow officers, pointing toward something on the TV in the back of the van. "Not now, man," Pete says. "We got better things to do."

But the officer is insistent, so we walk over. On the television is a press conference, with a breaking-news banner across the bottom.

"FBI: Arrest made in Hamilton Village arson murders."

Pete stares at the screen, and I would know what was going through his mind even if I didn't see the look on his face. I let him deal with it for a full minute, during which time he never takes his eyes off the screen, and doesn't even seem to blink. Laurie knows what is happening as well, so she doesn't say anything either.

Finally, "Come on, Pete," I say. "We're going to be late."

"Go ahead without me," he says. "Enjoy the game."

20

The game is proving tough to enjoy.

There are a number of reasons for this, the first being that the temperature here on the sidelines makes the parking lot feel like Cancún. My hands are so cold that if I were Eli Manning I wouldn't even be able to grip the football.

Which brings me to the second reason I'm miserable; Manning has thrown three interceptions and Kenny Schilling, our host, has fumbled twice, once inside the Eagle five-yard line. The Giants are losing 21–3.

They're probably pleased that the game is only in the early third quarter. I'm not.

Laurie seems to be enjoying herself, so I don't want to suggest we leave. I keep inching over toward the heaters behind the Giants bench, but the equipment manager is giving me dirty looks.

At least people in the stands can turn to alcohol to keep warm; on the field it's prohibited. If I had some I'd drink it anyway; the worst that could happen is they'd throw me out or send me to a warm jail. Either result would be fine with me.

I instinctively feel that if I can keep my mind active, it will prevent it from freezing. So while the Eagles continue what will no doubt be another time-consuming touchdown drive, I think about Pete, and the news report we saw in the parking lot.

The Hamilton Village murders date back six years, and it was one of Pete's first cases after achieving lieutenant status. It was a fire, quickly determined to be arson, in a small apartment building in a low-to middle-class Paterson neighborhood.

The fire started just past midnight on a winter morning, and the building was quickly engulfed in flames. By the time the fire department arrived there was nothing they could do, except listen to the last of the screams of the people inside.

There was no way to be sure how many of them might have escaped, had the exit doors not been locked and bolted from the outside. Twenty-six people died that day, including six children, and their death was ensured by the arsonist. It was not done to destroy a building; it was designed to

22

destroy the inhabitants of that building.

Newspaper reports at the time quoted fire officials as saying that certain chemicals were used in setting the blaze that made it the most intense fire they had ever had to combat.

Pete quickly determined that one of the apartments had been used as a base from which to sell drugs, and therefore the theory was that those people were the targets, while everyone else had the misfortune to live in the wrong place at the wrong time.

But there was no way to confirm that theory, because despite an enormous police effort, the killers were never found.

They say that every homicide cop has at least one unsolved case that haunts him. The Hamilton Village case is Pete's, and it's twenty-six for the price of one.

"You're thinking about Pete?" Laurie has just come over, though I hadn't noticed.

"How did you know?"

"The Giants just got a pick-six, and you didn't even look up."

Among the great things about Laurie is the fact that she knows a "pick-six" is an interception returned for a touchdown. Having said that, it's not her best quality. Not even close.

"I tried to look, but my neck was frozen."

"It will be a weight off of him," she says.

"But he wanted to solve it himself."

She nods. "I know. But this is better than nothing. Way better; it puts the slime who did it off the streets."

"The alleged slime."

She smiles. "Even in your frozen state you remain a defense attorney."

The Giants recover a fumble on the kick-off, and Kenny runs twenty-one yards for a touchdown. Then with thirty-one seconds on the clock, Manning hits Steve Smith in the end zone for the game-winning touch-down.

By this time I'm no longer cold; I'm screaming as loud as anyone in the stadium. And when it's over, Kenny comes over and gives me the ball he scored the touchdown with.

He expresses his gratefulness for probably the fifty-thousandth time for my proving his innocence and keeping him out of jail. Then he signs the ball, "To Andy Carpenter, the reason I'm here." It's a poignant, heartfelt moment, and my eyes fill with ice chips.

I don't think about Pete or the murders again until we're on the way home and listening to the radio. The arrest is all over the news, and for the first time I hear the accused's name.

Noah Galloway.
Noah-Goddamn-Galloway.

Noah Galloway broke into my house almost seven years ago.

Actually that may be overstating it. He didn't actually get into the house, but he tried to. Fortunately, he was so filled with prescription medication that he passed out at the rear door of the house.

I was married to Nicole at the time, though we were approaching our first separation. She was from an incredibly wealthy family, a woman of privilege who for some bizarre reason married me, a guy who represented people she felt belonged on another planet altogether, in special colonies.

Noah Galloway was the last straw, or at least he was the last straw until we reconciled the following year, at which point there was no shortage of straws. But Nicole believed that Noah and the break-in were somehow connected to my defense-attorney practice, and it both frightened and infuriated her.

Noah was arrested, and my curiosity led me to check into his life. He was a graduate of Stanford, with the unlikely educational résumé of holding a Ph.D. in chemical engineering and a master's in sociology. He also had been a walk-on defensive back as a sophomore for the football team, but in his third game he hurt his back.

Three operations and years of agony later, he was addicted to prescription pain medication, and his life unraveled. He had no family to lose, only a sister who tried to stand by him, but there was really no one to cushion his fall. And he fell to the bottom.

The night I told Nicole that I wasn't pressing charges against Noah was the night we decided to separate. It started as a screaming match, prompted by Nicole's certainty that once he was freed, he would come back and break into our house, this time successfully, and murder us.

"Nicole," I said patiently, "this is a guy whose life has fallen apart. He's a Stanford graduate, a brilliant guy. This is a first offense. I just think Noah Galloway deserves another chance."

"I DON'T CARE ABOUT NOAH-GODDAMN-GALLOWAY!" It was a stunning sentence, if not eloquent, simply because for Nicole the word "goddamn" was the equivalent of a barrage of profanity from anyone else.

So Nicole went off to live in one of her family's homes, and Noah Galloway went free. I checked up on him a couple of times from a distance. He left the New York/New Jersey area, and when he came back I heard he had licked the disease, and in fact had become a drug counselor.

Within a couple of years he was running an antidrug program for the city, and gaining significant recognition for his innovative techniques. He was being consulted by other cities for his expertise, and I had heard he was taking a job with the federal government.

I was glad that I had played a small part in helping the man I knew as "Noah-Goddamn-Galloway."

Until today.

"That's the guy?" Laurie asked.

I nodded. "That's the guy. I don't remember exactly when the fire was, but I think it was after we found him at the back door."

"Don't go there, Andy. This has nothing to do with you."

She thinks I'm blaming myself for allowing him to be out on the street, and being available to murder those people. She knows me better than I know me.

"Maybe."

"What do you think? If you had pressed charges on a first-degree trespassing that he would be sent away for life? He didn't even get in the house."

"Laurie, I know I didn't light the match, all right? But things might have been different, who knows?"

The truth is, I'm not exactly racked with guilt, at least not yet. I need much more information before I'll get there. But I am very capable of getting there.

"So look into it if you have to," Laurie says. "Talk to Pete; he'll find out everything about this. Maybe it happened before the break-in, and then you'll let yourself off the hook."

"Good idea."

"Just don't find out too much about Galloway. You'll wind up defending him."

"No chance. Nohow."

"Good," she says. "That wouldn't go over too well with Pete."

"It isn't possible, Noah. It simply isn't possible."

Noah knew that she would react this way, by vehemently denying what was right in front of her. She would get angry, not at him, but at the injustice. It was a coping mechanism, made stronger by the fact that she truly could not believe him capable of such an atrocity.

"It's true, Becky. Believe me, I wish more than anything it wasn't."

She flinched at his confession, which he had just made for at least the fifth time since she had arrived at the prison meeting room. Becky was not concerned that they would be overheard; she had registered as his attorney, so there would be no microphones or cameras eavesdropping on them.

"Have you said that to anyone else?"

He shook his head. "No, but I'm going to. I've known for years that I needed to be punished; I'm just sorry you and Adam have to go through this as well." When he mentioned Adam he started to choke up, but quickly stifled it. Noah was going to be strong for her; he was going to be a strong, despicable mass murderer.

"Please, Noah. Don't talk to anyone; do that for me." Becky's law practice dealt with family matters — divorce, custody, adoption, etc. — but she was more than confident in her admonition for him to remain silent to all but her.

He nodded. "Okay. For now."

Then they were quiet for a while, and she tried to come to terms with what was going on and where they were. But it was beyond surreal; this man that she loved, this wonderful man who would never hurt anyone, was sitting in a drab, barren room, handcuffed to a metal table.

"We have to get you a top criminal attorney," she said.

"Becky, you need to face what this is. Perry Mason or Clarence Darrow couldn't help me. They shouldn't help me."

"Noah, you tell me that you did this."

"Yes."

"Then tell me why."

"Because I had no money, and the people that were selling me drugs refused to do so," he said. "It was revenge. Pathetic, sick, horrifying revenge."

"But you have no recollection of actually setting the fire?"

"No, but there's plenty of things I have no recollection of in those days. The evidence was there, so I ran."

"Have they indicated what evidence they have?" she asked.

He shook his head. "No."

She thought for a few moments, an idea forming in her mind. She knew what his reaction would be, but she decided to go ahead with it. She wasn't going to let him go down this way.

"I'm going to talk to Andy Carpenter."

He laughed, a more derisive laugh than she deserved, and he immediately regretted it. "Come on, Becky. No. There's no way."

"He's as good as they come."

"No one is good enough to help me," he said.

"You don't know that."

"And why should he do it? We don't have enough money to pay him, and what we do have is going to stay with you and Adam."

"Because of Hannah," she said.

"Becky, come on. This is a time where we need to be realistic. This is not going to have a happy ending, and you are going to have

to walk away sooner or later. And the sooner you do it the better."

"I'm going to talk to him."

He couldn't talk her out of it, but it didn't really matter. Her conversation with Carpenter would give her a needed dose of reality, the first of many to follow.

And at some point, he knew she would realize that nothing she said or did was going to matter.

And then she and Adam would start a life without him.

It isn't the best of nights at Charlie's.

The greatest of all sports bars is at its least great on Monday nights during the NFL season. The burgers are just as thick, the fries just as crisp, the beer just as cold, and the televisions just as plentiful and prominent, so it's not any of that. The problem on Monday nights is the crowd.

I come here and sit at our regular table with Pete Stanton and Vince Sanders three or four nights a week. Sometimes Laurie joins us, the only outsider that Pete and Vince, or I for that matter, would consider tolerating.

Usually most tables are taken, primarily by regulars, but the atmosphere is low-key and reasonably quiet. The patrons are knowledgeable sports fans, there to watch the games while enjoying the food and drink.

But on Monday nights in the fall, the

place turns into a zoo, with a standing-room crowd that seems to consider it proper sports bar etiquette to scream and go nuts at every play, no matter how insignificant. There are even times that cringeworthy chants of "Defense! Defense!" erupt, as if the players in Dallas can hear them.

Pathetic.

Most offended by these displays is Vince. Vince is the editor of the local newspaper, a well-respected newsman with the best contacts of anybody I have ever met. He is also the most disagreeable person on the planet, and though we consider each other close friends, I have never seen him in a good mood. Were Vince to interview Osama bin Laden, within five minutes Osama would be whispering to an aide, "What's *his* problem?"

The Jets are playing the Cowboys tonight, and Pete is late in arriving. I'm hoping he shows up, because I want to ask him about the Noah Galloway arrest, but mainly because I don't want to be alone with Vince. Even surrounded by two hundred cheering maniacs, I don't want to be alone with Vince.

There's a guy, maybe mid-forties, who is pacing around the place, wearing a Cowboys hat and Tony Romo jersey, screaming at whichever TV screen he is nearest. He is shouting instructions to the players, predicting which play will be called, and constantly saying things like, "Time to step up! Time to step up and make a play!"

Sports fans who are not knowledgeable, and even some of the weaker TV analysts, seem to feel that all deficiencies are due to a lack of effort, and "stepping up" is the all-encompassing solution to all competitive problems.

This particular guy is driving Vince nuts, because of his antics, but especially because he's a Cowboys fan. "If I smash this asshole over the head with a beer bottle, what are my chances of getting off?" he asks.

"Depends if the judge is a Jets fan, but I would say twenty percent."

"That's if you were defending me," he says. "But what if I had a decent lawyer?"

Before I have a chance to answer, Pete mercifully shows up. He takes one look at the TV, sees the Jets are down 7–0, and says, "Shit."

Vince says, "You got that right."

We are an eloquent group.

By halftime the Jets are down 14–3, and I ask Pete what is going on with the Galloway arrest.

"Why? You going to represent the son of a bitch?"

"No chance," I say. I'm independently wealthy from a large inheritance and some big cases, and since I basically don't like to work, I haven't taken on a client in months. I also insist on only representing those accused that I consider innocent, and there are not many of them around. "How'd they get him?"

He shrugs. "I don't know. The Feds are too important to confide in us locals."

There is a constant friction between federal and local authorities, and information is only passed between the two when it's in the interest of both sides to do so. Clearly this is not one of those cases. "Why are they involved at all?" I ask.

"Interstate commerce."

His meaning is clear. The FBI has long used the interstate commerce clause of the Constitution to involve themselves in pretty much anything they want. As long as they can demonstrate that the criminal activity has even incidentally crossed state borders, they're in. In drug cases, since the drugs have clearly not originated in the opium fields of Passaic, the burden of proof is particularly low.

"Why now?" I ask, since the crime took

place so long ago.

Pete looks annoyed with the question. "Did I mention the fact that they're not telling us shit?"

"Had you been working on it? Was there anything new that they could have picked up on?"

"I've been working on it since the day it happened. I thought we were on to something recently, but it turns out it was in the wrong direction."

" 'Dumbass cop says he's been going in the wrong direction,' " Vince says. "That's my headline for tomorrow's paper."

"That will get you strangled," Pete says.

Vince points to the Cowboys fan. "You'd strangle me and let that asshole live?"

Pete disregards Vince, which is pretty much the only sane way to handle him, and continues talking about Galloway. He admits that, while he's glad to see Galloway go down, in fact he'd "strap the guy into the chair" himself, he would much prefer to have made the arrest. It's understandable; the perpetrator of this crime has been Pete's "white whale" for years.

That is the limit of Pete's self-reflection on this subject, at least for the moment. The second half starts, and we all turn back to the game.

Never let it be said we don't have our priorities straight.

For Danny Butler, it was the turning point.

It wasn't his first; he'd had a series of momentous moments in his life, moments which dictated his direction for at least a few years to follow. The difference was that this time he was pointed in an upward direction.

Danny had been hooked on prescription drugs, on and off but mostly on, for almost twenty-one years. Like so many other cases of this kind of addiction, it began with debilitating neck pain, the kind that required months of bed rest and three surgeries.

The difference here was that it wasn't Danny whose neck was in pain; it was his father's. But the poor guy was so drugged up, and filled so many prescriptions, that it was easy for Danny to take more than his share. And for a seventeen-year-old already on a constant diet of alcohol and marijuana, that was the promised land.

There had been four trips to the "bottom" since then, followed by four rehabs. The longest any of the rehabs worked was fourteen months, but none of the failures was a particular surprise to Danny.

The problem, as he figured it, was that he had nothing to fall back on, and "nothing" included money and a good job. His family had long ago discarded him, he dropped out of high school, and his one serious girlfriend had braces the last time he saw her. So using drugs, Danny introspectively reasoned, was his fall-back position, for lack of anything else.

But this time was going to be different, which was why it was clearly a turning point. This time he would have more money than he ever had before, and a good job. Women wouldn't be far behind.

Things were pointing upward.

They showed up at Danny's apartment almost a month ago, though he had no idea how they knew where he lived. It wasn't even an apartment, just a room without so much as a kitchen, that he rented by the week. That was only his second week there, and he certainly never told anyone about it. Who was there to tell?

So they must have been following him.

They gave their last names, Loney and

Camby, and described themselves as concerned citizens. He was sure the latter part was true; it's what they were really concerned about that remained a mystery.

Loney was obviously in charge, and he was the one who presented the proposition. Danny was to go to the FBI and tell them that when he was in a homeless shelter, the one in Clifton almost six years ago, he became friendly with Noah Galloway.

That much was actually almost true; he remembered Galloway and some of the talks they had together. Galloway was easily as screwed up as Danny was, but he talked to Danny like he was trying to help him, like he was his father or something. It pissed Danny off something fierce.

In one of their little chats, Danny was to report, Galloway had confided in him that he had set the Hamilton Village fire. He swore Danny to secrecy, but it had bothered Danny ever since. Now Danny was fully sober, and he was setting the record straight on everything, including Noah's confession.

The payment for this was one hundred thousand dollars, in cash. Fifty would be paid when Danny agreed to do it, and the other fifty after Galloway was arrested.

Additionally, Danny would be given a job as a driver for Loney, at a salary of eighty thousand dollars per year, plus overtime. The only condition was that Danny stay completely sober, since Loney's family would occasionally be among his passengers.

Danny would have done what they were asking for half of what was offered, but since the conversation with Galloway never actually happened, he instinctively felt like he should pretend to have some reservations about lying.

"Did he really set the fire?" Danny asked.

"Absolutely," Loney said. "And there is evidence that can prove it."

"So what do you need me for?" Danny asked, and then immediately regretted it. He was afraid he was coming on too strong, and the last thing he wanted was to convince these guys that they didn't need him.

Loney nodded, as if the question were perfectly reasonable. "Because the evidence can only be uncovered with a search warrant. And there's no probable cause for one to be issued."

"You know what 'probable cause' is?" Camby asked, and Danny thought he saw Loney look over at him, as if he was annoyed that Camby asked the question. In fact he didn't get the feeling that Loney had much use for Camby at all.

Danny nodded, even though he wouldn't know probable cause if it walked into the room and bit him on the ass. "Sure. Makes sense."

"Good," Loney said. "Because once the evidence is found, a mass murderer will pay for his crimes. And you'll be well compensated. It's a win-win for everyone."

Danny had to that point lived a life with very few wins, so a "win-win" sounded really good. He spent twelve hours over the next few days rehearsing exactly what he would tell the FBI, and the exact manner in which he would tell it. Lying was not exactly new ground for Danny, and he had no doubt he could pull it off.

And he did. Once they paid him the fifty thousand, half in hundreds and half in twenties, he made an appointment with an FBI agent named Neil Mulcahy, and told him everything. It went off like clockwork, and over the next week Mulcahy had him repeat the tale four times, to at least six other agents.

For a while Danny heard nothing, until he saw on the news that Galloway was arrested. Then he waited for Loney's call. He wasn't fearful that his benefactors would renege; they would be afraid that he could recant his testimony and implicate them in the bribe.

In fact, Danny thought he might be able to hold them up for more money, in return for his silence. That would certainly be preferable to a crummy job as a driver.

He would play it by ear and decide just how to take the most advantage of the turning point.

I need to be entertained.

I've never been into quiet, reflective thinking, or meditation, or introspection, or any of that stuff.

I can be alone; that's no problem at all. But if I am I want the TV on, or a book to read, or someone to talk to, or something, anything, to do. My best thinking comes when I'm doing something other than thinking.

But the time I am absolutely at my most comfortable, when I don't need or want outside diversions at all, is when I'm walking Tara. It's my version of yoga, but without the bending and chanting.

Tara is a golden retriever. I don't say she's my golden retriever, because that would reduce her to a possession, and I don't think of her in those terms. She is my partner, my friend, and the greatest living creature on the face of the earth, bar none.

I'm over the top about dogs, that's pretty much a given among everyone I know. My ex-client Willie Miller and I run the Tara Foundation, through which we rescue dogs and place them in good homes. It takes up most of Willie's time and much of mine, as well as a decent amount of money, but we love it.

I also have frequently handled cases involving dogs, some of which have been my clients. The fact that I've been successful at them has done little to reduce the sarcasm and ridicule I receive in the community. Nor has that reaction in any way deterred me.

But Tara is on an entirely different plane, even from other great dogs. I rescued her from the animal shelter at two years old. She's getting up there in age now, with white showing in her face, and I have been thankful for every day I have had with her. And today is no different.

We plan to head out for our walk at eight in the morning, like always. That gives me time to watch the first hour of *The Today Show,* which is when they cram in the real news of the day. It's a perfect time for me to watch TV while getting in my exercise on the treadmill, and some day I'm actually going to get a treadmill to try out the theory.

Of course, the show would have more time for news if they'd leave out the fake "good mornings." Matt or Meredith start the show by teasing the upcoming stories, then they turn to Anne Curry at the news desk, always including a "good morning, Anne." She responds with "good morning, Matt, good morning, Meredith," and then launches into her news recap.

Now, it's not like the news desk is in Iowa; it seems to be maybe fifteen feet away from the anchor desks, in the same studio. Are we to believe that these people have been beamed into place an instant before going on the air, without having had the opportunity to wish each other a good morning? Or is it at all possible that the "good mornings" are in fact contrived by some TV executive, who has decided it would be appealing to the audience to see the warmth and politeness between these talking heads?

The mystery is always solved when the show comes back from the seven-thirty break, and everybody goes through the same "good morning" routine again. I wonder if I'm the only one who is annoyed by this. Perhaps they have market research that shows that the rest of the audience has their collective eyes filled with tears at these heartwarming exchanges.

After they wish Al Roker a heartfelt "good morning" and he gives the weather, the first story is not surprisingly about the arrest of Noah Galloway. Unfortunately, since the FBI is being typically tight-lipped about details, there is little of substance that is added, and it's basically a rehash of the fire and its devastating and tragic effects. Substantial attention is given to what is known about Galloway, and the potentially serious political ramifications for an administration that was about to place an apparent mass murderer in a position of power and influence.

Dylan Campbell, a county prosecutor that I detest, is shown on camera saying that he is confident the case against Noah is strong. I'm not surprised that the Feds are letting the case be tried locally, and I'm also not surprised that Dylan angled to get the assignment. He would relish the publicity.

While I am not that interested in the skimpy report, Tara seems quite taken with it, barking and moving around in an animated, excited fashion. More likely she is anxious to get started on the walk, so we start out twenty minutes early.

We have three possible routes that we take through Eastside Park and then around to Broadway, where we eat bagels at an outside table, no matter how cold it is. I put butter on my bagel; she eats hers plain. I get coffee; she gets water.

A few people either nod or say hello to me, but everybody stops to pet Tara. She accepts the petting with a smile and a wag of her tail, and has the good manners to stop chewing during the process.

I'm not sure why, but I do my best thinking during these walks, and much of my trial strategy is planned that way. But today thinking is not a priority; I have no current clients, and no desire to get any.

We get back around nine-thirty, and I'm mildly surprised to see a car in front of the house. It's the only car parked on the street; there's an ordinance that during the night all cars must be in driveways or garages. The fact that this one is parked in front of my house leads me to the possibility that someone is visiting me, or Laurie, or Tara. Or not.

I am Andy Carpenter, deducer supreme.

Tara and I walk in the front door and immediately see Laurie in the kitchen with a woman, once again validating my intuitive powers. We walk toward them, Tara leading the way.

The woman gets down on one knee to vigorously pet her, and says something

50

which is hard for me to make out. It sounds something like "henner."

When I reach them, Laurie says, "Andy, I'd like you to meet —"

The woman interrupts, holds out her hand, and says, "Becky."

"Hi, Becky," is my clever retort. Never let it be said that Andy Carpenter doesn't keep a conversation humming.

"Becky has a story to tell you," Laurie says, in a way which leads me to think this is not going to be just any story.

"I love a good story," I say, though I'm not sure I'm looking forward to hearing this one. When strangers tell me stories I usually wind up with clients, and when I wind up with clients it means I wind up doing work.

"Then you're in for a treat," Laurie says.

"So you've heard the story?" I ask.

She nods. "Just now. You want some coffee?"

I say that I do, though at this point I think I'd prefer scotch on the rocks, or an arsenic spritzer. I've got a feeling I should have prolonged the walk with Tara, like until August.

We settle down with our coffees, and Becky starts telling me what she already told Laurie. "I've been married for four years, and I met my husband a year before that,"

51

she says. "So what I'm going to tell you is what he's told me over the years.

"He's led a very difficult life. I won't bore you with the details, at least right now, but some of those difficulties have been of his own making, though most have not. He reached his personal bottom, as they call it, about six years ago."

The way she says "personal bottom" causes me to ask, "Drugs?"

She nods. "Yes. And alcohol. And anything else that can take away one's connection to life."

I'm trying hard not to cringe; is this woman asking me to somehow defend her husband on some resurrected drug infraction? I doubt that's where this is going, because Laurie has reacted strangely to the visit. It's somewhere between a gleam in her eye and a worry about what might come next.

Becky continues. "About a year and a half prior to that, in an effort to bring some normalcy to his life, he had gotten a dog."

There is a two-by-four bearing down on my head, but I don't have time to duck. "This dog," she says, petting Tara. "Her original name was Hannah."

I don't know what to say, and I want her to get through this story as quickly as possible so I can find out where it's going. Wherever it's going, Tara is not going anywhere.

"My husband came to understand that with his problems, and his complete lack of sobriety, he couldn't care for her. He loved her very much, and he was afraid for her safety."

"So he dumped her in a shelter?" I ask. I have always felt that the person who did that to Tara had to be the lowest sort of vermin on earth.

"He had nothing else to do, or at least that's what he believed. He had lost all his friends, and his newer acquaintances were certainly not likely to give her the home she deserved.

"So he took her to the shelter, and then he went back there every day, to make sure that nothing bad happened to her. If her stay there was prolonged, he would have taken her back rather than subject her to the cruelties of the system."

She is obviously referring to the fact that dogs not adopted after a period of time are put down, usually because of overcrowding.

"It was only three days later that you came and adopted her. He was there at the time, and he followed you home from a distance.

He wanted to see where she was going to live."

"Why didn't he introduce himself to me?" I ask. "He could have told me things about her."

She shrugs. "I don't know. Hopefully you can ask him that. But for a period of time after you took Hannah . . . Tara . . . he watched you with her, to make sure you were treating her well. On one occasion, when the drugs made him careless, he entered your property and tried to peer into your house."

All of a sudden I know where she is going, and I have a pit in my stomach the size of Bolivia.

"Noah Galloway," I say.

This has disaster written all over it.

If what Becky Galloway is saying is true, that Noah was Tara's original owner, then it's a secret that they have kept for seven years. The fact that she's making the revelation now, when he's just been arrested, is no coincidence.

And the fact that I am a defense attorney who doesn't want a new client, especially this one, is where the disaster potential comes in.

I'm trying to remember if Tara's strange, excited behavior before our walk this morning was connected to footage of Galloway on the news, but I just can't be sure. I hope it wasn't, because she certainly seemed happy, and if there was a growl involved, I didn't hear it.

"Would the fact that you're choosing to reveal this now be in any way related to the fact that I'm a criminal attorney?"

She nods, without apparent embarrassment. "Very much so. I'm hoping you'll consider representing Noah."

"Because he used to own Tara?" I ask.

"Yes. Because you both love her. It's a connection that I'm trying to use," she says. "I'll do whatever I can to help my husband."

"He put her in a shelter," I say. It's a fact that I simply will never be able to get over.

She nods. "I know; he says that it was the hardest thing he had ever done. But he used every penny he had to get her the leg operation, and at the same time he felt powerless against the drugs. He couldn't take care of himself; and therefore he couldn't take care of her. He knew she would be better off." She looks around the room, then pets Tara's head. "And she is."

"How did she hurt her leg?" I ask. Tara has a plate in her leg, which was always a mystery to me. The operation would have been expensive, and I don't often see shelter dogs that had received such good care. It's inconsistent for an owner to spend that kind of money on a pet, and then to throw them away like that.

"I'll let Noah tell you all that; he knows all the details. Will you at least meet with him?"

I look over at Laurie, but she's not providing any relief. "Becky, I'm really sorry about your situation. And I'm sure your husband is innocent, but —"

She interrupts me. "He says he did it."

The surprises are coming in rapid-fire here. "He does? Is that how he's going to plead?"

"I'm not sure what he'll do. But he didn't do it, Andy. No matter what he says."

I nod, trying to digest this. It doesn't sound like it will go to trial, so Galloway's lawyer might simply be called upon to plea-bargain. Less time, less effort, but I still don't want to get near it. We're talking about twenty-six people locked in a burning building.

"He says he did it, but you say he didn't?" I ask, my incredulity showing.

"He believes he did it; he doesn't specifically remember it. But there is no chance that he did."

"How do you know that?"

"Could you believe Laurie burned twenty-six people to death?"

"No." I could point out that I wouldn't believe Laurie spent years strung out on drugs either, but I don't. I just want this to go away.

"Maybe I could speak with him, maybe with Hike," Laurie volunteers. "And get

some more information, to help you decide."

Laurie's talking about the other lawyer in
my two-person firm, "Hike" Lynch. I'm
sure Laurie is aware that I've already decided against getting involved, so her saying
that means she's on Becky's side in this one.
Or at the very least she's saying, what's the
harm in talking to the guy?

Of course, there is no harm in it, other
than the disappointment Becky would feel
when I tell her I'm not taking the case.
"Becky, if it means that much to you I'll
talk to him. But I want to be really clear; I
don't want to take on any new clients."

"I understand," she says.

"I can recommend other lawyers that are
terrific."

She nods. "Let's talk after you and Noah
meet."

I turn to Tara. "That work for you?"

She doesn't answer, remaining her normal
noncommittal self. I'll have to ply her with
biscuits to find out what she really thinks.

These guys did what they said they would do.

That's a pretty terrific quality, Danny figured, especially when it belonged to guys who promised to pay him money.

The morning after Noah Galloway was arrested, Loney was at his apartment with the payment of the other fifty thousand, again in cash. He was alone this time, without Camby.

Danny had decided that while he might strong-arm them with threats to reveal their role to the police, there was no hurry for that. The trial was a long way off, and he could come forward at any time before then.

Loney did throw him a bit of a curve ball, though. The job as driver for him and his family was still his for the asking, but it was in Vegas, not New Jersey. That was where Loney was going to be for at least the next six months, and the increased cost of living that Danny would face there would be recognized with an increase of twenty thousand in the agreed-upon salary.

This was getting better all the time. Danny had only been to Vegas once, almost fifteen years ago. On his thirtieth birthday. It probably would qualify as his favorite place on earth, but it was a city you didn't want to be in if you had no money.

Which was okay, because Danny had plenty of money.

Loney gave Danny a plane ticket, one way, to leave that night. The fact that it was a coach fare was slightly annoying, but at least it was an aisle seat.

"You can leave tonight?" Loney asked.

Danny smiled and made a hand motion to show Loney the room he was standing in. "Why not?"

Loney said that a car would pick Danny up at five o'clock, to take him to Newark for the eight o'clock flight. "Don't get too comfortable out there," he said. "You're coming back here for the trial."

"No problem. One day on the stand is all it will take."

Loney nodded. "But that's an important day. We're going to rehearse you for it."

"Piece of cake," Danny said. "So when I get there, where do I go?"

"A driver will take you to the Mirage; you've got a prepaid reservation there for two weeks. During that time you're going to need to get an apartment."

Danny said that he thought that was a really good idea, though at that point apartment hunting was the last thing on his mind. He had a hundred grand and two weeks at the Mirage, and he was going to enjoy every minute of it.

"Don't blow this, Danny," Loney said, possibly reading his mind.

"You don't need to worry about me," Danny said.

"Okay. See you in Vegas."

"You going to be there?"

Loney smiled. "See you in Vegas."

"Who are you guys?" Danny asked. "Come on, level with me."

"Concerned citizens."

"Connected concerned citizens?"

Loney didn't answer, but he didn't have to. Danny was smart enough to know that these guys were not people to mess with, and he immediately discarded the idea of holding them up for more money. Instead he was going to make himself indispensable to them, until they brought him into the club.

The flight out to Vegas was pretty comfortable, considering Danny was in coach. The seat next to him was empty, and Danny utilized the tray in front of the empty seat to rest his bloody marys. He had six of them, and only stopped when the good-looking flight attendant told him he had had enough.

He could have told her there was never enough.

A driver met Danny at baggage claim. He called Danny "Mr. Butler," and asked how his flight was, and a lot of other meaning-less kind of stuff. Danny kept up his side of the conversation as best he could, but his mind was on the bar at the Mirage.

The driver took Danny's bags and led him out to the curb. He then spoke into a walkie-talkie kind of device, and Danny realized that this wasn't the driver, that he was only calling for the car. These guys had their act together.

The car pulled up, and they loaded Danny's bags into the trunk. Danny half climbed, half fell into the backseat, as the actual driver welcomed "Mr. Butler" to Vegas.

They drove off, and Danny was asleep before they got out of the airport. He woke up a short time later, as the parking attendant at the Mirage opened the door.

Except it wasn't the parking attendant at the Mirage; it was somebody else, who got into the backseat next to Danny. And Danny barely had time to realize that they weren't at the hotel at all, they were on a dark street, in front of what looked like a vacant warehouse.

Within three seconds the man had a device around Danny's neck, but it took almost thirty seconds to make sure he was dead.

After which they drove off again.

I decide to take Hike with me to the jail.

On one level, it seems to make perfect sense. It's a depressing place, colored grey and filled with people who have for the most part moved past desperate into hopeless. Hike is a depressing person, an incurable pessimist who himself sees the world through grey-colored glasses.

I wouldn't be surprised if he makes an offer on a cell, maybe with a watch-tower view.

"So you owned the same dog?" Hike asks, moments after he gets in the car.

"Yes."

"That's it?" he asks.

I nod. "That's it."

"I'm not missing anything?"

"Nope."

"Why do you care about that?" he asks.

"Hike, you don't have a dog, right?"

"No way. I'd wind up with the mange, and I'd break out in rash pimples, filled with pus. I hate pus."

"Really?" I asked. "I love pus. But the thing is, him owning Tara creates sort of a curiosity, like a bond in some way. It's like if you were married, and you met your wife's first husband, you'd be curious, right?"

"No."

Hike has a law degree from Yale, and an M.B.A. from Harvard, but curiosity is not his thing. He figures that the more he finds out about something, the more depressed it will make him. He's probably right.

Once we get to the county jail, it takes about twenty minutes to get through security, and we spend another twenty waiting in a small visiting attorneys room for Galloway to be brought in.

I've seen him on television a couple of times, but he looks taller and thinner in person. He also wasn't handcuffed in those TV appearances, but he certainly is now.

"Mr. Carpenter, I'm sorry about this," is the first thing he says.

"About what?"

"My wife asking you to come down here. I didn't want her to do that."

"She's trying to help you," I say. "This is my associate, Eddie Lynch."

"Hike," is how he corrects me. "How's

the food here?"

Galloway shrugs. "It's okay."

"Watch out for bugs in the salad. I accidentally ate a couple of bugs once, I think at a rest stop off the Jersey Turnpike. They wound up taking a stand in my gut; I couldn't get rid of them. They turned my intestines into the goddamn Alamo."

"Thanks for sharing that, Hike," I say, and then turn back to Galloway. "So what can I do for you?"

"Not much."

"Do you have an attorney?" I ask.

"They assigned the public defender to me for the purposes of the arraignment. He seemed to handle it well enough."

The sense I get from Galloway is very different from every other recently arrested person I have ever met, and I've met a lot of them. Usually they are afraid, especially those who've been arrested for the first time. They don't know what is ahead of them, but they know it's going to be awful.

Some of them, the more experienced ones, are angry. Angry at themselves for getting caught, and angry at the authorities for catching them.

A lot of people claim to be able to judge someone's emotional state by looking in their eyes. I don't make eye contact, so it's a talent I've never perfected. When I talk to people, I generally look at their mouth, so while I can't judge emotions, I'm pretty good at identifying cavities.

But there is no mistaking the vibes that Noah Galloway is giving off. He is tired, maybe even a little relieved, and wearily resigned to his fate. It's depressing, and being in a room with Galloway and Hike, in a prison no less, is about as dreary as it gets.

I want to get out of here as fast as possible, so I quickly make a verbal agreement with Galloway that, for the sum of one dollar, Hike and I will serve as his lawyers for the next two hours. I'm hoping that two hours from now I'll be home walking Tara, but I use it as an outside amount of time. Galloway has no money on him, so I accept his promise to pay. We do all this so that anything he tells us will be covered by attorney-client privilege, though he seems unconcerned by it either way.

Once that's accomplished, he quickly tells us that he has always known that he set the fire, but that he has no recollection of doing so. It comes as no surprise, since Becky had said the exact same thing. But it still makes very little sense, so I ask him to explain his feelings of guilt.

"I had hit bottom," he says. "Except I

didn't bounce off the bottom; I stuck to it. My entire world revolved around drugs, pretty much every dollar I had went to pay for them. And I didn't have many dollars.

"I would have blackout periods, sometimes lasting for a day or more. When I would wake up, I had no idea what I had done, or how I had gotten to the physical place I was in. It was scary, but not as scary as you would think."

"Why not?" Hike asks.

"Because I really didn't care that much if I lived or died, so there was nothing to be scared of. And if I did live, dealing with blackouts was not important; getting drugs was the first and only priority."

Galloway is saying all this in a fairly dispassionate way, with no apparent embarrassment, or emotion. It seems he has long ago come to terms with what he was in those days.

He continues. "So I woke up one day from a two-day binge, in my apartment. The drugs hadn't worn off, not even close, but it was the pain that brought me out of it."

"What kind of pain?"

"I had burns on both of my arms. Chemical burns."

For the first time, I'm seeing emotion in Galloway as he gets closer to talking about the fire that killed all those people. I don't want to ask him anything yet; I find that when a story is pouring out voluntarily, questions can be a distraction.

He goes on to describe how the people in one of the apartments on the first floor of the incinerated building were his suppliers, and how they had cut off his credit, little as it was, earlier in that week. Though he doesn't know where, he says he must have gotten the drugs elsewhere, but they were likely of lower quality, and he reacted badly to them.

"I was terribly angry at them for doing that; I had been buying from them for over a year, and they knew how badly I needed it . . ." He shakes his head at the memory. "There's no doubt I wanted them dead. I wanted them worse than dead."

He goes silent for about twenty seconds. Silent time in a prison interview room is interminable, treadmill time zips along by comparison. I obviously need to get him back on track. "You mentioned chemical burns, as if that were significant," I say.

He nods. "I have a graduate degree in chemical engineering. The mixture that was reported to have caused the fire is something I am very familiar with. Most people aren't."

I ask Galloway if he knows what the police

uncovered so many years after the fact to lead to his arrest, but he professes to have no idea.

"Whatever it was," he says, "I feel glad it finally happened. It was long overdue."

This is the kind of stuff they should include in the orientation.

That's what Senator Ben Ryan thought about as he sat at the bar, and it brought a smile to his face. The rest of the night, he knew, would bring quite a few more smiles.

Incoming freshman members of Congress are subjected to long, boring meetings about what life in the halls of power is like, and how to successfully navigate this "new world." The focus is on understanding the rules, whether they be legal, political, financial, or ethical, and dealing with the press and constituents.

That was all fine, and Ben had heard it, internalized it, and used it to his advantage in the eleven years since. But what he never learned back then, and which he felt should be required, was anything about places like Chumley's.

It was his third time at Chumley's, a bar

in the lobby of the Newcastle Hotel in Amsterdam. Ben wasn't staying at the Newcastle, he was staying at the much nicer Plaza Victoria, with the rest of the delegation. There was a meeting scheduled for the next morning at ten A.M. and he'd make it, but not by much.

The orientations, Ben felt, should have included long sessions on delegation trips, and the value of them. Not value to the government or the people, since most of them were boondoggles. But rather value to the elected representative, in this case none other than Ben himself. It had taken him a while, but he had learned where the value was, and how to find it.

The key was in getting on the right committee, and he had certainly accomplished that. He was the ranking minority member on the Europe subcommittee in the Senate Committee on Foreign Affairs. It was aptly named, though in Ben's case he thought Committee on Foreign One-Night Stands would have been even more on point.

Ryan was also the ranking minority member on the Senate Committee on Energy and Natural Resources, which provided different opportunities. The travel was less, but those energy companies certainly knew how to provide campaign cash.

He'd been looking forward to this night for a while. His two previous times at Chumley's had more than lived up to expectations, and there was no reason to think this time would be any different. He knew the drill, and the great-looking woman at the other end of the bar, the one who had been staring at him, knew it even better.

It was showtime.

He walked over to her and sat down, then asked if he could buy her a drink.

She smiled and shook her head. "No."

"No?" This was a turn of events he didn't expect.

She pointed to her drink, sitting mostly full in front of her. "I've already got one, and there are plenty more in the minibar in my room upstairs. Besides, you've got better things to do with your money. Much better."

"Sounds good to me," he said.

"What's your name?"

There was obviously no way he would ever use his real name in this situation, and fortunately his face was not even widely recognized back in the U.S. "Harrison Ford."

She smiled and stood up. "Nice to meet you, Harrison. Let's go."

"Why don't we negotiate the terms first?" he asked.

"How about you get a look at what you're buying first?"

There was certainly no harm in that, and he went with her up to her room. He had no way of knowing if anyone else had been there with her that night, but he knew for sure that he would be the last one. Once he got going, there was no stopping him.

The woman turned out to be right; showing him the "merchandise" was her best way of negotiating a good deal. As was the custom, that merchandise also included premium-grade cocaine. Ryan eagerly agreed, and as also was the custom, paid her half in advance, with a promise to pay the rest when the "session" had concluded.

It proved to be by far the best time he had ever had on one of these trips, and when it was over he vowed to be back soon. Our European relations, he figured, needed much more hands-on attention from dedicated senators like himself.

He was a country-first kind of guy.

He was dressed by eight o'clock in the morning, giving him just enough time to get back to his hotel, shower, and grab some coffee. He gave the woman the remaining cash, and told her to look for him in a couple of months.

It was obvious to the woman that he was not on the Intelligence Committee, because he had never noticed, or looked for, any of the five tiny hidden video cameras and microphones that had recorded every moment of his stay in the room.

Once he was out the door, the woman picked up her cell phone and dialed a number. When the call was answered, she simply said, "Done."

"Why did you put Tara in a shelter?" I ask.

I've gotten all the information Galloway seems to have about the arson and arrest, and I'm not anxious for the conversation to move into the area of his legal representation, so I might as well satisfy my curiosity.

"Because I loved her," he says, "and it was the best I could do for her. She was the greatest thing in my life; in some ways she was the only connection I had to the world. But she deserved so much better than me, so I had to give her a chance to get it."

"She could have been killed."

"No, I would have prevented that if it came to it." He doesn't seem sure about anything else, but his commitment to protecting Tara he is certain about.

I ask him a bunch of questions about Tara as a puppy, and with each question I can hear Hike unsuccessfully try to stifle a moan. I enjoy hearing about it, but it's the

76

opposite of what I had pictured.

"Where was she born?" I ask.

"I don't know. I found her lying on the side of a two-lane highway outside of Dayton, Ohio. She had obviously been hit by a car, and her leg was broken. She didn't have a collar on, and there was no way to tell who she belonged to."

This qualifies as stunning news to me; the image of Tara lying on the side of the road, badly injured, is one I will have trouble getting out of my mind.

He continues. "I put her in my car and took her to a shelter nearby, but they told me that with her leg like that, she'd never get adopted, and they'd wind up putting her down. So I worked out a deal with a vet, and he did the surgery for less money. Nice guy . . ."

He continues talking about how, when he descended further into his drug use, Tara had been his crutch. It's funny, but my hope had always been that Tara had been well taken care of, until some perverse twist of fate had led her to her temporary imprisonment in the shelter. The truth now is that her life nearly ended early, and once she was rescued, it turned out that she had been the caretaker. It was a task she is well suited for.

"You know," Galloway says, "on my good days I would go to that coffee place on Broadway, because I knew that you and Tara would stop there for a bagel during your walk."

"Did you ever come over to us?"

He shakes his head. "No, I stayed off to the side so she wouldn't see me. I didn't think that would be fair to her."

Hike is pacing; he wants to get the hell out of here. But I'm starting to enjoy myself; here's a guy who understands and loves Tara. In fact, of all the mass murderers I have ever met, I think I like Noah Galloway the best.

But this is a prison, so I finally and reluctantly get back to the matter at hand. "I've got to be honest with you, Noah. I'm not inclined to take on a murder trial right now."

He nods. "I understand, but this is not going to trial."

"They'll only plea-bargain if they have weaknesses in their case."

"That's okay; I'm not bargaining. There's no way I'm going to see the light of day again. I just want this over with; the less Becky has to go through . . . the less Adam has to hear as he grows up . . ." He starts to choke up, and stops speaking.

78

"Why did you plead 'not guilty' at the arraignment?" I ask.

"The public defender said it was a formality. That it was best to do it that way, even if I was going to change my plea."

The PD was right, and I tell Noah that. Then, "Would you like me to talk to the prosecutor on your behalf?"

He nods. "I would appreciate that very much."

"Okay. I'll do what I can."

"Just make this go away," he says. "Make me go away."

If you asked my assistant, Edna, what is the greatest invention ever, she would say, "Caller ID."

Of course, in order to ask her the question, you'd have to be able to get her on the phone, which is almost impossible. If her office is her castle, then caller ID is her moat.

It's not that Edna doesn't like people; she has an extended list of family and friends that is miles long. When any of their numbers pop up, she happily takes the call. It's that she likes work even less than I do, and any unfamiliar number that she answers is a potential assignment.

My cell phone number is one of the chosen few, and she answers on the fourth ring. "We've got a client," I tell her, and I can feel her physically recoil through the phone.

"Really?"

"Really. His name is Noah Galloway."

"Noah Galloway? The Noah Galloway on TV? The mass murderer?"

"The very one."

For most people, cringing is a physical act. For Edna it is verbal; I can hear it in her voice. "Do you think that's a good idea?"

"I do."

"Well . . . okay . . . but you know I have a vacation planned."

Edna spends seventy percent of every day doing crossword puzzles, and she is an unmatched genius in that area. The other thirty percent she spends planning vacations with her family that they never take. When she adds up all the nieces, cousins, and the like, there are seventy-two people, and they won't go away until all of them can make it. Suffice it to say that seventy-two schedules don't ever match up that perfectly.

"Where are you going?"

"Either on a cruise to the Caribbean or Mount Rushmore," she says.

"Six of one, half a dozen of the other."

I ask Edna to call Dylan's office and make an appointment for me to see him regarding Noah's case. How quickly he sees me will be a sure indicator as to how strong he considers his position. Fast means he's confident, slow means he doesn't completely

81

have his act together, and there are holes to be plugged.

Edna calls me back five minutes later, to tell me that Dylan is available now if I'm so inclined. I'm not at all inclined, but I suck it up and tell her to advise him that I'm on the way.

There is pretty much nothing I like about Dylan Campbell. For one thing, he's at least six foot two, maybe two hundred pounds, and in outstanding shape. He probably gets up at three-thirty in the morning to do calisthenics and eat wheat germ.

He was a quarterback at Duke, which is why I bet against them every chance I get. Unfortunately, this childishness extends to my betting against their basketball team, not a very profitable thing to do.

He's got one of those cleft-things in his chin, which I've never trusted. Even his teeth, which I would like to knock out of his mouth, are pure white and perfectly spaced.

To my knowledge, only two things really bother Dylan. One is that his ambition has been at least temporarily thwarted. He has always seen his job as prosecutor as a stepping stone for his political career, and even made noise about running for Congress last year. His party establishment chose a different candidate, and Dylan was said to be livid about it.

The other source of pain for Dylan is the fact that he has faced me in two major cases and lost both times. This not only damaged his reputation, but particularly galled him because he hates me. Most prosecutors hate me, but Dylan's hatred rises above the others'.

The distressing topper to all of this is that Dylan is smart and tough. He comes in prepared and focused, not a good combination for us inhabitants of the defense table.

Dylan is of course all fake smiles when I arrive, and he comes out to the corridor to greet me. He shakes my hand with a powerful grip and says, "Andy, good to see you. It's been too long . . . way too long."

"Really? You think? I thought it felt just right."

He laughs, as if I'm kidding, though he knows I'm not. I silently admonish myself; for Noah's sake I need to be on my best behavior, since Dylan holds all the cards.

He brings me into his office, and he gets right to the point. "You've got a tough one here, Andy."

"Not the way I see it."

"Then you're not looking too carefully. This guy is going down with a thud."

83

"What have you got?" I'm going to see what he has in detail when I get the discovery documents; I'm just looking for a preview now.

"Twice as much as we need, including a confession."

"He allowed himself to be interrogated?"

Dylan shakes his head. "No. But we've got someone he confessed to a few weeks after the crime."

"Who might that be?" I ask, cringing.

"A friend of his at the time. Galloway told him chapter and verse how he did it. The chemicals he used, how he set it off, locked the doors, and who he was after."

A key part of lawyering, both in and out of the courtroom, is to never look surprised. It's even better never to actually be surprised, but if that's impossible, then appearance will have to do. What Dylan has just said is stunning to me and makes little sense. How could Noah have remembered something in such detail then, but have no recollection of it now? Could it be a result of his drugtaking?

"When will I get discovery?" I ask.

He shrugs. "Day or so. We're putting it together."

"Can I get the documents relating to this witness now? Seems like it would be an important piece in deciding which direction to go with this."

"No problem." He picks up the phone and gives directions to his assistant to copy those particular documents right away.

All kinds of theories are going through my mind, but I put them on hold to finish this conversation. There is still information to be gathered, and impressions to be left.

"So what are you looking for on this?" I ask.

He smiles an annoying smile. "Justice."

"Aren't we all?"

"Andy, twenty-six people died a horrible death. The guy who did it is never going to see the sun again. Life . . . no parole."

It is exactly what I expected, but I don't tell him that. I also don't tell him that Noah would be fine with that outcome. There's nothing for me to say until I see the witness statement.

Dylan's assistant brings in a folder with the statement documents in it, and I thank him, make some noises about talking to my client about all this, and leave.

Your mother was wrong, Brett Fowler would tell you.

Breakfast is not the most important meal of the day.

Lunch is where the action is. It's where deals are brokered, alliances are forged, careers are made, lies are told, backs are stabbed, and lives are ruined.

And then it's time to get the check.

Fowler was not someone who would be considered to be at the center of the political world. He wasn't an elected representative; he never ran for office, introduced a bill, or voted on an amendment. He was an outlier, an appendage who contributed to the process, and certainly profited from it.

He was a political consultant.

Political consultants, especially in Washington, D.C., have gotten a bad name as a group. Not quite as bad as lobbyists, or lawyers, or politicians themselves, but pretty bad nonetheless.

The truth is there are few things one can be in Washington and still have a good name, since the city itself has become the subject of scorn. Politicians who've served in Washington for twenty years try to reinvent themselves as "outsiders," and they go home to give speeches that decry "Washington politics."

So the bad-mouthing that was done of political consultants didn't bother Brett much. In fact, it didn't bother him at all.

The trend in political consulting was toward large firms, but Brett had long ago decided he would never go that route. He believed in operating on his own, no restrictions. If was better for himself and for his clients. Especially for himself.

Of course, that was when political consulting was his main occupation, when helping people succeed was his stock-in-trade. That was before he became an executive in another operation, which also helped people, but which then owned and used them from that time forward.

Almost everybody, even the wealthy or powerful, reached a point in their lives when they needed or wanted something that they couldn't get. Very often accomplishing that goal would be very embarrassing, very illegal, and nearly impossible. So Fowler's "team" provided the money or the muscle necessary to make it happen.

And from that moment they owned that person, as surely as anyone can own anything.

It reminded Fowler of that line from *The Godfather,* which he considered the best movie ever made. Don Corleone had done a favor for a man, an undertaker, and he said to the grateful man, "Someday, and that day may never come, I will call upon you to do a service for me."

That is how Fowler saw his own situation, with one difference.

That day always came.

Lunch that day was with Joseph Chesney, congressman from the Fourteenth District in Central Kansas, one of Brett's second-tier clients. Chesney was mulling a run for the Senate the following year. At least that's the story he was putting out in the press; the truth was he was doing far more than "mulling." He had already made the decision to go full speed ahead.

It was not an easy call. Chesney's district was a safe one, and he probably could have remained in Congress for many, many years to come. But in the class system that is the U.S. government, the Senate is on a much higher level than the House, and that's where Chesney wanted to be.

The problem for Chesney was that the incumbent senator that he would have to take on in the general election was Ben Ryan. Ryan was finishing his second term, and if anything his star was on the rise. He won his last election five years ago with an unheard-of seventy-one percent of the vote, and polls showed him at least as popular now.

Chesney's own private polls showed him getting swamped in a proposed matchup with Ryan, and most people would consider his entry into the race to be political suicide.

Which is why he hired Brett Fowler.

The purpose of the lunch was for Brett to provide a report on "campaign operations," but instead Chesney had to endure an hour of conversation, consisting mostly of political gossip about what was happening in Washington. Mostly it was a recitation of who was up and who was down, and the two always evened out. Washington is a zero-sum city.

It wasn't until Brett asked for and received the check that he addressed himself to the one thing that Chesney wanted to hear. "Your senator just got back from Amsterdam yesterday. Another example of his tireless efforts to help the people of Kansas."

Chesney was immediately on alert. "And how did his trip go?"

"Apparently he had a wonderful time," Brett said. "I didn't talk to him directly, but I spoke to a friend of a friend of his."

Chesney cast a wary glance at the other people in the restaurant, in the unlikely event that this apparently bland conversation was being overheard. Satisfied that what they were saying was private, he asked, "So it went well?"

Brett looked at Chesney, who thought he was in the process of cementing a bright future. He had no idea that he was just a backup, to be used only in case Plan A went very wrong. Which didn't bode well for him, since a Plan A in this operation never went wrong.

Brett just smiled and raised his water glass. "It went fine, Senator."

The Tara Foundation is how I want to spend my declining years.

Which is just as well, since my body started declining a while ago, and it's not like it started from that high a peak.

When I don't have any clients to take up my time, I spend much of my day at the foundation building, located in Haledon. But I never put in the effort that Willie Miller, and his wife, Sondra, do. It is their sole focus, and for them it's a total commitment and a labor of love.

We've been doing it for five years, and in that time have placed close to three thousand dogs in homes. It would have been more, but Willie has rather rigorous criteria for what constitutes a home worthy of having one of our dogs. I'm strict about it, but Willie is over the top.

The operation costs us a lot of money, but that is not exactly a major problem. I am the undeserving beneficiary of a very large inheritance, plus a few enormous financial victories on behalf of clients. Willie is also very well off, since he was one of those clients, earning ten million in a wrongful-imprisonment lawsuit. It's a lot of money, but not worth his spending seven years on death row for a murder he didn't commit.

Outside factors have caused Willie's time commitment to the foundation to waver lately. Being a national hero can be a time drain, and that is what Willie has been for the last four months.

It was part of a case that I was working on. Willie insisted on helping out, and I reluctantly gave him minor assignments, since Willie can be a bit of a loose cannon. Not only did he wind up catching the bad guys, but he heroically thwarted what would have been a devastating terrorist attack on a natural-gas tanker.

Willie's resulting national celebrity was very much deserved, and he became the target of every interviewer in America. If he turned one down, I'm not at this point aware of it.

I was supposed to be here this morning to spend the day working and hanging out with the dogs, but my involvement with Noah and his case prevented it. I characteristically forgot to call Willie and tell him, and I know he will just as characteristically think nothing of it.

Sondra is in the reception area when I get there. "Sorry," I say, "I got tied up with some work stuff."

She smiles. "No problem. It's been slow here today anyway."

"Thanks, Sondra. Willie here?"

"In the back. He's anxious to talk to you about something."

"What is it?"

"I'll let him tell you. But after he does, please talk him out of it."

Willie is somewhat volatile, and more than somewhat impetuous, so this could be anything from wanting to remodel the foundation offices to enrolling in astronaut school. I'm not going to know until I know.

When I get into the back, which is where the dogs are, I find Willie in his normal position, rolling around on the ground, playing with six of them. I love dogs in a way that most people consider well north of eccentric, but Willie makes me look normal.

When he sees me, he jumps up, gives each dog a chewie to occupy them, and heads over to me. "Big news," he says.

"I'm ready."

"They want me to write a book."

"Who does?"

The question throws him. "I don't know . . . some book guy."

This is already not going well. "A book guy? That's all you know about him? Was he a big book guy? An old book guy?"

"Hold on a second," he says, and walks over to his desk, opening the drawer. "He gave me his card."

Willie hands me the card, which was given to him by Mr. Alexander Downey, the managing editor at a publishing house in New York. It seems legit, but who knows.

"So what exactly did he say?"

"That I should write a book, like my life story, and they'd put it out there. You know, print it out and stuff."

"Anything else?"

"That they'd give me a lot of money. And I'd get it as soon as I say I'll do it, before I even write the thing. But if I don't write it, I have to give the money back. He wants me to have my agent call him."

"Who's your agent?" I ask, dreading the answer.

"You."

"Willie, are you up for writing a book?"

"Sure. What's the big deal?"

"Well, just to make sure, maybe you should read one first, so you'll know what

94

you're getting into." The only reading I've ever seen Willie do are his own press clippings.

"Come on, Andy, I told you a million times, I can't do that. I get bored real easily; I read a ketchup bottle and I fall asleep."

"It's a big deal, Willie, a lot of work."

"They said they'll give me somebody to help. He's helped other, you know, writers . . . like me."

"I'm sure they will."

"Hey, I'm gonna need some pens, and a lot of paper. You think maybe the helper guy will get me all that?"

I hold up the card. "Why don't I call this guy, and then we'll go from there."

He nods. "Good idea. Hey, how many words are there in a book?"

"I don't know, maybe eighty, a hundred thousand, or so."

"How many words have we said? You know, since you got here and we've been talking."

"Maybe a few hundred," I say.

He's clearly not pleased by my answer. "That's it?"

"That's it."

He ponders this for a few moments. "Make sure they give me a good helper."

"Do you know a man named Daniel Butler? People seem to call him Danny."

Noah's face shows no hint of recognition, and certainly no concern about my reason for asking the question.

"No, I don't think so," he says. "Should I?"

"Danny Butler is the reason you were arrested."

He shakes his head. "I'm the reason I was arrested. But who is he?"

"He went to the FBI and told them that you confessed setting the fire to him. The conversation supposedly took place a few weeks after the fire."

"That's not possible."

"How can you be sure of that? Maybe it was during one of your blackout periods?"

He shakes his head, more firmly this time, as if adamant. "No, when I realized what I had done, I went cold turkey. I still lived in

homeless shelters for a while, but I have not put a drug into my system since that day."

"So you don't know him at all? He claims that he had breakfast with you at a homeless shelter, and that you were bragging about it."

"I had breakfast with plenty of people at homeless shelters, but I never talked about the fire with anyone, at any time, until I got arrested and told Becky. And then you."

I believe Noah is telling the truth. For one thing, he sounds sincere, though that is not terribly important. Plenty of sincere-sounding people have lied to me through their teeth. More significantly, he has no reason to lie. He's already planning to admit his guilt and plead accordingly, so he gains nothing by denying his connection to Danny Butler.

"In his deposition, Butler goes on to say that you told him exactly how you had done it, where you set the fires, and the kind of chemicals you used. He said —"

"He's lying, Andy." For the first time, I hear something other than resignation in Noah's voice. I hear a little anger.

"Why would he be lying?"

"I don't know, but he's lying. I've never had the slightest recollection of anything from that day. There is no possible way I

97

accurately described to him what h
pened."

"His story matches up with the foren
investigation."

He thinks for a moment, frustration evi
dent on his face. "I don't know what to say."

I hesitate before I continue. I'm crossing a
bridge, and when I get to the other side and
turn around, the bridge is going to be gone,
and there won't be any going back. And the
problem is, I don't want to get to the other
side at all, and I absolutely dread getting
stuck there.

"Noah, it's important that you think about
the implications of this. Let's assume that
you're right, that you never had this incriminating conversation with Danny Butler."

"I'm definitely right about that," he says.

"Okay. Then how did he know the details?
You couldn't have had an accomplice, could
you?"

He shakes his head. "No."

"So somebody else told Butler everything
that happened, or he set the fire himself."

"I set the fire."

"You think that you did, I know that," I
say. "And maybe it's true. But how did
Butler find out about it? And why did he
wait six years to come forward?"

Noah thinks about it and comes up with

an explanation that is not completely out of left field. "You said his statement matched the forensics report. Well, maybe someone gave him the report. He read it, and attributed the information to me."

"So he read it, and then framed someone he never met, you, while you were coincidentally hiding a belief in your own guilt."

By now I'm pacing around the room, trying to make sense out of this. I'm sure Noah would be pacing as well, if he were not handcuffed to the metal table.

"Where does this leave us, Andy?"

"Well, I'm sorry, but what I should have already told you is that the prosecutor will not settle for anything other than life without the possibility of parole."

He nods; it's exactly what he expected, and probably what he wants. "I understand."

"So there's no rush to pleading guilty," I say. "It's not going to change your sentence."

"I told you, I don't want a trial."

"Noah, in any negotiation, even one in which you hold no cards of any value, there is always time to make a bad deal."

"What does that mean?"

"It means at any point you can interrupt the process and plead guilty, and that will

99

put a stop to everything, and you'll go away for the rest of your life. But I'm suggesting you hold off for a while, at least until we can explain what's behind this Danny Butler situation."

"You're going to do that?" He rattles his handcuffs. "Because I'm sort of tied up."

I nod. "I've got some free time."

"You might regret that choice of words. Because I have no money to pay you."

"You gave me Tara. I owe you one."

"How do I get myself into these situations?"

Laurie and I are in bed; she's reading, and I'm watching a *Seinfeld* rerun. I don't actually have to "watch" *Seinfeld,* since once I hear a single sentence of any episode, it triggers my memory bank, and I know everything that is going to happen from that moment on. So this way I'm able to enjoy the show and obsess about life simultaneously.

Tara lies in the corner, on a large, puffy dog bed. She used to sleep in bed with us, but now prefers to be able to stretch out by herself.

"Which situation might that be?" Laurie asks.

"I have absolutely no desire to have a client, and I'd rather have a root canal without Novocain than take on a trial, much less a murder trial. So I accept a client for no reason at all —"

Laurie interrupts, pointing to Tara. "You

did it as a favor to her."

That doesn't seem worthy of a response, so I don't give her one. Instead, I continue. "But I catch a break. This client doesn't want to go to trial; he wants to confess to anyone who will listen. So what do I do? I talk him out of pleading guilty, so that maybe we can have a trial."

"Andy, you did the right thing. Now if you are finished beating yourself up, I'm trying to read this book."

"How many words are in it?"

"How many words are in what? This book?"

"Yes, a publishing house wants Willie to write a book, but he's afraid it's going to take too many words."

"God help us," she says.

"Let's get back to my situation," I say. "Do I now have to investigate this thing?"

"You know you do."

"Full scale, or a sweep-under-the-rug job?"

"Full scale," she says.

"Will you help?"

"Now?"

"You know what I mean." Laurie is an ex-cop, who when she's not teaching college-level criminology, serves as my lead investigator. That's obviously only when I have a client, but because I'm an idiot, I seem to have one now.

"Of course I will," she says. "Now can I finish my book? I'll count the words later; it might be distracting to do it as I read."

"What are you reading?" I can't tell, because she's got one of those e-book readers.

"*War and Peace,* by Willie Miller," she says.

I want to get back to obsessing about Noah's case, so I say, "I'll call a meeting of the team for tomorrow morning. With any luck we can find out that Noah is guilty as hell by the end of the day."

"Mmmm," Laurie says, not really listening because she's started reading again.

"You know, we're at an impasse here," I say.

"How is that?"

"Well, you're reading, and I want to have a conversation."

She puts the book device down. "That is quite an impasse. How about a third choice? We could make love."

"Sex?" I ask, not quite believing what I just heard.

She nods. "I believe there will be some sex involved. Consider it a reward for doing the right thing and helping Noah and Becky

Galloway."

"I see injustice and I need to right the wrong. That's just who I am." I'm undressing as I talk, to cut down on the time Laurie has to change her mind. It doesn't seem like she will, because she has her clothes off faster than I do.

"Here's to winning the trial," she says.

"Don't kill the mood."

It's been a while since the team has assembled.

Not as long as I'd like, but right now I don't seem to have a choice. Any slight hope I had of backing out ended with my acceptance of Laurie's "reward" last night. Not only wouldn't I have given it back, but my intention is to perform just as nobly in the future, so as to get more rewards.

Present at this meeting, in addition to Laurie, Hike, Edna, and myself are Sam Willis and Marcus Clark. Sam is my accountant, but that is not his role here, especially since our client can't afford to pay us. He is here because of his talent as computer hacker supreme. If we need to find out anything at all about anything at all, Sam can find it, so long as it resides in some computer, somewhere. Which is good, because pretty much everything in recorded history is in some computer, somewhere.

The fact that much of the information is illegally obtained is something that has never kept either Sam or I awake at night.

Marcus Clark is an outstanding investigator, and an even better bodyguard. To perform both functions, he takes full advantage of the fact that he is the scariest and toughest human being on the planet.

He hardly ever talks, and when he does Laurie is the only one who can understand what he is grunting. But occasionally he seems to listen, so the goal is not to say anything that might make him angry.

In fact, no one in Marcus's presence wants to even look at him; it seems the safest way to stay alive. So everybody just acts nonchalant, as if no one is terrified. It's as if Godzilla walked through the streets of Tokyo, and the citizens just sauntered along, whistling and chatting amiably, as if nothing was amiss.

I grab some coffee and come into the room. Hike is telling Sam how the world is soon to end from an asteroid strike. "There are more asteroids out there than we have grains of sand on our beaches," he says. "We're like in a shooting gallery."

"We're not getting hit," Sam says. He is the optimistic opposite of Hike.

"That's what the dinosaurs said. You see

106

any of them on the bus coming in this morning?"

"So you're saying we're all going to die?"

Hike nods solemnly. "If not this week, then next. Law of averages."

I call the meeting to order. "We've got a client," I say. "His name is Noah Galloway. We haven't received the discovery yet, but Edna will pass out copies of the information we have so far."

Edna looks stunned. "I was supposed to make copies?"

I nod. "Now that you say so, that's probably a good way to do it. That way we'll each have our own."

She stands, folder in hand, and makes the trudge to the copy room. When she's finished, we are going to have one exhausted Edna on our hands.

I give them the basic outline, which they can supplement by reading the documents, should Edna succeed in copying them. Then I lay out the individual assignments.

"Hike and I will go through the discovery, which I'm told we'll have by close of business today. Sam, you should focus on digging up all available information on the fire, the victims, and Danny Butler."

He seems disappointed. "That's it? Did I mention I got a gun permit?"

"Yes, I believe you did. And if we need to shoot anyone, you're our man." Sam feels inhibited by being assigned only computer work; he wants to be out on the street gunning down bad guys.

"Laurie, you'll be in charge of the investigation itself, and Marcus will work with you." I briefly look over at Marcus to see if he has any reaction, but he doesn't. He likes Laurie, so I use her as a buffer whenever I can.

Edna comes back into the room and announces, with obvious relief in her voice, that the copier is out of toner. I wouldn't have the slightest idea how to rectify that technical a problem, so Sam says he'll reload it when the meeting is over.

"We don't have a lot of time on this," I say, trying to get things back on track. "If it goes on too long, our client is going to preempt us and plead guilty."

"Is he guilty?" Sam asks.

"He thinks so, but I'm not so sure." I take a few minutes to explain my doubts. "If we find out he's right, he pleads guilty and we ride out of town."

The phone rings, and everybody looks at Edna, waiting for her to answer it. By the third ring, she gets the idea and reluctantly picks it up. After a brief hello, she holds the phone toward me. "It's Pete Stanton."

"Tell him I'll call him back," I say, partially because we're in the middle of a meeting, but mostly because I'm afraid to talk to him. He may have found out that I am representing Noah already. I had planned to tell him personally, but hadn't yet summoned up the guts. I was thinking three years from Tuesday might be a good time to do it.

Edna gets back on the phone, repeats what I said, and listens for a few moments. She then holds out the phone to me again. "He said that if you don't take the call, whatever you are doing will be the last thing you ever do."

I nod and turn to the others in the room. "Maybe I should take this."

They get up and start to leave, with the exception of Laurie. I pick up the phone and say, "Hey, Pete old buddy, what's going on?"

"Tell me why," he says.

That sounds like a song lyric to me, and I'm feverishly searching for a joke to tell about it, something to lighten the mood. But this mood probably shouldn't be lightened, so I hit it head-on.

"Two reasons, least important first. He saved Tara's life."

"The second one better be a beauty," he says.

"There is very substantial doubt in my mind that he is guilty."

"What a surprise, a defendant who claims he is innocent." Pete has what I would call a healthy disrespect for defense attorneys, which is no great surprise. But I'm not hearing bitterness or intense anger in his voice yet, which surprises me.

I do realize that I've got to be careful here; I can't say anything that Noah told me, including his own belief that he committed the crime. It would be an obvious violation of attorney-client privilege.

"I'm talking about in my mind, Pete. What I have seen so far doesn't add up."

"Depends on who is doing the math. And whether they're using lawycr-math."

"I'll make you a promise," I say. "If I think he's probably guilty when we're done with the investigation, I won't take it to trial."

It's an easy promise for me to make, since Noah doesn't want to go to trial anyway, but I'm sure it comes as a surprise to Pete.

He doesn't say anything for maybe twenty seconds, probably trying to figure out what to make of it. Then, "That works."

"It does?" I ask, unable to conceal my surprise.

"But I'll make you a promise," he says. "If you wind up getting a guilty party off the hook, you will wish you had been in that fire yourself."

Click.

I hang up the phone and Laurie asks, "What did he say?"

"He threatened to burn me alive."

"That's it?" she asks. "I've heard him threaten worse than that fifty times at Charlie's. How angry was he?"

I nod. "That's the weird part. I know Pete really well, and I don't think he was angry at all. I think he wants me to do this."

You would never know that twenty-six people died here.

It's a vacant lot now, actually cleaner than some of the other vacant lots in this neighborhood. I guess when rubble includes a lot of charred bodies, the city pays more attention to the cleanup. Generally, a dead-end street like this would not get much attention, and the other vacant lots are evidence of that.

Laurie and I are on Chapman Street in Paterson, not far from Eastside High School, which is my alma mater. The area was rundown then, and is worse now. It's late afternoon, so students are walking home, regarding us curiously but not overly so.

We like to start a case by going to the scene of the crime, but the value is certainly limited in this case. The crime itself, to say nothing of the years since, has literally wiped away the scene.

The discovery documents started coming in a few hours before we came here, and I took the time to look at the ones relating to the scene, so I've seen contemporaneous pictures, and read a few witness reports. I'll go over them in far more detail later, but doing the little that I did helps me to understand what we're looking at.

"Certainly wasn't a random crime," Laurie says. "They chose the house to hit."

"How do you know that?"

"Random criminals generally pick targets that allow for an easy getaway. It's why there are more drive-by shootings than walk-by ones."

I know what she's getting at, but I don't interrupt.

She points. "This is the seventh lot in on a dead-end street. Even allowing for wanting privacy in the commission of the crime, which might therefore eliminate the corner house and maybe the one next to it, there is no reason they would have come this far down the block. Not unless they were targeting this particular house."

"I agree, but it doesn't help us," I say. "The allegation is that Noah was targeting his drug suppliers, and had been to this house before to purchase his drugs. So he certainly would have bypassed the first six houses and gone after this one."

"Do they think he drove here?"

"I don't know what they think, but I can't imagine he did. He had lost everything, so I doubt he had a car."

She nods, and walks toward one of the other buildings. We stare at it, and I wait until she tells me what I'm supposed to be thinking.

"Three floors, maybe three apartments to a floor? Maybe an average of at least three people per apartment?"

I nod. "Sounds right That's twenty-seven people, close to the number that died."

"Fifteen buildings on the street, both sides, so maybe four hundred people living on this street. What time was the fire?"

"Just after midnight," I say

"And it happened in the summer, right?"

"July fourteenth."

"We need to check the weather that evening," she says. "If it was a hot night and not raining, some people might have been outside, even at that hour. Someone should have seen something."

"And it was a chemical fire. The perp would have had to be carrying the materials to start it. Might have made them stand out some. We'll have to canvass the neighborhood, and identify people that have moved away."

"The perp?" she asks, mimicking me.

I nod. "It stands for 'perpetrator,' which means bad guy. It's crime talk; sorry, I sometimes lapse into my native tongue."

I'm trying to find some humor in this, but it's hard, because it's not going to be fun. It's going to be a long, painstaking investigation, essentially duplicating Pete's failed one. And he and his colleagues had the advantage of working when the crime was fresh.

And when it's all over, one of two things will happen. Either a guy I like will go to prison for the rest of his life, or I'll be devoting months of my own life to something I have absolutely no desire to do. Or both.

We head back to the office, and I call Hike on the way, asking him to head down there, so that we can go over the discovery documents. It's a difficult process; by definition it will show the odds to be heavily stacked against the defendant, which is why they arrested him in the first place.

Hike agrees to meet me at the office; he would agree to meet me in a swamp in the Everglades if he could bill by the hour. "None of my business," he asks, "but are you getting paid for this?" He knows that I have taken a few cases in recent years with clients that had no money.

"No."

"Let me put it another way. Am I getting paid for this?"

"Yes."

"You cut a lot of classes in law school? Maybe the ones where they went over compensation and client billing?"

I've just realized that as dismal as this looked a few minutes ago, it's actually worse. I'm doing all of this for nothing, and I'm doing it with Hike.

The most important courtroom in America, at least for financial matters, is in Delaware.

Most people are surprised to hear that, since Delaware has never been confused with Wall Street as a center of high finance.

It's called the Delaware Chancery Court, and it has been home to some of the most significant financial trials in American business history. Many of them have gone completely unnoticed by those outside the business community, but the verdicts have on some level affected everyone.

Delaware's achieving preeminence in this area was the result of design. Favorable state tax laws attracted companies from all over the country, not to make Delaware their corporate headquarters, but rather to make it the state in which they incorporated. So when those same companies are involved in lawsuits, that is naturally where those suits are tried.

Over time, the court has also come to be known for its competence. It is a place where decisions are rendered by its judges strictly according to the law. Lawyers don't have to worry about renegade judges making unsupported decisions, and surprises are a rarity. And lawyers hate surprises.

This outstanding legal reputation frequently brings "business" into Delaware by mutual agreement of companies that are not even incorporated there. When these companies enter into contracts with each other, they often agree in advance that if they eventually have a dispute, it will be settled in Delaware.

So Judge Walter Holland, chief judge of the Chancery Court, had a very important job, and he took that job very seriously. Blessed with an outstanding legal mind, and having earned a reputation for impeccable integrity, he had long been considered a lawyer's judge. That is, he would decide cases strictly according to the law, and he possessed a keen understanding of that law.

No surprises.

On this day Judge Holland sat in his courtroom moments before he was to hear opening arguments in a dispute concerning an attempted takeover of Milgram Oil and Gas. In his position as chief judge, it was

118

easy for him to arrange to hear the case himself, and that's what he did.

As companies in the energy field go, Milgram was a relative pygmy, with a market capitalization of less than a billion and a half dollars. The company attempting the takeover was Entech Industries, a smallish energy firm, based in Philadelphia and run by CEO Alex Bauer. Entech Industries had owned about three percent of Milgram, but then suddenly bought another fifteen percent.

Milgram, correctly anticipating a takeover move by Entech, adopted what is known as a poison pill defense. Simply put, the measure said that if any outside investor bought enough shares to own in excess of twenty percent of the company, then all existing shareholders had the right to buy more shares at a discount.

This maneuver would have the effect of diluting Entech's shares, and making an ultimate takeover difficult, if not impossible. So Bauer and Entech sued, claiming the poison pill defense in this case was illegal.

It was a fairly complicated case; Judge Holland knew that from his reading of the submitted briefs. But complicated cases were nothing new to him; he faced that every day.

It was also a typical case, in that it was not even close to the public consciousness. Mentions could be found of it on the financial pages, but they focused mainly on the impact that the case would have on the stock of the parties involved.

The lawyers representing the companies were from the finest firms in the country, and Holland knew that they were worth the exorbitant fees they charged. They would prepare meticulously, and they would know every single fact and element of the law that might bear on the outcome.

But Judge Walter Holland knew certain things that the lawyers did not.

He knew that it was not important how well the lawyers were prepared, or how persuasive they would be. None of that would matter, for one simple reason.

Judge Holland already knew who was going to win.

And he knew that twenty-six people had burned to death to ensure it.

Alexander Downey is going to regret his decision.

He's the vice president and assistant managing editor of Henderson Publishing, and after trading a few phone calls, we set up a meeting to talk about the possibility of Willie Miller writing a book about his heroic exploits.

I'm too busy with trial preparation to go to his midtown Manhattan office, and I suggested we have our discussion over the phone. But Downey wanted to meet in person, and offered to come to my office. That's the part he's likely to regret.

My office is located on the second floor of a three-story building on Van Houten Avenue in Paterson. Directly below us is Sofia Hernandez's fruit stand, which is sort of the community center of the neighborhood. People from surrounding blocks come there to squeeze cantaloupes and discuss the pressing issues of the day.

Downey arrives and climbs the twenty-two creaking stairs to the office. Once inside, he runs into Edna, who reluctantly puts down her crossword puzzle to usher him into my office. She doesn't offer him coffee, probably because if he said yes, she'd have to make some.

Downey is wearing a dark, pin-striped suit, which, if he auctioned it off, could pay our rent until the end of hockey season. He introduces himself with, "Mr. Carpenter, it's a pleasure to meet you. I'm a longtime admirer." This guy is no dummy.

I offer him a seat, and he picks the cleanest one and sits down. We exchange small talk for a while, an easy thing to do once I learn he's a Giants fan.

I need to move this along, since I've got a lot of work to do, so I say, "I understand you want Willie Miller to write a book for you."

He nods. "Very much. He's got an amazing story to tell, and I'm sure he will tell it colorfully. He has a unique voice."

"That he does. Until now, I'm sure you understand, that voice has been verbal. This would be Willie's first book."

Downey smiles. "Not a problem, we understand that he is not an established writer.

We want him to speak from the heart, in his own words."

"In his own words . . ." I repeat, wondering if he's actually heard any of Willie's words.

"Mr. Carpenter —"

"Andy."

"Thank you, Andy," he says. "We . . . I . . . understand Willie's capabilities as a wordsmith. When I told him I wanted his story told truthfully and unembellished, that there was no need for anything fallacious, he said, ' 'Course not, man, I'm married.' "

I can't help laughing at this recounting, and Downey joins in. From there the conversation goes smoothly, and Downey claims to have the perfect person to serve as Willie's ghostwriter.

When I ask about compensation, he gives me a piece of paper he has prepared as a proposal, and suggests that I study it. "It calls for an advance of five hundred thousand," he says, "but I'm confident that with royalties he will earn considerably more than that."

We reach a basic agreement; the money is obviously good, and since Willie wants to do it, I see no reason to stand in his way. Downey says that he will prepare the contracts and send them to me. We shake hands on it, but it appears that the meeting is not yet over. He tells me that he'd like me to write a book as well.

"Willie knows much more about what happened than I do. He was there."

"I'm not talking about that case, at least not specifically," Downey says. "You've been part of quite a few high-profile cases, including Galloway. This could be the story of your life, and especially your career."

"I don't think so," I say.

"There would be a substantial audience for it. We do a lot of these books, some written by the subject, some not. Some authorized, some not."

I think the only thing I would dislike more than work is writing about work, so I say, "Let's focus on Willie for now."

He smiles. "Fine."

"Thanks for coming all the way here," I say.

"Happy to do it. I think I'll pick up a watermelon downstairs as a remembrance."

What if they gave a town and nobody came?

That's what the residents of Jean, Nevada, would be asking themselves, if there were any residents of Jean, Nevada. But there are none, not a single one.

Another thing Jean obviously does not have is a city planner. Set up to be a gambling community, it stands on Highway 15, on the route into Vegas from Los Angeles. That might ordinarily be a good place to be, the theory being that anxious gamblers from L.A. might stop there to get a blackjack fix before driving on to Vegas.

The problem with that is that Primm, Nevada, is located just over the state line between California and Nevada. In fact, the original name of Primm was Stateline. Primm's casinos are larger than Jean's, which is just as well, since people actually go there. If they want to gamble before getting to Vegas, they stop at Primm. If not,

125

they go on to Vegas. Either way, there's no reason to stop at Jean.

None of this deterred Billy Klayman from making a one-o'clock-in-the-morning stop at the Gold Strike Casino in Jean. Having lost almost all of his money in a disastrous two-day trip to Vegas, Billy was driving back to his home in Anaheim a broke and hungry man. The broke part was going to be tough to solve, but the hungry part he could deal with. That's because the sign in front of the Gold Strike was advertising "24 hour all you can eat — $6.99." At least one of Billy's credit cards should be able to deal with that.

So Billy parked his car in the nearly deserted lot and went in to the Gold Strike. It was a "serve yourself" buffet, utilizing small plates and difficult-to-reach entrees to deter patrons from overdoing it.

None of that had any effect on Billy, nor did the fact that the food had very little taste. He had arrived starved, and he was going to leave stuffed.

It took Billy forty-five minutes to have the meal, which included nine trips back to the buffet line. So full that he could barely get out of the chair, he left the restaurant, made a stop in the men's room, and then another one in the bar adjacent to the casino.

He could only afford one beer, so that's the exact number that he bought. He lingered over it for a half hour, not anxious to get back onto the road for the rest of the dreary ride home. Once he got there, he would have to explain to his wife where the rent money went, a conversation he did not relish at all.

Billy briefly considered taking a room in the hotel, but rejected the idea when he realized that it would cost money to do it. So instead he waddled out to the parking lot, and headed for his car. He was still depressed and miserable, but he was no longer hungry.

It was only about a hundred yards from the hotel entrance to Billy's car, and Billy later remembered noticing how dark it was, and thinking that someone who left the casino flush with cash could be an easy target for a predator. Then he laughed to himself at the concept of someone leaving the Gold Strike Casino flush with cash.

Billy unlocked the driver's side door and got in the car. More accurately, he tried to get in the car, but was stopped by the fact that there was already someone in the driver's seat.

In the dim interior light of the car, Billy saw that it was a man's body, wrapped tightly in what seemed like cellophane, but with an empty space where the head was supposed to be. The body rolled back and forth from the impact of Billy's jostling it, then fell to the left and out of the car and onto the asphalt. In the process, it covered up the note that was taped to the body's chest.

And then Billy screamed, loud enough to wake the residents of Jean, Nevada, if there were any.

128

Discovery documents are the New York Yankees of the criminal justice system.

Before the baseball season, all the experts look at the various rosters of the teams, and say that the Yankees are by far the best, and that there's no way they should lose. And then supporters of the other teams bravely say that everyone should just wait until the season is played, and that although the Yankees may have the best team on paper, the season isn't played on paper.

Discovery documents are the prosecutor's version of events, and they chronicle in excruciating detail the results of what are usually intensive investigations by law enforcement. Obviously it is all incriminating to the accused, since it all resulted in the poor sucker getting arrested.

So as evidence "rosters" go, the discovery always shows that the prosecution's is by far the best. Of course, in this case it's a two-

team league, which leaves the defense in second, meaning last, place.

But, like baseball games, trials are not "played on paper"; they are won or lost in the courtroom. Unfortunately, once they get off the paper and into that courtroom, the evidence included in discovery usually carries the day, and the prosecution winds up winning.

Just like the Yankees.

Considering the fact that this case was at least partially put together six years after the crime, the evidence-gathering against Noah has been impressive.

A number of neighbors identified Noah as a frequent presence in the area, and it was understood that he was purchasing drugs from the people in one of the first-floor apartments. He was also seen and heard earlier that evening engaged in an angry dispute with those same pushers, no doubt over their refusal to extend him credit.

It gets worse from there. Soon after the fire a paint can had been found in a trash can three blocks from the burned house. Testing showed it to have contained residu from the chemical compound identified having caused the fire. There was DNA the can, including a tiny piece of ch? skin.

Noah's DNA.

Noah's skin.

Of course, the trigger that set this whole process in motion was the deposition given by Danny Butler. It makes for a devastating read, if you happen to be Noah's defense attorney, which unfortunately I am, at least for the time being.

Hike and I go through the material together, exchanging documents when we're through with them. I can hear him audibly moaning as he reads, which is not terribly significant, since Hike spends most of every day moaning.

When we're finished, he says, "Well, at least we've got a client we can believe. When he says he did it, he did it."

"So says the prosecution."

"So says the evidence. Come on, Andy, that paint can is the goddamn murder weapon, and Galloway's DNA is on it. The only thing they don't have is a deposition from God saying Galloway set the fire. And they'd probably have that by the time we went to trial."

"We haven't developed our own evidence yet," I say lamely.

"What are you talking about?" he asks. "We've already got the key piece. He saved your dog. All we have to do is present studies proving that dog-savers do not burn down houses."

Hike is annoying me by not playing the game. A defense attorney is supposed to disbelieve and discount everything the prosecution says. "Have you ever read discovery that didn't make it look like your client was guilty?"

"No, but my clients are always guilty."

"And maybe this one is also, but we start by assuming he's not, and we try to make the pieces fit. Maybe the real killer set him up to take the fall."

Hike frowns, which is what he does when he's not moaning, though he is able to do both simultaneously. "Interesting frame. They plant the evidence, and then wait six years to bring it to light. We're dealing with some very patient framers."

Hike is right, of course, but the more he talks, the more obstinate I feel. The problem is that my obstinate feelings have nothing to do with whether Noah will spend the rest of his life in jail.

The phone rings, and since Edna is either not in the office or hiding, I pick it up. A woman's voice says, "Mr. Carpenter?" and I confirm that it's me. She then tells me to hold for Mr. Campbell.

Dylan picks up moments later. "Andy,

glad I got you," he says. "There's been a new development in the case, which is obviously not included in the discovery yet. It's pretty important, so I thought I should tell you right away."

Based on Dylan's calling me like this, and the upbeat tone of his voice, the chance that this is bad news for Noah is exactly one hundred percent.

I don't ask Dylan what it is, because he's going to tell me anyway, and I don't want to give him the satisfaction. So without prodding, he continues. "A body was found in a parking lot in Jean, Nevada, just outside of Vegas. The deceased is Danny Butler."

"Cause of death?"

"Well, the autopsy hasn't been done yet, but it shouldn't be too difficult. Butler was decapitated, and the head hasn't been found."

"That's it?" I ask.

"That's it."

"Nice chatting with you, Dylan."

"Damn, I forgot, there's one more thing. They found a note on the body. It says, 'Talkers die.' "

The death of Danny Butler is a major problem for Noah.

Not as big a problem as it is for Danny Butler, but it's a serious blow, at least if Noah's case goes to trial. No trial, then no harm, no foul.

The damage is on two levels. First of all, the timing of the murder, along with the note on the body, makes it look like it is a revenge killing for Danny's squealing on Noah. While Noah's presence in jail obviously disqualifies him as the actual killer, his possible connection to criminal elements in the drug world would suggest that he could have requested it be done.

At the very least, it suggests that perhaps Noah has substantial influence with, and connection to, murderers. That is never a good thing for a murder defendant to have on his résumé.

Even more serious than that is the potential legal impact. If there is a trial, there will be a legal battle, and I'll be arguing that the statement Butler gave to the police should not be admitted.

I will cite the Confrontation Clause in the Sixth Amendment to the Constitution, which states that the accused "shall enjoy the right . . . to be confronted with the witnesses against him." Though I certainly would not agree with the use of the word "enjoy," it's a crucial part of our legal system.

It insures that everything comes to light, and most importantly, that a defendant's lawyer has the right to cross-examine the witness. We lawyers think we can break witnesses down, and reduce the impact of the negative things they have to say about our clients.

In Danny's case, we would have had a minor advantage, in that everything he had to say was committed to a statement, which he signed. If I could have gotten him to deviate in any way from that statement, and I almost always can do that, then the jury might tend to disbelieve him.

So I would make all these arguments, citing the Constitution, and I would lose. Because over time, judges and lawyers have carved some holes in that document, and

Noah is about to fall into a big one. In fact, two of them.

There are two reasons the judge will admit Butler's statement. First of all, it represents a confession. Not by Butler, of course, but Butler was reporting Noah's alleged confession. That is admissible, and represents an exception to the Confrontation Clause, as well as to the hearsay rule.

The other factor insuring our legal defeat is that the law says that witnesses can be exempt from testifying, with their prior statements being admissible, if that witness is legitimately unavailable.

When you're wrapped in cellophane and missing your head, that's about as unavailable as it gets.

Hike and I discuss this new development. As big a pain in the ass as Hike can be, he's got a brilliant legal mind, and I'm hoping that he can come up with something we can use.

"Anything at all you can think of?" I ask.

"Nope."

Thanks, Hike.

The more I think about it, the more I see a silver lining, albeit not in any legal cloud. The only reason I opened this investigation at all was that I believed Noah when he said he didn't confess the arson to Butler, and wouldn't have been able to supply the details of the crime even if he wanted to.

So, assuming Butler didn't wake up one day and decide for no reason to randomly pick Noah as the person to lie about, then he was put up to it.

His subsequent murder, which I refuse to believe is a coincidence, confirms the existence of an evil third party here. The people that used Butler decided they didn't need him anymore, and that his knowledge of their involvement could be risky for them. Killing him put another nail in Noah's legal coffin, and shut Butler up in the process.

A twofer, wrapped in cellophane.

I call Becky Galloway. It's easier to get in touch with her than with Noah, since Noah is behind bars, which are in turn behind walls.

"Has Noah ever been to Vegas?" I ask.

"Of course."

"Why of course?"

"He was born there. That's where he grew up."

I'm talking to Becky, but I can hear Dylan salivating. He's going to talk about how Noah knows people there, people with whom he learned to do drugs, and they killed Danny Butler at their friend Noah's behest.

He won't have any evidence of it, or at least I hope he won't, but he'll have one advantage. It will sound true, and the jury will think it makes logical sense that it's true.

And unfortunately, as trials go, that's all that matters. Because the idea that trials are a search for the truth is just a myth. Trials are a search for that which the jury will believe is the truth.

"Senator Ryan, this is Brett Fowler. Thank you for taking my call."

"You told my assistant it was urgent," Ryan said, though the truth was he would have taken the call anyway. Fowler was very well connected in Washington, and though Ryan never used him in his role as consultant, he was always worth talking to.

"Yes, I'm afraid it is," Fowler said. "I'm afraid it is."

"What's the problem?"

"Well, please understand that I am simply acting as an intermediary here, but I have some instructions for you."

"Is that right?" Even though Ryan was worried about where this could be going, he wasn't about to let a political flack start issuing instructions to a senator of his stature.

"Yes, sir. When you leave the office tonight, you'll find a package on the passenger

139

seat of your car. Don't open it until you get home, but when you do please examine it carefully."

"What is it?" Ryan asked. "What the hell is this about?"

"Please, Senator, just do as I say. Believe me, it's better for both of us if you do. After you are familiar with the contents of the package, we will need to meet."

"I don't like this," Ryan said. "I don't like the mystery, and I don't like the way you're talking to me."

"Senator, it is what it is. You'll see that soon enough. Just call me when you are ready to meet."

The package was waiting in the car, just as Fowler had said. But Ryan was not about to wait until he got home to open it, and he did so before he even pulled out of the parking lot.

It was a DVD, unmarked, and the thought of what might be on it made Ryan sick to his stomach. And with no DVD player in the car, all he could do was as he was told — to go home and play it.

When he arrived home, he realized that he had forgotten that his daughter and future son-in-law were over for dinner. After saying hello to them and his wife, Linda, he said that he had to make an important call.

He went into his office, locked the door, and watched as his worst fears were realized. There he was, in the Amsterdam hotel, having sex with a prostitute and ingesting cocaine. He was looking at the end of his career, his marriage, and life as he knew it.

He called Fowler, who answered the phone with a calm, "Hello, Senator. Thanks for calling."

"You stinking son of a bitch."

"I see no reason for name-calling, Senator. For instance, I didn't address you as a cheating, cocaine-snorting pervert, even though the evidence certainly would support such a characterization."

"What do you want?" Ryan asked.

"I'll tell you at breakfast tomorrow. Believe me, it won't be nearly as bad as you think. By next week this can all be behind you."

They met at the restaurant in the Madison Hotel, on Fifteenth Street Northwest, a perfectly normal spot for a senator to be having breakfast. Fowler was already there when Ryan arrived, which was to be expected considering their relative status.

An outside observer would never have thought there was anything wrong, or that Ryan was not in charge of the meeting. But of course to Ryan something was very wrong, and he most definitely was not in charge.

Fowler tried to make small talk at first but Ryan was having none of it. "Just tell me what you want," he said.

"It's not what I want, Senator. But the people I represent do have a request."

"Who are those people?"

Fowler laughed. "I'm afraid that's privileged, Senator. Very, very privileged."

"I'm waiting," Ryan said.

"You have a bill coming out of your committee this week. I believe it is number D427967, regulating certain mining activities. It is not a terribly significant piece of legislation, and is expected to be passed easily by both houses and signed by the President. No controversy at all, which in this political climate is remarkable, don't you think?"

Ryan obviously knew of the legislation, and knew that Fowler was characterizing its certain passage accurately. "What about it?"

"Certain amendments, also enjoying widespread support, will be added in the next two days. There is an additional amendment that you will add in your capacity as ranking minority member. It will seem insignificant, and in fact is of little importance, and should sail through by acclamation."

"And what if I don't?"

Fowler shook his head, as if saddened. "Senator, please . . . don't embarrass yourself."

"Then what if I do as you ask?"

"When you do," Fowler said, leaving no doubt that "if" was not the correct word for this situation, "then the content of the video will never be disseminated, and you will not be called upon in this manner again. You have my word; I work for honorable people."

"What is the amendment?"

Fowler took an envelope out of his pocket and handed it to him. "It's in here."

Ryan did not want to wait to see what was in there, so he opened the envelope and took out the piece of paper. It was four paragraphs of legislative language, so he read it closely and carefully. Then he turned to Fowler.

"Done," he said.

Sam Willis has spent three days online learning as much as he can about the victims.

In my experience, three days is enough time for Sam to fully chronicle every event that has happened in the history of the world, with special attention to New Jersey.

But as research projects go, this one is proving very difficult. That's because for the most part the people who died lived on the fringe of society, many not in the workforce, and had done little to document their impact on the world.

We know how they died, but the challenge we face is finding out how they lived.

"Twenty-six people," Sam says. "Twelve men, eight women, six kids, four of them boys. One survivor, a twelve-year-old boy who jumped out a window. He lost three family members that day."

The images that my mind conjures about

that fire are horrible, and obviously the jury will feel the same way. They will also want to be able to assign blame, to at least partially right the wrong. And Noah will be the one sitting in the crosshairs.

I look quickly through the information that Sam has assembled, long enough to know it won't help us, and I say, "This isn't enough. I've got to know more about them."

"There's very little out there about these people, Andy. We're not talking about CEOs, you know? Even the ones that I could find out where they were employed, some of them had given fake documentation."

"What about other family members, friends, friends of friends? I need to know these people, Sam, so I can know if they could have been the targets."

"I'm trying, Andy, but so far it's not there. I don't even have three names."

"What do you mean?"

"Three of the victims were never identified. No one came forward to say who they were, and the cops assumed they were transients. They figured the targets were the guys in 1-C, and they were probably right."

I agree with Sam; the police probably were correct about that. But once again we butt up against the reality of courtroom life; it doesn't matter if it's true. It only matters if the jury buys it.

"We're going to need to get out in the field for this, Andy. Pound the pavement. Shoe-leather time."

"Shoe-leather time?"

"You know what I mean."

"Yes, I do, and you're probably right. But that's why we have Laurie, and it's especially why we have Marcus. They go out in the field and get information."

"You don't think I can do that?" he asks.

"Absolutely," I lie. The image of Sam loose on the streets with his gun is not a pretty one. "But your special gift is to get information by working a computer key-board. Fingertip time."

I finally get Sam to leave, and I call Pete. He's not in, so I try him on his cell. When he answers, I can hear street noises in the background.

"Hey, Pete, what's going on?"

"What's going on? You calling to chitchat? I'm out arresting lowlifes and criminals, so you can put them back on the street."

"Always happy to help. I've got a question about the Galloway case."

A few moments of silence, and then, "Yeah?"

"Danny Butler knew all the facts behind

the arson, stuff that forensics confirmed."

"So?"

"So I want to know if he could have gotten a look at the police documents, the murder book." The investigatory record that detectives keep when investigating a homicide is called the "murder book."

"You want to know if a slimeball like Danny Butler saw my murder book?" Pete asks, obviously insulted by the question.

"Yes."

"Definitely. We posted it on scumbag.com so Danny and his friends could familiarize themselves with it."

"So it's not possible?" I ask, knowing his answer but still needing to hear it.

"No, it's not possible. For the last two years that book has been in my wall safe at home. It's been bedtime reading. You think Butler broke into my house? Or you think he read it, and then waited two years to talk about it?"

"I don't suppose you have any idea how Butler found out the details?"

"Maybe your client told him."

"He didn't," I say. "I'm sure of it."

"So prove it."

"I'm trying to, but I'm six years late to the party. You've been there all this time, dancing and drinking the punch. I need a road map, or at least a place to start."

Pete is quiet for a few moments, then seems to make a decision. "Start with 'Double J.' "

"Who is 'Double J,' and why should I talk to him? Or her."

"You'll find him, but you'll need Marcus to talk to him."

"Why?"

"Just take my word for it. If you deal with this guy, make sure Marcus is there. No matter what. You send him a letter, have Marcus mail it. Am I making myself clear?"

Pete is insulting my manhood, fragile as that may be. "You don't think I can handle myself?"

"Andy, you so much as ask this guy what time it is without Marcus around, and Laurie will be going to singles bars."

Neither Laurie nor Marcus has ever heard of the guy Pete called "Double J."

So Laurie instructs Marcus to ask around, a process which works slightly more than ninety-nine percent of the time. When Marcus wants anything, especially answers, people have a tendency to want to accommodate him. It's called a "self-preservation instinct."

So I'm not surprised when Laurie reports six hours later that Marcus has not only found Double J, he's already learned quite a bit about him. He's a drug dealer whose base of operations six years ago was the ill-fated house which was burned to the ground.

Apparently Double J has stepped up in the world, because he now lives and works in the big city, New York. He's located in the Bronx on Andrews Avenue, an area that will never be confused with Park Avenue.

I need to talk to him, even though I don't quite know why. Pete implied that he had information that was helpful, or at least relevant, to Noah's case, and I'm sure that must be true. Pete also described him as extremely dangerous, and Pete's a pretty good authority on that kind of stuff.

"I need to ask him some questions," I tell Laurie. "I don't suppose Marcus got his e-mail address?"

"No, I don't suppose he did," she says. "You're going to have to go see him, and I'm going with you."

"Pete said I needed to bring Marcus."

"Of course we'll bring Marcus."

Laurie asks Marcus when the best time would be to go, and he says Double J is apparently always there at around eight P.M., before he goes off to do whatever it is that comprises his nightly ritual.

The idea of barging in on a dangerous drug dealer at night in that neighborhood runs counter to every instinct I have. "It's dark at night," I say.

"Wow," Laurie says. "You don't miss a thing."

We head off at seven o'clock in my car, with Laurie in the passenger seat and Marcus in the back. It's about an hour's drive, and Marcus doesn't say a word. If we drove to New Zealand, Marcus wouldn't say a word.

This is a very rundown, very tough area of the city. Vacant lots abound, strewn with rubble, and some of the houses are boarded up and unoccupied. If there are streetlights, they're not working, and the moonlight is not doing the trick.

If Marcus were not with us, I wouldn't get out of the car if it was on fire.

I park in front of the house that Marcus identifies as Double J's. If there are any lights on inside, they're not visible from the street. Just as I'm getting out of the car, I realize too late that I should have written out questions for Marcus to have given Double J, sort of like an essay test. Then he could have brought it home to me, and I could have graded it.

Marcus leads the way along the concrete path to the house. Laurie and I stay a few steps behind, and I notice that her right hand is at her side, slightly behind her leg. I think, but I'm not sure, that she's holding a weapon there.

I hope she is. I hope it's a bazooka.

We reach the front door, and Marcus opts not to knock or ring a bell. Instead he opens it and goes in. He doesn't hesitate; it's as if he's just come from the office and has headed home to the little woman for a home-cooked meal.

Marcus is amazingly quiet for a man his size. Laurie and I follow his lead and are quiet as well, though I'm afraid that whoever is in the house can hear my heart pounding. When I set out to become a lawyer, I never imagined myself in a situation like this, and suffice it to say I'm not going to run into any of my law school buddies in this house.

"Should we wait out here?" I whisper to Laurie.

"No," she says, in a tone that indicates the issue is not really debatable.

So we follow Marcus through the now open door. I don't close it behind me; there is not enough money in the world to make me do anything that would impede my escape route out of here.

There is a staircase directly in front of us, and a source of very dim light coming from near the top of it. On the entry floor seems to be a hallway with a few closed apartment doors, though there is no light coming from underneath them.

Marcus still seems to know where he is going, and that is up the stairs. Laurie and I start to follow him, though it's too narrow for us to walk side by side. I graciously allow her to go first.

Suddenly there is a noise from above, and the sound of an angry, unfamiliar voice. I can't make out the words, but from the tone, I don't think it's "Make my home your home."

I'm straining unsuccessfully to see what's happening, but I can't do it. I sense some quick motion above us, and I hear the word "Hey!" Then there is a thumping sound, a shriek of pain, and something seems to come out of the darkness, heading down toward us.

Actually, it is flying above us, so high that we don't even have to duck to get out of the way. It's very large and it's making a disgusting noise, so I think it's a body. I also feel a slight spray of liquid, and I don't even want to guess what that might be.

It lands with a sickening thud on the floor at the bottom of the stairs, and doesn't move.

"What the hell —"

My question is cut off by what seems like another human missile fired from the top of the stairs. It's pretty much the same as the first, but mercifully without the spray. It doesn't go quite as far, and seems to land on the first step. Marcus must be getting tired. Maybe he threw some bodies a few days ago, and he's pitching on only three days' rest.

"Marcus, are you all right?" It's Laurie's voice, probably confirming that Marcus was not one of the flying bodies.

"Yuh," Marcus says, always at his most eloquent in a crisis.

"I'll stay down here and watch them. You want Andy to come with you?"

"Yuh."

Just because Marcus said "Yuh," it doesn't mean I have to obey. I take orders from no one; I dance to my own drummer. I have never been accused of being a "Yuh-man."

On the other hand, if I stay down here and send Laurie up, I'll be in the dark, watching over two enormous goons who are going to be rather pissed if and when they wake up. If I go up the stairs, at least I'm under Marcus's rather large protective umbrella.

While I'm deciding, Laurie says, "Andy, are you going up?"

"Yuh," I say, always at my most eloquent in a crisis.

I trudge up the steps, feeling my way along the railing in the dark.

When I'm about three quarters of the way there, I hear a click and turn around. Laurie has snapped on a small flashlight, the kind that might go on a key ring. She is shining it on the two motionless masses at the bottom of the stairs, and holding a gun on them in case they move.

I have no idea whether they are alive or dead, and I'm not going to spend much time worrying about it.

As I near the top of the steps, I hear a crashing noise, and I think that Marcus must have broken down a door. Sure enough, down the hall there is an apartment with no door, and light emanating from inside. I hear scuffling noises and grunts coming from that direction, and then silence.

"Marcus?" Before I walk through that

door, I want to know that Marcus prevailed. If he didn't, there's no way I could.

"Yuh."

I take a deep breath, walk to the open door and enter the apartment. It is completely unlike what I expected. It's a nicely decorated, very comfortable living room, complete with trinkets on the tables and pictures on the walls. The furniture is comfortable and welcoming; this could have been the living room in *Leave It to Beaver.* Add some stockings, a tree, and seventy-two chairs, and Edna could invite her extended family here for the holidays.

There is a large sofa, complete with throw pillows, and Marcus sits at one end of it. He looks at ease and comfortable; the only thing missing is slippers and a pipe.

Double J is nowhere to be found, although the gasping noises I hear make me believe that Marcus has hidden him somewhere. I scan the room, and sure enough, a head that I assume belongs to Double J sticks out from under the couch, on the side where Marcus is sitting. I further assume the rest of him is under the couch, though I could be wrong.

Double J's face shows his obvious panic over the fact that he is not able to get any air into his lungs, so I say, "Marcus, get up.

He's gonna die."

Marcus thinks about it for a moment, as if weighing the pros and cons, and then gets up. He turns and lifts the couch off its captive, as if it were a toy. He then picks Double J off the floor by his collar, and puts him on the couch, in the same place that Marcus was sitting.

I wait a few minutes while Double J keeps gasping and writhing. Feeling more secure, I call down to Laurie to make sure she's okay, and she assures me she's fine.

Finally, Double J is able to speak, and he croaks, "Who the hell are you?"

"I'm a lawyer," I say, and then I point to Marcus, who is sitting on what looks like a dining room table. "He's an intern in my office. Helps out with collating, copying, that sort of thing."

He just looks at me, not knowing what the hell I'm talking about, so I continue. "I want to talk to you about the fire in Paterson, six years ago."

"What about it?"

"I'm trying to find the guilty party, and I have reason to believe you have information that could be helpful to me."

He looks incredulous. "That's it?"

I nod. "That's it."

"Are you shitting me? That's what this is about?"

"Yes."

"So why did you come in like the goddamn Marines?" he asks, pointing at Marcus as well. "And why the hell did you have to bring the Incredible Hulk?"

"Your associates weren't welcoming enough. So am I to assume you're willing to talk to me about the fire?"

"Shit, I'll talk to anybody about the damn fire. Three of my people died in that thing, man. I was out, or I would have been charcoal-broiled myself. You think I don't want to find the son of a bitch that did it?"

"So help me find the guilty party."

"Don't be an asshole," he says, glancing over at Marcus to make sure he's not offended by the name-calling. He doesn't seem to be. "If I knew anything, I'd have caught the prick myself. And he'd have been dead ten minutes later."

"Do you know Noah Galloway?"

He laughs derisively. "You mean the guy they just arrested? Yeah, I knew him. He was a customer, the little shit."

"Could he have done it?"

He shakes his head. "No chance."

"Why not?"

"First of all, he wouldn't have had the

158

balls, and if he did have the balls, he was always wasted. No way he could have pulled it off."

"It was a can of fluid and a match," I say. "He couldn't have done that?"

He looks at me like I'm an idiot, then points at Marcus. "You needed him to get in here, and this ain't where I work, you know? Where I work, nobody gets in. I got more to protect."

"Somebody got in," I point out.

"Maybe."

"What does that mean?"

"It means I think it was somebody that was already inside; that's the only way," he says.

"But you don't know who."

He nods. "Lucky for whoever did it."

"You haven't convinced me it's not Galloway."

"You think I give a shit if you're convinced?"

I seem to have gotten all I can get out of Double J, which isn't much.

"Why do they call you Double J?"

" 'Cause my name's Jesse Jackson. I got sick of the 'Reverend' jokes."

"That's the first thing you've said that makes sense. Let's go, Marcus."

But Double J is not finished. Despite his

claim that he doesn't care if I'm convinced, he takes another shot at it. "You like money?" he asks.

"Why?"

"Just tell me, you like money?"

"I've got more than I need."

He stifles a moan. "Damn, you're a pain in the ass. If you liked money, more than anything else in the world, and a whole shit-load of it was sitting on this table, would you set fire to it? Or would you take it?"

I see where he's going with this, and not only does it make perfect sense, but it's something I should have seen long ago. Maybe I should hire Double J to write my closing arguments. "So there were drugs in that house?"

"Enough to keep Galloway wasted for a hundred years."

"And he would have known that?" I ask.

"Absolutely. And there's nothing he wouldn't have done to get it. He would have burned the house down, but to get the shit, not to destroy it."

"So who could have done it? Who were your enemies?"

"They weren't after us," he says. "We were what you assholes call 'innocent bystanders.' "

"How do you know that?"

"Because I ran my own little investigation, you know? It wasn't nobody after us. No way."

"Maybe you didn't investigate that well," I say.

He frowns. "I'm the top guy in my operation, you understand? It starts and ends with me. If there was somebody out to get us, they wouldn't have done it when I wasn't there. If someone was pissed off, I'd be the guy they were after. And if they left me alive, they'd know they'd be in deep shit."

The argument makes sense, though of course the arsonist might have believed Double J was in the apartment. In any event, while his logic is surprisingly compelling, it's nothing that advances the ball for me, and certainly nothing I can use in court.

Marcus and I leave and head back downstairs, where Laurie is still watching over the two unconscious morons who messed with Marcus.

"They're both breathing," she says.

"Is that meant to be good news?" I ask. "You think they might come after us?"

"Nunh," Marcus says.

Well put.

I've never been on a jury.

Since I vote in every election, I've been called for jury duty a bunch of times, but I've never made it on to a panel. There is more chance they would take an admitted Islamic terrorist than a defense attorney.

One time I went through voir dire on a DUI case, and the defense attorney pronounced that I was acceptable to their side. The prosecutor, a friend of mine named Norman Trell, said that he was rejecting me "for cause." When the judge asked him to state the cause, Norman laughed and said, " 'Cause he's a defense attorney!"

But at this moment I know how jurors feel, because it's verdict time in the Noah Galloway trial that's been taking place in my mind. For me to take the case, or at least to try and convince Noah to plead not guilty, I have to be able to find reasonable doubt in my own mind, which is pretty much what juries have to do in order to acquit.

Of course, in this case I can impanel whoever I want as my fellow juror, and since I'm thinking about this in bed, the logical candidate is the woman I sleep with, Laurie Collins. As a former police officer, she's generally more of a prosecution-favoring witness, but if I don't use her, there's no alternate to choose from, since I'm monogamous.

Laurie and I go over what we've learned about the case so far. Within ten minutes she says, "I've got doubts. I think you should go to trial."

"That was quick. I was hoping we could deliberate a while longer, maybe even sequester ourselves."

"No reason," she says. "I'm sure."

"How can that be?"

"Beam yourself," she says.

Laurie often employs a rather unique decision-making technique. She imagines beaming herself into a future situation that will result from her decision. She goes on to imagine how she will feel, and if it is intolerable, then she'll beam herself a second time, with the decision variable reversed. Often the second beaming results in a more palatable situation.

163

"I don't think I'm in a beaming mood," I say.

"Try it. It'll clear things up."

"Okay. Where am I beaming myself?"

"The courtroom. You've just watched Noah enter a guilty plea, and the judge is in the process of sentencing him. He's calling him the perpetrator of an unbelievably heinous act, and he takes pleasure in sentencing him to a maximum security prison for the rest of his natural life."

I'm going along with this, imagining myself in that situation, and it truly does feel awful. But beaming myself into months of a difficult, probably futile murder trial doesn't brighten my mood either.

"Let me speak to juror number three," I say, and I get out of bed and walk over to the corner of the room, where Tara is sound asleep on a bed of her own. She has a contented smile on her face; maybe she's beaming herself to the biscuit aisle at Petsmart.

I wake her by petting her head and saying, "Bark if you think I should take this to trial."

Stunningly, shockingly, she sits up and barks. I turn around in amazement to see if Laurie has seen this, and Laurie is grinning and holding up a rawhide chewie where Tara

164

can see it. The prospect of chewies gets her to bark one hundred percent of the time.

I get up and head back to bed. "Doesn't matter what Tara thinks; Galloway saved her life, so she's biased. I'm rejecting her for cause."

Laurie goes over to give Tara the chewie, and says to her, "Don't listen to him. You can be the jury forewoman."

Visiting Noah in jail is unlike visiting any client I've ever had.

The trappings are the same . . . the security routine upon entry, the dreary grey room with the metal table, the sullen guards, and the strict attention to routine. The change begins when Noah is brought in.

He seems genuinely happy to see me. He even seems happy to see Hike, as counter-intuitive a reaction as I can imagine. But that in itself is not unusual. The incarcerated, especially those who haven't been convicted, always like it when their lawyers show up. The reason for this, simply put, is that there is always the possibility they are bringing good news.

Noah doesn't really seem to care what kind of news we're bringing, if any. He has accepted his fate, and considers it just and fitting. He welcomes our arrival not because we might change that fate, but rather because he's looking forward to a conversation with people he regards as new friends.

I'm about to shake up his world, and I'm not sure I should.

We exchange pleasantries, though pleasantries with Hike are fairly difficult to achieve. Noah mentions that he has a cold, which sends Hike off on a diatribe about attracting diseases in close quarters.

"That's the problem with airplanes," he says. "You're in a close area, sucking down everybody's germs. And cruise ships, they're the worst. If you take a plane to a cruise ship, your chances of winding up in a hospital with tubes down your throat are like eighty percent."

Noah is not quite sure how to respond to this, so he makes a joke and says, "Maybe I should try and get into the prison hospital. It's probably nicer in there."

Hike practically snorts his disagreement. "Yeah, I'm sure it's great. You probably have to cut through the bacteria with a machete and a blowtorch."

"Maybe we should talk about your case," I say to Noah.

"Sure. Have you talked to the prosecutor again?"

"No, we've been doing more background work about the fire, and your potential involvement in it."

"Potential involvement?"

"Right. I told you that I wasn't comfortable with where we were, that Danny Butler's detailed knowledge of the crime didn't seem to fit with the theory that you set it."

He nods. "Right. I guess I thought we'd be past that by now."

"Noah, I can't get past it. At least not yet."

"What does that mean?"

"It means that I, Hike and I, have real doubts that you did this at all. So unless you have anything more to add, I can't help you plead guilty. If I'm to be your lawyer, we're going to trial."

"Andy, you know how I feel about this," he says.

I nod. "I do, and I respect that. And obviously you know that you can give in and not fight this. We just won't be here to watch."

"The public defender could guide me through it?" he asks.

"Absolutely."

"I can't put Becky through a trial."

"A trial is what Becky wants."

He doesn't answer for a minute or so, so I plunge ahead. "Noah, when you were using drugs, when it was really bad, how important was it for you to get them?"

168

"I hope you never understand how important it was," he says. "Getting what I needed became everything. Every day was an urgent day."

"And that room, in that house, was where you would get your drugs?" I ask.

"Yes."

"And there were always drugs in that room?"

"To my knowledge, yes."

"So you set fire to it?"

He seems to recoil from the jolt. It was right there in front of us, him and me, but neither of us had seen it.

Finally, "Nothing could have made me do that. Nothing in the world."

I smile. "Then let's get to work."

The key to finding this killer could be learning who he meant to kill.

That's not usually the case, and it's a sign of how dismal our situation is. Usually the intended murder victim is obvious; he's the one in the wooden box.

Not this time.

So we need to learn everything we can about who was in the house that night, and what they were doing there. Of course, we can't ask them, because murder victims are notoriously tight-lipped.

Sam has provided us with as many details as he can about the occupants of the house, but they're sketchy, as evidenced by the fact that three of the victims remain unknown to this day. I assign him the equally difficult task of finding friends and relatives of the deceased so that we can interview them.

In the meantime, I need to speak to the one person who escaped the house that night. His name is Antonio Esperanza, and he was twelve years old at the time of the fire. I'm particularly interested in talking to him, not only because he's the sole survivor, but because he lived on the third floor.

The fire department reports show that the chemical mixture was spread on the first and third floors. The first floor makes sense, because the fire obviously burns up. Setting it on the third floor would not really have been necessary, since with the intensity level and heat of the blaze, the upper floors would have quickly collapsed anyway. It leads me to wonder if someone or something on the third floor could have been a target.

Antonio had jumped from a window and fractured both his legs, but lived to tell about it. Hopefully he'll tell us about it. He proves easy to find, mainly because his last known address is listed in the police reports. He doesn't live there anymore, but it provides a simple way for Sam to track him down.

Antonio, who Sam learns is not surprisingly called "Tony," lives in Clifton but works at a Taco Bell in Elmwood Park. I decide that I'll talk to him at work, since if I go to his home I'll have less chance of having a steak quesadilla after the interview.

Laurie insists on going with me for another reason, though she is also a major Taco Bell fan. She thinks that whenever I go off to interview a witness it could be dangerous, and she has no confidence whatsoever in my ability to deal with danger. It doesn't matter who the prospective witness is; I could be questioning Mother Teresa, and Laurie would fear for my safety.

Laurie and I arrive at the Taco Bell, which has recently added a small Pizza Hut menu, apparently for diversity. "See, I don't approve of that," I say.

"Why not?"

"Because tacos are tacos and pizza is pizza."

"Wow, that is profound," she says. "Have you got a pen? I want to write that down."

We've gotten here at ten-thirty in the morning, the time that they open, to reduce the likelihood that Tony would be too busy to talk to us. There is one car in the drive-thru lane, but we are the only ones in the restaurant itself.

We ask the young woman behind the register if we could speak to Tony, but she doesn't take the time to respond. All she does is immediately yell out, "Tony!" It's obviously a fast-talk, as well as fast-food, establishment.

A young man comes out from the back,

and says, "What's up?" The young woman, perhaps afraid she's going to use up her word quota for the day, simply points to us. So Tony comes over to us and asks, "What's up?" — a phrase he has apparently mastered.

"My name is Andy Carpenter," I say. "This is Laurie Collins We're investigating the fire."

Tony physically pulls back from the words. "Oh, man, again? I told that cop everything I knew. All of a sudden everybody wants to talk to me."

"I'm sorry, but someone has been arrested, and we need to determine if they have the right person." I'm skirting the issue, trying not to identify myself as Noah's attorney. Since three of Tony's relatives were killed in the fire, and he himself was injured, he might not be too inclined to talk to someone on Noah's side.

"It may not be him?" Tony asks.

"We're just trying to make sure," I say.

We go over to a table near the window, and I ask Tony to tell us whatever he remembers about that night.

He takes a deep breath and says, "I was asleep; it was after midnight. This really loud noise woke me up; it sounded like I was in a wind tunnel, or something. Or maybe one of those big storms, like a tornado.

"But when I looked around, everything seemed to be okay. I thought I heard yelling over the noise, but I couldn't be sure. So I went to open the door, and the handle . . . the doorknob . . . burned my hand. But it was too late, the door opened just a little bit, and all these flames and air came flooding into the room. I think the air was hotter than the flames.

"I wanted to go through the door, my mother and two sisters were in there, but there was no way I could. I swear, there was no way. By then my room was on fire; there were flames everywhere. So all I could do was jump out the window, and hope they had made it out okay.

"They didn't."

He says all this without much apparent emotion, almost as if he's reading the words from a script. Some self-preservation instinct has enabled him to deal with this and continue to function in society.

"We're so very sorry," Laurie says, and I echo those sentiments. It's almost impossible to imagine what this young man has been through.

"Did you know a lot of people in that building?" I ask.

174

"No . . . not too many. A lot of people would move in and out, and then there were some people my mother warned my sisters and me to stay away from."

"Who were they?" Laurie asks.

"There were two apartments on the first floor; my mother said they were drug dealers."

"Do you think they were the targets of the fire?" I ask.

He shrugs. "I guess. No way for me to really know."

"Who did you know?"

"There was a kid my age on the second floor . . . I forget his name — maybe William something. I was in his apartment a few times. I met his mother, but I don't think he had a father, at least not one that lived there."

"Anyone else?"

"Not really. I met the lady who lived across the hall a couple of times. You know, just to say hello in the hallway. She only lived there about a year. Once she had the baby, I didn't see that much of her. But people came to see her, sometimes they were dressed in suits."

"Do you know her name, or what the people wanted?" I ask.

"No. And then there was a lady on the

second floor, Charisse. My mother warned me about her too. I didn't know why at the time, but now that I know more . . ." He looks at Laurie, as if trying to decide to continue. "I think she was probably a hooker, you know? Maybe the lady across the hall was as well."

"Is there anything you can think of, anything at all, that would lead you to believe that someone in the apartment building had terrible enemies who might have done this?"

"No. I'm sorry, but no."

"Where did you go after the fire, Tony?" Laurie asks.

"Well, I was in the hospital for a while, maybe a month, and then I went to live with my aunt."

"Are you still with her?"

"I'm in her apartment. She died a couple of months ago."

"I'm sorry." Laurie and I both say it simultaneously. We could say we're sorry to Tony for the next ten years, and it wouldn't cover it. Nor would it help him any.

"Andy, make a right into that 7-Eleven."

"Why? What do you need?" I ask, but Laurie doesn't answer. She seems to be focused on something in the mirror.

"Laurie?"

She still doesn't answer, at least not right away, and I pull into the strip mall parking lot and turn off the car.

"Go in and buy something. Take your time about it."

"What am I supposed to buy?" I ask, more confused than normal.

"Doesn't matter. I think we're being followed, and I want to make sure."

I get out of the car and go into the store, and I notice that Laurie is starting to make a call on her cell phone. Once inside, I start to wander the aisles, pretending to be looking for something. Since there are only two aisles, and since I'm the only person in the store, the cashier starts to look at me a little strangely.

"Can I help you?" she asks.

I give her my most charming smile, for which there is no known defense. "Just browsing; everything looks so good." The fact that I'm standing in front of laundry detergent and bleach may be one reason why she doesn't return the smile or seem at all captivated. Instead, she stays silent and keeps watching me.

I look through the window and see that Laurie is off the phone. She and I make eye contact, and she shakes her head slightly, telling me she's not ready for me to come back to the car.

I'm not feeling too significant to this process, but there's really nothing I can do about it right now. I take a bottle of bleach and a loaf of whole wheat bread, and bring it to the cashier. "How's it going?" I ask, pulling out all the conversational stops.

"That it?" is her response, referring to the two items I'm getting.

"You know something, give me a minute. I should get some sodas . . . to wash down the bread." I leave my items there and head back to the refrigerator case filled with drinks. I pretend to agonize over them, but don't take any because Laurie finally nods to me that it's okay for me to come out. I go back to the cashier, pay for the original items, and leave.

When I get back in the car, Laurie says, "What did you get?"

"Bread and a bottle of bleach. You mind telling me what's going on?"

"There's somebody following us; the car is parked diagonally across the street . . . don't look in that direction. I think it's just one male in the car, but I can't be positive."

"Are you sure about this?" I ask.

"Andy . . ." is how she admonishes me. She has spent most of her life as a police officer; this is her area of expertise.

"Okay, I believe you. What are we going to do about it?"

"It's already done. Marcus just got here; he's going to follow the guy following us. And then he'll learn whatever there is to learn."

"How?"

"By being Marcus," she says.

"So I should just drive home?"

"Yes. Normal speed. Don't look in the rearview mirror any more than you normally would."

"It's under control," I say. "You can count on me."

"We really didn't need any more bleach."

"I was under a lot of pressure."

It takes us another fifteen minutes to get home, during which time I don't see any sign of the car following us or Marcus. Neither Laurie nor I can think of any reason why we'd be under surveillance by anyone.

"But it's got to be related to the Galloway case," I say. "That's the advantage of having only one client; it's easy to narrow these things down."

Once we get into the house, Laurie peeks through the window to see if our stalker is on the street, but if he is, he's nowhere to be found.

Now all that there is left to do is wait for Marcus to call. I'm anxious for him to do so, but not so anxious that I'm going to answer the phone when it rings. One thing I don't need now is a conversation with Marcus, during which he utters undecipherable one-word grunts.

I'll leave that to Laurie.

Loney got lucky.

He was uncharacteristically late in arriving at the motel for the meeting with Camby, and therefore was able to see Carpenter's investigator enter the room. The guy didn't knock, or pick the lock; he just lowered his shoulder and almost casually forced the door open. As someone who had bashed in a few doors himself, Loney was impressed.

But more than lucky, Loney was smart. He was smart enough to have researched Carpenter and his team thoroughly, and he knew all about Marcus Clark. And one thing he knew for sure; Ray Camby was not going to stand up to him.

Recruiting Camby was a mistake; Loney had felt that from the moment he met him. But Camby had been recommended, and he did have some virtues. He would do what he was told, he had no hesitancy whatsoever

181

to break the law, and most important, he was expendable.

Loney could see through the window, and it was easy to tell that Camby was scared. Clark was going to force him to talk, and the problem was that Camby had plenty to say. At the top of that list were the dealings that he and Loney had had with Danny Butler.

Loney had the ability to remain calm and think clearly in a crisis, and it served him well here. His first idea was to shoot Clark; he had a clear view into the room, and a weapon that could easily bridge the distance.

But Clark seemed to be smart enough to stay out of the line of sight, and Loney could only get brief glimpses of him. Also, killing Clark would attract a lot of unwanted attention to Carpenter and the Galloway case.

The other option was to kill Camby before he could talk. Camby was visible through the window and Loney could pick him off with ease. Certainly, Camby's death would not be a significant loss to the operation, especially since his identity was now compromised.

The other key factor that Loney considered was that he was soon going to have to kill Camby anyway. He knew far too much, and when the ultimate task was accomplished, it would be far too risky to let him live. A lot of people would be dying, and Camby was to be one of many.

Now he would lead the way.

Once he had made the decision, Loney didn't hesitate. He took out his gun and in one smooth motion aimed and fired. The bullet made surprisingly little noise as it went through the motel room window, and it hit Camby square in the chest. The unnecessary second bullet went through his skull, and he went straight back and down.

Loney didn't see Clark after the shooting; he was obviously taking cover in anticipation of more shots. Loney retreated to a position farther from the motel, from where he would be able to see Clark's car leave, without being seen himself.

It was only three or four minutes before the car went by. Loney had not detected any other commotion; it seemed likely that the shooting had gone unnoticed.

Loney headed back to Camby's room for what would be a cleanup operation. He was not unhappy with how things turned out, and recognized the element of luck that had helped in the process.

But he also knew that intelligence and

resourcefulness were the qualities that had prevailed. They would continue to do so, right up to the time that the goal was reached, and everyone in the way was dead.

We wait almost five hours for Marcus to call us.

I'm so bored that I actually go on Facebook, something I probably haven't done in six months.

I understand that it's a social network, and that people feel it brings them together, but I just don't get it. People fill it with boring, uneventful moments in their day, I assume believing that other people care about it.

Why should I care if Sylvia Swathouse is "having a cup of tea"? But as dreary as that stuff is, the responses are even worse, and completely cloying. "Oh, Sylvia, that sounds so warm and wonderful." Or, "Is it chamomile, Syl? That's my favorite."

But everybody is doing it, even Hike. Though last time I looked, I was his only friend.

Laurie answers when Marcus finally calls,

and for the next three or four minutes, just listens, not saying a word. Since I know from past experience that Marcus is not exactly verbose, it's possible that the line has gone dead and neither of them knows it.

Finally, Laurie says, "Marcus, are you all right?"

Another minute goes by, and she says, "Okay. Right away," before she hangs up.

"The situation has taken a somewhat surprising turn," she says.

"Surprising good, or surprising bad?"

"You can make up your own mind about that. The guy tailing us waited down the block from here for about an hour, probably making sure we weren't going to leave. Finally he left, and made some stops around town, with Marcus following him all the way."

"Not too surprising thus far," I say.

"I'm getting there. Eventually he stopped at a motel on Route 4, where he apparently was staying. Marcus decided to intercept him at that point, and he entered the guy's room to question him."

"The guy let him in, or he broke the door down?" I ask

"I don't know, but one way or the other he got in. He was conducting an interrogation when two bullets came through the window and hit the man. Marcus took evasive action and was unharmed, and the sniper apparently fled the scene."

"Dead?" I ask.

She nods. "Very much so. Marcus was quite impressed with the killer's marksmanship."

"So what did Marcus do?"

"He grabbed some of the deceased's stuff, and then left. The room was in the back, and there was significant noise from the highway. The bullets went smoothly through the window, and no one seemed to notice. Marcus said there was no sign of the police being called."

"Where is Marcus now?"

"On the way here."

I suppose if I had normal human emotions, I would be reflecting on the tragic loss of life I just heard about. Fortunately, I'm not burdened with them, and I'm going to assume for the time being that the loss will be something that society can successfully recover from.

Instead I'm worried about Marcus, and whether he left traces of himself in the dead man's room. Those traces could be fingerprints, DNA, or a witness who saw him enter the room. I don't want to have to defend Marcus in a murder trial; juries would take one look at him and decide this is a person who should be taken off the streets. The trick would be to try and get twelve wardens on the jury, all of whom would greatly prefer Marcus stay on those streets and out of their jails.

Marcus arrives at the house, and indicates that he wants to talk to us in the kitchen. This allows him to be close to the refrigerator, which he clearly intends to empty. Marcus has the most amazing capacity to eat of anyone I've ever seen, and he's going to demonstrate it now.

If Marcus is shaken by today's events, he's hiding it well. The stress of the ordeal has him babbling at the rate of one word every few minutes, and his relating of the story takes what seems like a couple of days, with extra time for chewing.

Marcus is positive that he left no trace of himself at the scene, and seems slightly put off that I would suggest such a thing. Since Marcus is the person in the world I least want mad at me, I resist asking, "Are you sure?" If he's wrong, we'll find out soon enough anyway.

Marcus had looked around the room before he left for papers that might identify the dead man, but could find none. The guy was also not carrying a wallet; obviously his identity was to be kept a secret.

Marcus took the man's cell phone, which he places on our kitchen table, since that gives us the opportunity to know who he has been in touch with. He also took an empty beer bottle that was in the room for possible fingerprints. Marcus's mother did not raise a stupid child.

The man was carrying two handguns, which Marcus left at the scene. It scares the hell out of me that a heavily armed person was following Laurie and me, but it doesn't seem to bother her. To Laurie and Marcus, this is just another day at the office. I was clearly born with a defective courage gene.

With nothing left to tell, and absolutely nothing left to eat, Marcus leaves to go wherever it is that Marcus goes. I call Sam Willis and ask him to come over right away.

"What's going on?" he asks, probably wondering if he should pack his gun.

"I need your help tracing some phone records." Sam has amazing ways, none of which could possibly be legal, of finding out information like this on the computer.

"Oh."

Sam is at the house in fifteen minutes, and I give him the cell phone. "I want to know everyone he's called, and everyone who has called him."

"Going back how far?"

"The Revolutionary War." I also give Sam the motel name and room number and ask if he can check what calls were made from that room.

He nods. "Going out, but not coming in. They would come in to the main switch-board, and there's no way to know where they're directed from there. It's not like the motel was going to bill him for incoming calls."

"Sam, it's very important that you don't leave any trace of yourself in this."

"Of course not. Why?"

"Because the person who owned this phone and stayed in that room was mur-dered today."

Sam lights up like a little boy who's just been given a lollipop. "He was? Was he a bad guy or a good guy?"

"A bad guy."

"That is so cool . . . did you kill him?"

"Of course not."

"Did Marcus?"

"No."

He nods. "Cool. I'm on the case."

Once Sam leaves, my next call is to Pete. "I talked to Double J," I say.

"Good for you."

"He doesn't think Noah did it."

"Maybe you should try and get him on the jury," he says. "Are we nearing the point of this call?"

"I need your help."

"That is the sole reason for my existence."

"I have a beer bottle. I need it dusted for fingerprints, and then run through the computer for a match."

Pete is going to give me a very hard time about this, and I considered getting the information from a few other sources available to Laurie and me. But Pete is the only one I trust to do it quickly and discreetly, so I'm willing to endure the abuse.

"Does this relate to the Galloway case?" he asks.

"It does."

"Give me the beer bottle at Charlie's tonight," he says. I wasn't planning to go, but now I will. "You can give it to me in the parking lot, but keep it separate from the cases."

"What cases?"

"The two cases of beer you're going to give me for doing this for you. American beer, none of that stick-your-pinkie-out-when-you-drink stuff."

"You're demanding a payoff?" I ask.

"I am."

191

"I thought all you cared about was getting to the truth."

He pauses for a moment. "I see nothing about receiving beer that is inconsistent with the search for the truth."

"I'll see you at Charlie's," I say.

"I'm looking forward to it."

For the first time in the entire operation, Loney was worried.

He had made a couple of mistakes, and made some tough decisions, and they seemed likely to come back to haunt him.

His first mistake was hiring Camby, and then having him follow Carpenter. He had no respect for Camby's smarts or ability, and should have realized that Carpenter would realize he was being followed. Beyond that, there was little value in watching Carpenter at all, and certainly not enough to justify the risk.

Mistake number two, and a much bigger one, was in giving Camby a cell phone, and letting him use it to call Loney. Once Marcus Clark had left, Loney had gone into the motel room and done a quick search. Camby's phone was missing, and Loney assumed that Clark had taken it with him. That was a real problem.

Loney didn't feel in any personal jeopardy, at least not from the police and certainly not from Carpenter. Nor was he worried about the people who ran the operation; they were businessmen and weren't personally dangerous. They hired people to be dangerous for them, which was why Loney wound up in their employ.

No, the man Loney was worried about was his real boss, Carmine Ricci. Carmine provided the muscle for the operation; Loney was the prime example of that. Loney didn't know if Carmine got a piece of the action, or just a healthy fee, and it really wasn't Loney's business.

But whatever the arrangement, it was all predicated on Carmine being kept well out of it. Anything that came back to him personally, or caused him a moment of worry, was something that Loney was not to have happen.

This situation with Camby and the cell phone, while a couple of layers removed from Carmine, was still a cause for concern. And the first decision Loney had to make was whether to tell Carmine about it.

If he didn't tell him, there was always the chance that the phone records could lead to Loney's phone, and then eventually to Carmine, or people close to him.

But Loney knew something about the law, and he knew that Carpenter did not have subpoena power. Therefore the phone records would be difficult, if not impossible, to obtain, and in any event the process would be very time-consuming.

Loney decided that it was a risk worth taking not to tell anyone, at least for the moment. He would be alert to problems as they came up, and he'd handle them the way he always handled problems.

By killing the people who created them.

But at the moment he had something else to do. He had a trial to stop.

Judge Anthony De Luca is the judicial version of me.

Just as I'm a lawyer who doesn't like lawyering, Judge De Luca is a judge who avoids judging whenever he can. I can respect that.

The way De Luca does it is to call the parties to the dispute before him, and ominously warn that a settlement is in their best interest. Since most cases result in a winner and a loser, it's a testament to De Luca's persuasiveness that he can make each side panic and feel their interests are in great peril. He served as an officer in army intelligence in his younger days, which may be where he acquired some of his talent for making people cave.

Of course, De Luca's tactics are more effective in civil cases than criminal ones, but while he used to operate mostly in that area, in recent years he has moved to almost exclusively handle criminal matters.

The reason for that is simple. De Luca comes from a very prominent local family, and they have long been fixtures in the legal and business communities. There have been Judge De Lucas as far back as the eighteen hundreds, and those De Lucas who haven't been judges have been practicing lawyers and leading businessmen. There are few major law or business schools in the country that haven't graduated a De Luca.

The problem with that is the fact that with their enormous extended family, it seemed like some De Luca, somewhere, had an interest in most civil matters that came before the court. Either a De Luca lawyer was representing one of the parties or a De Luca businessman was suing or getting sued.

If you stand in front of the courthouse and throw a dart, you'll hit a De Luca.

All this meant that Judge Anthony De Luca was constantly having to recuse himself, which on one level fit in with the deficient work ethic that he and I share. But it was getting embarrassing, so he switched to criminal court. There were far fewer De Lucas to be found there.

He still tries to intimidate the lawyers into settling their cases without a trial, but has far less success in criminal court. Most resistant to his strong-arm tactics are cases which are very public and in which there are political considerations.

Both of those things are very prevalent in the Galloway case, so it is unlikely that the hearing he has convened today will have any effect. Of course, Dylan doesn't know that, and he probably still believes we may cave and avoid a trial.

I bring Hike with me, since for all his personality issues, he's as smart an attorney as I've ever met. Dylan brings four lawyers from his office, all young and fresh-faced and carrying identical briefcases. They represent the cream of the crop from the law school at Cookie Cutter U, but I'd bet Hike could wipe the legal floor with them.

The gallery is empty, because De Luca has dictated that the hearing was to be closed. He is planning to cajole or intimidate, whatever is necessary, and he wants to do it in private.

There are a lot of press gathered outside, which is very unusual for a pretrial hearing with a defendant not named Simpson. It's a sign of what will be intense interest in the actual trial.

Once we're all seated, Judge De Luca asks, "Where are we, gentlemen?"

Dylan just about jumps to his feet. "The

state is ready to proceed at whatever trial date Your Honor sets." He's acting like he's hoping for a positive report on "parent-teacher night."

De Luca turns to me. "Mr. Carpenter?"

"We're ready as well, Your Honor," I lie. "The sooner the better."

I can see a flash of surprise in Dylan's face, which quickly turns into a confident smile.

In any event, Judge De Luca is not smiling. "Have you had settlement discussions?"

"We've talked," Dylan says. "I was waiting to hear whether the defense wanted to proceed to trial."

"Well, now you've heard," I say. "Your Honor, an innocent man is sitting in prison, waiting for his vindication. The sooner the truth comes out in this case, the better."

"It sounds like you're playing to the jury, Mr. Carpenter, but I don't see one here."

I smile. "I'm practicing, Your Honor."

"Do it on your own time."

"Yes, Your Honor. But there is no chance that we will accept any arrangement that leaves Mr. Galloway incarcerated. We would, however, support a motion by Mr. Campbell to dismiss the charges, provided it were accompanied with a gracious apology."

De Luca pushes and prods a bit more, but

even he can see there is no room for compromise here. Dylan has no intention of making a deal, and with his evidence, he shouldn't. I won't make a deal because there's no way I'm going to allow a client to plead guilty when I don't believe it to be the case. Noah would have to find another lawyer for that, and right now he doesn't want to.

Dylan must be surprised that I've exercised our right to a speedy trial. It's counterintuitive; the defense usually seeks as many delays as possible. But Noah's deal with me is that we move quickly, due to a probably misguided belief that it would be easier on Becky. What would actually be best for Becky is for Noah to be acquitted.

De Luca asks if there's anything else to discuss, and I refer to the brief that we have submitted requesting a change of venue. Hike wrote it, and it was a solid presentation that should prevail on the merits, but in the real world doesn't have a chance. Dylan has submitted an opposing brief, no doubt written by one of his devoted minions.

"I've read the briefs," De Luca says. "I'll issue a ruling shortly."

"Thank you, Your Honor. We believe it effectively points out the dangers inherent in conducting the trial in this jurisdiction." I believe what I am saying; this was a heinous crime, one of the most notorious in local history. The press coverage was overwhelming then, and shows signs of being so now. There is no doubt in my mind that it would be easier to impanel an unbiased jury, if there is such a thing, elsewhere.

Dylan quickly and confidently sums up his opposition. My goal in the trial will be to wipe that confident look off his face, and I'll goad him to do so. Dylan has a thin skin, and is prone to mistakes when angry. As Laurie would be the first to say, I can irritate anyone.

But Dylan is going to emerge from today's hearing a winner, and De Luca revealingly says, "Perhaps I have more faith in our judicial system than you do, Mr. Carpenter."

"With respect, Your Honor, a change of venue is not a violation of that system." I'm going down in flames, and annoyed by it.

De Luca is dismissive. "As I said, I will issue a ruling shortly. But I would suggest you not purchase plane tickets just yet. Now, is there anything else?"

I object to the state's decision to charge Noah with four counts of murder. Technically, if Noah was acquitted, they could come back and charge him with the other twenty-two deaths, without violating his double-jeopardy rights. It's a chickenshit thing for Dylan to do, but I don't have a legal leg to stand on, and De Luca points that out.

When Hike and I leave the courtroom, we opt to walk right out the front door, into the waiting questions of the press that are camped out there. Our client is accused of being a mass murderer, a killer who burned twenty-six victims to death. People like that, even people alleged to be like that, are not usually favorites of the general public. The same general public from which we will choose our jury. The same general public we therefore need to suck up to.

I mouth platitudes about how anxious we are to get to trial and clear Noah's good name, and how confident we are that justice will prevail.

"No chance of a plea bargain, Andy?" The questioner is Dina Janikowski, a reporter who works for Vince at the *Bergen News.* Vince must like her, because when someone mentions her name in his presence, he doesn't snarl or spit.

I look shocked, as if it was absurd to consider such a thing. "Would you admit to killing twenty-six people if you had nothing to do with it?"

She smiles, knowing better than to get drawn into this kind of back-and-forth. "No one has accused me, Andy."

"Then you're very, very lucky. Because innocent people can be victimized by overzealous prosecutors. The fact that Noah Galloway is sitting in jail is proof positive of that."

It's a parting shot at Dylan that will anger him when he sees it on the news. There's even a chance he'll take me off his Christmas card list.

Sam Willis is getting frustrated.

When I give him an assignment to research something on the computer, he takes definite pride in giving me a complete, accurate report on a timely basis.

He couldn't do that, at least not to his satisfaction, when it came to learning who was killed in the fire. The information was vague, and three people are still unidentified. Sam also had trouble identifying surviving family members for some of the victims.

The problem is that the only information you can get from the Internet is information that has been entered into it. While that encompasses almost everything in recorded history, there are exceptions, and Sam has just hit on another one.

Sam comes to the office to report on the phone that Marcus took from the dead body in the motel. "It's registered to Buster

Douglas," he says.

"The fighter that beat Mike Tyson?" I ask.

"No, this guy couldn't beat Mike Tyson. He couldn't beat you."

"Because he's dead?"

Sam shakes his head. "No, because he doesn't exist, never did. Fake address, fake driver's license number, fake Social Security number, fake everything."

"Not a major surprise," I say. "Do we know who he called, and who called him?"

"Partially. He only made seventeen calls in the last month. Six were to a landline number in Missoula, Montana, and the other eleven were to a New York City cell number. He only received four calls in that time, all from the same New York number as the one he called."

"Why did you say 'partially'?"

"The number in Montana is to a Doris Camby; I've got the address. But the New York number is registered to Trevor Berbick."

"That's another guy that fought Tyson," I say.

Sam nods. "And he doesn't exist either. And both Berbick and Douglas paid their phone bills in cash, so there's no way to trace them back."

What Sam is saying is disappointing, but

not necessarily without promise. "You up for some more work?" I ask.

"Of course."

"Good. Then check out this Doris Camby; find out what she does, and whether she has any family. If she has any close male relatives, maybe a husband or son, try and find out where they are."

"I'm on it. Anything else?"

"Check out her phone bill; see who she's called. But most importantly, check out the phone bill listed in Berbick's name; let's find out who he called. If he's using a fake name, then he's likely somebody we'll be interested in."

"If I find out where he lives, you want me and Marcus to pay him a visit?"

"That's about as bad an idea as any I've ever heard," I say.

"Come on, Andy. I'm ready for some real detective work."

I nod. "Maybe you and Hike can work the streets as a team."

"Me and Hike?" he asks, panic in his voice. "I think I'd work better alone."

"He's really a laugh a minute when you get to know him."

"I know him."

"Sam, all kidding aside, what you're doing on the computer is really important. Believe it or not, it's the best thing we have to go on at this point."

He nods, resigned. "Okay, I hear you."

Sam leaves, and Mr. Barrel of Laughs himself comes in a few minutes later. I brief him on what Sam has found out, and Hike says, "Time to start focusing on the defensive side of the ball."

I know what he means. The investigation, the effort to find the real killer, represents the offensive side of the game plan. But we are defense lawyers, and we need to spend time refuting the prosecution's version of events. That is the defensive side of the ball, and almost always the most important side. We don't have to reveal the real killer, all we have to do is raise a reasonable doubt that it was Noah.

The first step in doing that is to become totally familiar with every single fact in the case. There can be no hesitation in court, no surprises. We must know everything Dylan and his witnesses are going to say and do before they say and do it. Stretching the football analogy a bit, it's like I am the quarterback, and when I get to the line of scrimmage, I have to be completely familiar with whatever formation the defensive team presents to me.

The only way to do that is to review the

discovery evidence repeatedly, until we know every nuance. By definition, there are dangers for us on every page; we must know them and counter them.

The preparation for a murder trial is intense and all-consuming, but there is no substitute for it, so Hike and I settle down for the long haul.

Fun time is over.

For Judge Walter Holland, the trial seemed surreal.

On the surface, it seemed to be business as usual. Two sets of lawyers arguing over minutiae that absolutely no one, other than themselves and the people they represent, cared about.

Both sides had positions that they repeatedly affirmed to be correct beyond question. Should their firms happen to have been employed by the other side, they would have taken equally passionate stands a hundred eighty degrees from where they were in this trial.

But for Judge Holland, things were anything but normal. He was trying to act impartial, to pepper each side with the same intensity and amount of difficult, probing questions. He was the "trier of fact," and personal bias or other considerations could have no part of his process.

Of course, he ordinarily didn't have to "act" impartial, since he had always been impartial. It was something he'd prided himself on, something he always took for granted. It's not that he hadn't had personal biases, everyone does, but until this trial he'd been able to check them at the courthouse door.

The irony was that he had no idea why he was being called on, why the marker was finally being cashed. The stakes in the trial were potentially significant, but certainly no more so than many other cases he'd presided over, and probably less than most. But he'd waited six long years for this to happen, and the hammer was being dropped for a very significant reason, even if he didn't know what that reason was.

He could only hope that this was the last time that hammer would be dropped. For that he was relying on the honor of people with absolutely no honor at all.

It was a terrible position to be in, and it was entirely his own fault.

After the lunch break that day, one of the lawyers reported that their next witness had taken ill, and they were requesting an adjournment for the day. In the morning, if that witness was still unavailable, they would have another witness there to take his place.

Judge Holland was happy to grant the request; he would have been happy to grant a year's adjournment. Every day in court was terribly painful for him, the culmination of six years of pain. This delay would give him time to get home and be with Alice and Benji.

Work had always consumed a great deal of his time, and more of his mind, but lately it had been even worse. Alice had been characteristically understanding, possibly because he had never confided the truth to her. Benji had been preoccupied with wondering what he would be getting for Christmas, and making out lists of possibilities.

It was on his way home that Judge Holland got the call on his cell phone. Somehow the man known as Loney only called when he was available to take it; it was as if he was watching him. Holland wouldn't put it past him.

"Short day today, Your Honor?"

Asking questions that he already knew the answer to was one of the eight billion things about Loney that annoyed him.

"Didn't feel very short."

"You were hard on our side," Loney said.

"I was hard on both sides. That's my role."

"Good. Because it's very important that you completely understand your role. Right through to the end."

"You have nothing to worry about," Holland said. "I'm going to do this the way we agreed, and then I'm never going to hear from you again."

"You don't enjoy our little chats?" Loney asked, the cold amusement evident in his voice.

"I don't."

"That pains me," Loney said, laughing a mocking laugh. "I cherish our time together. But you have a full life, what with Alice and Benji."

As it always did, the mention of his family sent a chill through him. "Don't call me again. I don't want to hear your voice ever again."

"You know something, Judge? Sometimes we don't get what we want." Then he laughed again. "Except for me. I always get what I want."

When he clicked off the call he was still laughing.

I haven't really been keeping Tara up to date on the case.

At least not as much as I should. After all, she's the reason I took it on, and she has an emotional investment in it. Filling her in is the least I can do.

The truth is, I consult with Tara a great deal on all my cases. I often find it helpful to verbalize my thoughts and ideas, and she is a willing listener. She's also discreet; when I tell her something, I can be sure she won't go barking it around the neighborhood.

So tonight I am planning to take Tara for a walk through Eastside Park, down near the ball fields, where nobody will overhear us. It's a setting that Tara loves; the park provides a seemingly endless supply of alluring scents.

I take out the leash, but then decide to check something in the case file, and we don't leave right away. Tara is not pleased

213

by the delay, and she barks at me a few times.

"Can you be a little flexible on this?" I ask her. "Don't forget, I'm only working this case as a favor to you."

Her look tells me she's not impressed by my argument, and she barks a few more times. I take the leash again, and we're off.

"Among the many things I don't understand," I tell her after we're about a block away, "is why this all started up now. Why would someone wait six years to have Butler go to the Feds with his accusations? Something must have happened, it might even still be happening now, that has put someone in jeopardy."

Tara's not barking a word; she knows better than to interrupt my train of thought at times like this. I almost wish she would; there's something in the back of my brain that I can't seem to get to come to the front where I can see it.

"I'm missing something," I say. "Actually, I'm pretty much missing everything."

We walk for another hour, during which time I get absolutely no clarity. I would stay out longer, but Laurie is home, and it's nearing bedtime. The outbreak of nuclear war would not be enough to get me to miss bedtime with Laurie.

Unfortunately, this particular bedtime is going to be somewhat delayed, as Pete's car is pulling up in front of the house when I get home. Whenever I visualize Laurie and me in bed together, Pete is nowhere to be seen.

"To what do I owe this rare pleasure?" I ask. "And how long will you be staying?"

"I ran the fingerprint from the beer bottle."

"Great, but you didn't have to deliver the news personally," I say.

"Oh yes, I did."

He says that in a somewhat ominous fashion, but I'll find out what's going on soon enough. "Come on in."

When we get inside the house, Laurie is in the den reading. "Laurie, honey, look what I found outside in the street. A pathetic urchin. Do we have any porridge we can spare?"

"Don't listen to him, Pete," she says.

"It's hard not to; he never shuts up."

"You want a beer?" I ask.

"I'm on duty."

"You want a Shirley Temple?" When he doesn't answer, I ask him who the print on the bottle belonged to.

"Guy by the name of Ray Camby. Local muscle, available for hire."

215

Camby is the name of the party that the phone was linked to in Montana. "Originally from Montana?" I ask.

"How the hell do I know? And who gives a shit?"

"Anything else you can tell me about him?" I ask. "Without being surly?"

"Well, there is one other thing, sort of a funny coincidence."

"What's that?"

"Well, it's the darnedest thing. Seems they fished Camby's body out of the Passaic River this morning. You have a beer with him, and then he turns up dead. What are the odds against that?"

"Poor guy," I say. "Do you know where the services are being held? I feel like I should send something."

"Boys, boys . . ." Laurie admonishes.

"How do you live with this pain in the ass?" Pete asks her.

"I stay heavily medicated," she says.

He nods and turns back to me. "You want to tell me what you know about Camby's death here, or you want to come to the station and answer the questions?"

"That's a tough one," I say. "Go down to the station with you, or stay here with Laurie and Tara. It's a coin flip, that's for sure."

"Playtime's over. Talk to me."

I nod. "He took a bullet in the head at the Castle Inn; it's a motel on Route 4. Room 131 in the back."

"You were there?" he asks.

"No, but I had inside information, which will remain inside."

"Did Marcus kill this guy?"

"No," I say. "Absolutely not. I would have much preferred Camby remained alive to answer questions. Not as grueling as these, of course. Camby had been following me; Laurie noticed him."

Laurie nods. "He was killed before Marcus could question him, Pete. That's the truth."

Pete nods. For some reason he believes Laurie and thinks I'm full of shit. It wounds me terribly.

"Why was he following you?" Pete asks.

I shrug. "It would have been nice to ask him that. But you can bet it had something to do with the Galloway case."

"You don't know that."

"Good point, Sherlock. It's just a co-incidence. Just like it's a coincidence that Danny Butler got killed, and that he came forward after all these years to talk to the Feds . . ."

As I'm saying this, what I couldn't think

of while I was walking with Tara hits me between the eyes. "Pete, why did Butler go to the Feds?"

"He said he had information implicating your boy."

I shake my head. "But why the Feds? This was a local case; you'd been working on it for years. In fact, the Feds had to drum up the Interstate Commerce thing to even get involved. Why would Butler go to them? Why not you?"

"Good question," he says, after thinking about it for a few moments.

"Maybe he didn't think you'd believe him," Laurie says.

Pete considers this for a while as well; he seems to be pondering something that he is not inclined to share with us.

The silence becomes interminable and I prompt him with, "Pete?"

He finally says, "Maybe."

"Any idea why that would be?" I ask. "And if you can answer in under twenty minutes, we'd appreciate it."

He just nods, turns, and leaves the house, leaving Laurie and me staring at each other. "What the hell was that about?" I ask.

"I imagine we'll find out eventually," she says. "I'm going to bed. You coming?"

"Is that a serious question?"

It's the routine that was getting Becky Galloway through the day.

Nothing exciting, just the normal chores in a life that would never again be normal. But she had come to embrace them, to focus on them, and it provided a small sense of security and calm, amid the chaos.

Going to the market, paying the bills, taking Adam to and from school . . . these were the kinds of things that filled Becky's day. And every moment she thought about them was a moment she didn't obsess over Noah's nightmare situation.

So Becky had learned that in fact life really does go on, and dealing with it could be a welcome distraction. But at night, in the dark with the lights off, well, that was another story.

Becky had decided to plant a wide array of flowers in the garden behind their house. The actual planting wouldn't take place until spring, but planning it now helped divert Becky's mind from real life.

So part of this afternoon was spent at the garden supply store on Route 17 in Paramus, trying to decide what plants would go best with each other, and which would thrive in the soil behind the house. She had long consultations with the very knowledgeable store employees, and she agonized over the decision as if it had the slightest consequence on her pain-filled life.

She finally made her choice, spent more than she should have, and only left the comfort and sweet smells of the place because she had to pick up Adam at school.

She went out to the parking lot, and loaded up everything in the trunk. Then she got into the car and looked in the rearview mirror, so that she could back out.

And saw nothing.

The mirror had no reflection, it was somehow empty, and even before Becky realized it had been covered with black tape, she felt the hand on her neck. She screamed and jumped in fright, but could not move, such was the power in the fingers that were holding her down.

"Calm down, Becky," Loney said. "Calm down and be quiet. You're going to get through this." He pressed tighter on the back of her neck, a not-so-subtle message that she was powerless to resist him.

"What do you want?"

"I want you to listen to me, very carefully. It will be quick, and then you can go pick up Adam at nursery school. You should be on time, but if you're not, Mrs. Dembeck will wait with him."

Loney's words sent a chill through her; this man knew where Adam went to school, and who his teacher was. The familiarity was the most frightening thing she had ever experienced.

"Okay? We understand each other?" he asked.

"Yes."

"Good. Your husband is a mass murderer, Becky. Everyone already knows that. All I want is for him to admit it to the world. Plead guilty, reject the travesty of a trial, and live out his life in prison."

She was not about to argue Noah's guilt or innocence with this man; she did not want to provoke him. "I'll talk to Noah about it," she said. "I will."

"Don't lie to me, Becky. Don't say what you think I want to hear to get rid of me."

"I swear, I'll talk to him. I'll try and convince him."

"Becky, Becky, Becky . . ." he said, as if

he was disappointed in her. "You haven't even let me convince you yet."

"Please don't hurt me." She would have added, "or Adam," but she didn't even want to give voice to that possibility.

"No need for that at all," Loney said. "I just wanted to point out that with Noah in prison, you're going to need money to live. If he pleads guilty, that will never be a problem for you. You have my word on that."

"Okay."

"Of course, if he goes ahead with the trial, you and Adam won't need money to live, because you won't be alive." He paused for a moment. "Becky, we can get to you both. Anywhere."

She tried not to let her voice reveal the terror she was feeling. "I understand."

"Good; understanding is important. Now get out of the car and walk back into the store. Do not turn around, or I will have to shoot you. Come back in ten minutes, and then go pick up Adam. Do not call the police, or neither of you will live until tomorrow. Do you understand all of this?"

"Yes."

There was some movement and she saw his gloved hand place something on the front passenger seat. It was a large box, gift-wrapped.

"Please accept this gift as a token of our understanding. You can open it when you get back."

Becky did exactly as he said, getting out and walking into the store, her legs shaking so much that it was hard to walk. When she came back out he was gone, but the package was still on the front seat.

She didn't open it then, instead driving toward Adam's school. But then she realized that she didn't want him in the car with it without knowing what it was, so she pulled over a few blocks from the school, took a deep breath, tore off the wrapping paper at the top, and opened it.

It was money, hundred-dollar bills spread out across the top. Sitting on top of the bills, bizarrely, was a CD labeled *Danny Boy,* by Bing Crosby.

Becky had never seen anything like it, and couldn't imagine how much money could be in the fairly deep box if it was filled with these bills. She started to dig into the box, pushing the bills to the side, until she hit something solid.

She moved all the bills to the side to see what was there, and that was when she screamed. She threw open the car door and staggered out, landing on all fours, throwing up in the grass along the sidewalk.

Left behind in the car was the box with the money. And underneath that money, encased in plastic, was the severed head of Danny Butler.

You could walk right through it, and not know anything was happening.

Of course, there would be no particular reason for you to walk through it, unless you made a habit of strolling through desolate, uninhabited land in east Texas.

There was some equipment there, a few machines and some deconstructed oil rigs, but that was to be expected. This was land that was owned by an oil company, just like millions of acres in this part of the country.

It was bought up cheap, and there was no certainty that it had oil reserves worth even that cost. But like much land both on and off shore, there was the potential for cashing in, so the companies bought it all up.

Only seven percent of such owned land was developed; the rest could sit there for a decade or more, waiting its turn. This particular piece, officially designated TX43765, held no more promise than any of the others.

Also, this land was owned by Milgram Oil and Gas, which was not exactly a behemoth in the industry. Milgram had to be careful with its resources, financial and otherwise, and was less inclined to drill on this kind of land than its larger competitors would be.

Milgram couldn't afford many dry wells, especially at this point, when they were being drained by an ongoing legal takeover fight. So they paid attention to the sites that were more likely to be moneymakers, and devoted the rest of their available cash to their wind-turbine program. That was the area that they hoped would save the company.

But while walking along the land would tell you very little, walking under it would be a revelation. Because down there was a series of underground mines and tunnels, built over the last six years. It was done without the knowledge of Milgram or any government entity, by people who literally came in under the cover of darkness.

As desolate as the land was, detection was always a danger. Milgram employed security, which patrolled the area on a random basis. As land leased by the government, federal agencies also had eyes occasionally open and watching. And the mining efforts themselves caused rumblings within the ground, detectable by instruments.

So the work was done in total secrecy, a little at a time, which was one of a number of reasons it was so time-consuming. Another was the danger inherent in the operation. Mining always came with its perils, but what these men were preparing to take out of the ground increased that danger many times over. To make it even more difficult, it was the deepest mine any of them had ever worked in.

But now the work was nearing a conclusion, and the men could only bide their time and wait for the signal.

The signal that would change the world forever.

If I'm ever in a foxhole, I want Becky Galloway in there with me.

Under the tremendous pressure and stress of the experience, she still acted intelligently and courageously. In a similar circumstance, I would have pissed in my pants and started calling for my mommy.

Her first concern was for Noah, and she didn't want to do anything that could impact negatively on his situation. So after calling the school and arranging for Adam to go to a neighbor's house, she called me. In a shaky, but remarkably calm voice, she told me what happened.

"Where is the package now?" I ask.

"Still on the seat of my car, in the grocery store parking lot. I put the lid back over it so no one can see in."

"Can you drive the car?" I'm not asking it literally, I mean is she emotionally able to get back in the car.

"It's not my first choice, but I can do it."

"Okay, then . . ." I start, then change my mind in mid-sentence. I am concerned that the guy who threatened her might come back. "Go in the store, but keep an eye on your car. Somebody is going to come there; he's going to be the scariest person you've ever seen, but he's on our side."

"What's his name?"

"Marcus. You get in the backseat, and he'll drive the car."

"Okay. Thanks," she says. Then, "Andy, I'm scared."

"I know, but it's going to get better."

I hang up and update Laurie on the conversation. She immediately calls Marcus and gives him his instructions. He's to bring Becky and the car to my house, where he will park it in the garage. Then we can figure out what to do.

Legally, our options are one and done. We are obligated to report what has happened, not so much because of the threat, but because of the severed head. We have knowledge of a crime, and even though that crime has long ago been reported in Vegas, it does not lessen our obligation.

Of course, I am not above disregarding legalities; it's part of my charm. My first concern is for my client, and a disclosure of this incident will not go well for him. Dylan is already planning to imply that Noah's friends disposed of Danny in a revenge killing; Noah's wife being in the possession of the missing head can only make the implication much stronger.

Then, of course, there is the matter of the threat to Becky and her child, and we will have to protect her. There is also the question of what we tell Noah, and how he will react. Knowing him as I do, he could decide to protect his family by pleading guilty, since that was his instinct in the first place.

Marcus pulls the car into the garage, and as I watch, he opens the back door for Becky to get out. Marcus with manners; the world must be spinning in the wrong direction.

He takes the box off the front seat, and he, Becky, and Danny's head come into the house. Laurie gives Becky a warm, comforting hug, and holds her as she breaks down crying. She kept her composure a lot longer than I would have.

Marcus puts the box with the decapitated head in it on the table. I take a quick look at it and instantly regret doing so. It is one ugly head.

Laurie examines it in a longer, more professional manner, and somehow deduces that Danny was strangled, and that his head was cut off after he was already dead. The fact that I sleep every night with a severed-head expert is a tad disconcerting.

"I'm sorry," Becky says when she's composed herself. "It was very frightening."

"Did you get a look at the man?" Laurie asks.

She shakes her head. "No. He was careful about that. But I think I would recognize his voice if I heard it again."

Under my prodding, she recounts everything she can remember about the incident. There is nothing in there that gives us a clue to his identity, and her mentioning that he was wearing gloves removes the chance of our getting fingerprints out of the car.

"Okay, first things first," I say. "We need to protect you and your son."

She nods. "I've thought about it. Adam and I can stay at my parents' house in Ohio. My father will come get us."

Laurie nods approvingly. "Good. Until he gets here Marcus can watch you."

"We need to tell Noah; he has a right to know about this."

Becky nods. "I'll do that, but it's not going to be fun."

"His reaction will be to consider changing his plea," I say.

"Maybe at first, but believe it or not, Noah is a fighter. He won't want these people to win. And the fact that they're out there will increase his belief in his own innocence. But there's one other problem."

"What's that?"

"Our dog. My father is allergic to her."

It's funny, but even though a dog was the reason I'm defending Noah in the first place, I never thought to ask if he has one now. I'm about to say that their dog can board at the Tara Foundation, when Laurie says, "She can stay here. What's her name?"

"Bailey."

"Is she a golden?" I ask.

"No. Thank you, Noah wouldn't have been able to stand it knowing she was in a dog run or a cage. He'll be happy she's here, with you and Tara, and so will I."

I tell her to bring the dog over any time, and then I look over at the box. "Okay, we all understand that any talk about this head cannot leave this room. But the head itself is definitely going to leave this room. Any thoughts about what we should do with it?"

"It's well preserved in the plastic," Laurie says. "I don't think we should bury or destroy it, in case we change our minds later and decide to report it to the authorities."

"And then there's the matter of the

money," I say. "It looks like a few thousand dollars, but I don't want to be the one to count it."

"Let's save it for a party when we win," Becky says.

Marcus, who hasn't said a word this entire time, picks up the box, and puts it under his arm.

"Sounds like a plan," I say.

Becky was not quite as persuasive with Noah as she had predicted.

She reported that he freaked out, so much so that the guard came in from outside the door to settle things down. Noah finally regained control; sometimes being chained to the table can do that for you. But he wouldn't agree to anything until he talked to me.

"Who is this guy?" he asks.

"I don't know," I say. "But I know what he wants; he wants to stop the trial."

"Why would it be so important for him for me to be convicted?"

"My guess, and it's just a guess, is that you're not the point here. It's the trial he cares about. He's afraid of what might come out; he doesn't want a spotlight put on this crime. Not after all these years."

"Then why send Danny Butler in the first place?"

"I don't know that either. But when we find that out we'll know the key to everything."

"And how are we going to protect Becky and Adam? I mean protect them beyond any doubt."

I explain the arrangements we are making, which Becky has already told him about. Marcus will watch her for the two days it will take for her father to get here, and they will bring the dog to live with us. As a recently retired police officer, Becky's father will have the friends and resources to protect her at his house in Ohio.

"Becky seemed to have confidence in this guy Marcus," he says.

"Marcus could beat up North Korea."

"Andy, you have no idea what it's like being in here, and having Becky and Adam in danger. It is the most frightening experience of my life."

"Noah, they will be safe, I promise you that."

"I can insure that by pleading guilty."

"Which would also insure Becky not having a husband and Adam not having a father, all because of a crime you didn't commit."

"You still believe that?"

"I'm positive of it. But we have to focus

on proving it."

"Okay. On one condition. You move the trial date up; I want it to start as soon as possible."

"It's already too early," I say. "It's not in your best interest."

"When the trial starts it takes away the incentive to threaten Becky; it would be too late."

"Noah . . ."

"Who'd stop you from moving it earlier? The prosecutor?"

"Are you kidding? Dylan would be happy to start in twenty minutes. It's the defense that benefits from delay. You, in case you were wondering, are the defense."

"What about the judge?" he asks.

I shrug. "His calendar is clear enough. He'd be willing to adjust the start date."

"How do you know that?"

"I checked; I knew you'd head in this direction."

He nods; his decision final. "Okay, let's do it."

"Noah, it can significantly impact your chances. We haven't nearly developed our case enough yet."

"I understand that, Andy, really I do. But I'm more worried about Becky and Adam. My eyes are wide open on this."

"I hear you," I say. "And I'll take care of it. But I've got a demand of my own, equally nonnegotiable."

"I'm not going to like this."

"Maybe, maybe not," I say. "But I'm going to take the steps necessary to get you put in solitary confinement."

"Why?"

"Because a sure way to stop a trial is to make it so that the defendant is no longer alive. That is something we need to avoid. For one thing, it would leave me alone at the defense table with Hike."

Noah laughs. "He can be a bit of a downer, huh?"

"He makes other downers look like uppers."

"Okay, solitary can't be any worse than this. But Andy, there's something I don't understand. Someone gets Danny Butler to come forward to accuse me, resulting in my arrest and trial. Then those same people kill Butler, and seem willing to do anything to prevent that trial. It doesn't make sense."

"Noah, I'm not the hardest worker in the world, and if I never had another case I'd be fine with it. But if there's one thing I like about my job, one thing I like about the system, it's that at its core it always makes sense. It's just up to us to find the sense in it. The answer is there; we just have to locate it."

"Are you always able to?"

"No. That's one of the parts I don't like."

"This guy spent a lot of time on the phone," Sam said.

He's talking about the owner of the New York cell phone that Camby called a number of times in the month before he took the bullet in the hotel room. The one registered in the name of Trevor Berbick.

"How many calls did he make?"

"A hundred and seventy-eight in the past month. To thirty-eight different numbers. And he called all over the country, New York, Chicago, L.A., San Francisco . . . eleven calls to Washington, D.C., and fourteen to Vegas. He made four calls to Camby's phone as well, including an hour before Camby died. And get this; he called Danny Butler three times."

"But we still can't identify him?"

"No chance; not from his phone records."

"What about Camby's motel room phone?"

"No calls went out; there's no way to know if any came in."

It's a sign of how grim our situation is that this is our most promising lead. Someone who followed me, and who was subsequently murdered, called a cell phone. We now have the records of numbers called by that second cell phone.

Big deal.

"I'm trying to attach names to the numbers that he called," Sam says. "It may take a day or so."

"Thanks, Sam. You're doing a great job."

He leaves, and I tell Laurie that I want to go with her today. She's been interviewing family and friends of the victims that Sam has been able to find. It's obviously unpleasant, and has so far yielded no significant information. I basically want to sit in on today's sessions because I have nothing else to do.

Our first stop is a small garden apartment on Garfield Avenue in Elmwood Park. It starts to snow as we pull up, not a blizzard but enough that it will stick if it continues like this. I love it when it snows, an emotional remnant of childhood days when snow meant the possibility of school being canceled.

When we get out of the car, I hear a voice

240

calling out, "Ms. Collins! Ms. Collins!"

The door to one of the garden apartments is open, and an elderly woman is standing there, frantically motioning us in. We head for the door, and I realize that she had opened the door and come out because of the weather, not wanting us to stay out in the elements a moment more than necessary.

When we get there, she ushers us in, muttering about how terrible the weather is. Before we even have a chance to introduce ourselves, we have cups of hot tea in our hands. I don't even like tea, but I drink it gratefully.

Laurie finally introduces me to Mrs. Martha Leavitt, who is probably pushing eighty. She lost her daughter, son-in-law, and grandson in the fire. I'm not sure how anyone gets through that, but she seems vibrant and alert, and has a warmth about her that makes her immediately likable.

"I'm sorry to have to talk to you about this," I say. "I'm sure you'd rather think about anything else."

She smiles sadly. "I think about it all day, every day, Mr. Carpenter. I even talk about it to myself, out loud. The only difference now is you're here to listen to me."

She goes on to talk about the family

241

members that she lost, showing us pictures and telling stories that are painful to listen to, and absolutely of no use to our case. The truth is that she knows nothing at all about the fire that wasn't in the papers.

Laurie says, "Mrs. Leavitt, one of the things we are trying to do is understand why that house was chosen by the arsonist. We believe that someone in that house was the target, but we don't know who that might be."

She seems surprised by this. "Oh my, I never thought about it in those terms." She is silent for a few moments. "I guess it didn't really matter; they were gone, and they weren't coming back, no matter the reason."

"Do you know of anyone who might have had a reason to hurt your family? Did any of them have any enemies?"

"Oh, no, that's just not possible. Not possible at all."

We ask her a bunch of questions to gently probe the matter, but there is no way she could ever entertain the thought that the people that she loved could have been the targets of such evil.

Our next stop is Morlot Avenue in Fair Lawn, where Jesse Briggs has agreed to meet us at a coffee shop. Laurie says that when she told him on the phone who we were representing, he was reluctant to meet at all. He finally consented to the coffee shop, and Laurie felt it was because he didn't want people who were on Noah Galloway's side in his house.

Briggs is in his early fifties, but looks older because his hair is completely white. He makes an effort to be polite to us, but it's clear that he resents the intrusion.

"All this time nobody talks to me about this, and now twice this month. Where's everyone been for the last six years?"

"Who else spoke to you?" I ask.

"A policeman."

I'm surprised and annoyed to hear this. I've read the discovery documents cover to cover a few times, and there was no mention of Mr. Briggs being interviewed recently, or at all, for that matter. I make a mental note to torture Dylan for holding out on me.

Briggs lost his daughter, Natasha, and his infant grandson. He is clearly still embittered about it, as I would certainly be. If something like that happened to me, I would try and burn down Earth.

"What about your daughter's husband?" I ask. "He wasn't there?"

"She didn't have a husband."

243

"Was the baby's father there?"

"Natasha never told me who the father was. But you can be sure he wasn't there. If I knew who he was I'd have killed him myself."

A few tears start to slip down his face, and he grabs a napkin from the dispenser on the table, quickly wiping them away.

"But it wasn't the father's fault that they died," he says, softly. "It was mine. I'm the one who told her to move back here. I'm the one who said I would take care of her and my grandson."

"It wasn't your fault either, Mr. Briggs. It was the fault of the piece of garbage who set the fire."

"The man you're trying to let walk free," he says.

"I don't believe that to be the case, sir. I truly don't."

He looks at me for a few moments, then, "I've got cancer, Mr. Carpenter. It's spread to places I didn't even know I had. The doctors said I had about six months, and they said that eight months ago. The only thing I've wanted for the last six years was for them to catch and put away the man that did this. So I hope you're wrong."

Laurie and I tell him that we understand, that we wish him well, and that we appreciate his talking to us. Then we pay the check, and leave.

This was a miserable way to spend a day.

The cell phone call list from our mystery man is surprising, to say the least.

There are seven prominent businessmen in New York, Chicago, and San Francisco; two judges, in Delaware and Missouri; six members of Congress; officers of various governmental agencies including the SEC and FDA; a Washington, D.C., political consultant; a customs officer in Galveston, Texas; as well as a number of other people whose names aren't so easily recognizable.

There are also a few numbers that Sam hasn't been able to track down yet, which causes him to view them with great suspicion. The only way that they could be so hard to identify is if they took great pains to make it so, and Sam feels that the reasons for doing that must be nefarious.

He may well be right.

Sam presents this information to Laurie and me in my office, and while it is certainly intriguing, it is far from clear how we should proceed.

"Let's confront these people, one at a time, and shake them down," Sam says. "We can split the names up three ways."

Laurie shakes her head. "Won't work. We don't even have an approach to use."

"What do you mean?" Sam asks.

I know exactly what Laurie is saying, so I take over from here. "It does us no good to go to someone on that list, and tell them they got a phone call from someone we can't identify, and then ask them what it was about. Even if they know what we're talking about, they'll laugh at us."

We kick it around a while longer, and then Laurie says, "We need to make them think we know more than we do. If there's any chance at all to get them to talk to us, it would be because they are afraid not to. Of course, the problem is that we're not really in a position to instill fear in anyone."

"Maybe we are," I say. "For the most part, these are public people. They run public companies, or serve in various areas of government. They are not going to want to deal with being dragged into this kind of spotlight."

"So maybe they'll talk to us quietly."

I nod. "Maybe. Or maybe the fact that

they were on this call list has nothing to do with this case. Maybe we're wasting our time."

"What else do we have to do?"

There's certainly no good answer to that, so we address ourselves to the question of how we can credibly make these people fear public disclosure, when we don't have the slightest idea what it is we're threatening to disclose.

By the time we're done, we're close to having a plan of attack. It's not brilliant, but it has a chance, and it feels good to at least have that.

With the trial about to start, I have to put on my lawyer hat, and leave the investigating more to Laurie and Marcus. But the way our plan sets up, I'm going to have to be the one to set it into motion, though I'm going to recruit some help.

At the moment I have to prepare for trial, to go over the evidence again, and again after that, until I know it cold. I also have to prepare my opening statement, though "prepare" may be overstating it. I think in general terms about what I am going to say, and what points it is essential that I make. But I never write it out, and I absolutely never rehearse. It cuts down on my spontaneity, and spontaneity is one of the few things I've got going for me.

So basically I have to think, which means Tara is about to go for another long walk. She's lucky I don't take on more clients, or at her age she'd probably have to get knee replacements.

We are in trouble on two fronts. The evidence is against us, but so will be the emotional factor, and in this case it will be incredibly strong. Tara is way more sensitive than me, so it's this aspect that I decide to talk to her about.

"Dylan is going to parade the families and friends of all the victims to the stand. They're going to talk about what wonderful people they were, and what a nightmare it was that they died an agonizing death in that fire."

Tara keeps sniffing the grass; I don't think I'm getting through to her. "They're going to hate Noah, because they're going to want somebody to suffer for it and he's the easy and obvious target."

More sniffing; as golden retrievers go she's as coldhearted as they come.

"I talked to some of those people with Laurie. Just listening to them made me want to vote guilty. I mean, the world moves on, but these people have had to live with it every day. And then suddenly they're harassed by cops and lawyers, and —"

Tara stops sniffing just as something hits me; I don't think the two actions are connected.

Jesse Briggs mentioned that he was questioned by a police officer recently, and it annoyed me that the interview report wasn't included in the discovery documents that Dylan had sent me. But Noah's arrest was as the result of a federal investigation; there were no documents at all relating to "policemen."

It could be just semantics, but I would think that if Briggs was questioned by an FBI agent, he would know the difference and speak more precisely.

More significantly, Tony at Taco Bell also mentioned something about talking to the cops recently. I didn't think much of it, and assumed he meant back near the time of the fire, or to FBI agents. But maybe that's not what he meant at all; maybe it was local cops that were doing the questioning.

If that's the case, I need to find out why they were suddenly active, and more importantly, when.

The "when" is everything.

Becky was right; Bailey is not a golden.

Becky says that she's a mastiff when she and Marcus drop her off, but I think she might be a horse. I even think I might have bet on her once.

She's enormous, at least a hundred and fifty pounds, and walks slowly, languidly, as if it's fine if she gets where she wants to go, but if she doesn't, no big deal either way. She's only three years old, but seems to have less energy than Edna.

As we always do when we introduce Tara to a visitor, we bring them separately to the backyard and have them meet there. Tara has no idea what to make of her; I'm sure she's never seen an animal this big. She wouldn't have to bend down much to walk under her.

Bailey, for her part, seems fine with Tara, though she doesn't seem to care one way or the other. She wags her tail a couple of times, and I'm glad I'm not standing in the way of it when she does. Godzilla knocked over buildings in Tokyo with a smaller backside.

"What does she eat?" I ask, hoping the answer is not "small children."

"Becky brought her food. It's the same as Tara's, only more. Much, much more."

"Okay, Bailey," I say. "This is Tara. She's in control here; you have a problem, you come to me. If I can't handle it, I go to Tara. We don't ask much of you, just make your bed in the morning, and don't make anything else in the house. And I handle the remote control at all times. You got that?"

I think she nods, although it could be that she's dozing off. I don't think she's going to be a problem.

When we get back in the house, Bailey walks over to the couch and lies down on it. It's amazing to watch; she doesn't jump on to the couch, or climb on to it. Her legs are so long that she walks on to it.

I'm still staring at her when Willie Miller comes over. He does a double take when he sees Bailey, and says, "Whoa, what is that?"

"That's Bailey. Tara's new friend."

"Oh, man, I want one of those." He goes over and hugs Bailey on the couch, who seems to take it in stride.

Willie is here to update me on the progress he is making on his book. "This writing stuff is not as hard as I thought," he says. "It's like talking, only somebody puts it on paper when I'm finished."

"Finished with what?"

"Talking. My helper has a tape recorder, and he asks me questions, and I answer them. Then he says, can we say it this way? Or that way? And I say, sure, whatever you want."

"Sounds easy."

"Well, not everybody could do it, but I'm picking it up pretty fast. You should try it; you can use the tape recorder when I'm done."

As jury selection gets more crucial, it gets more boring.

That's not to say it isn't both crucial and boring to start with; it's just that both aspects get magnified as it goes along.

The reason it's crucial is of course that a few weeks down the road twelve people are going to sit in a room and decide whether Noah goes free or spends the rest of his life in jail. And right now Dylan and I are in the process of choosing who is going to be in that room.

But it's also deadly dull, particularly now when we're in the second day. We've already asked the same tedious questions of at least fifty people, and listened as they've given pat answers that may or not be true.

People react to their being called for jury duty in different ways, but all of them show up with a plan. That plan could consist of a way to get excused, or a way to get on a panel. They then answer questions according to what they think will accomplish their goal.

When it's a high-profile trial like this one, the stakes get that much higher, both for the lawyers and the potential jurors. It increases the number of people who want to serve; instead of a lot of them seeing it as a few weeks out of commission, they often look at it as a potential book deal waiting to happen.

If you're a defense lawyer, as I happen to be, the peril is even greater in this situation. That is because people who want on the jury to make a name for themselves are more likely to convict.

The public wants someone to blame for this crime, and the jurors that identify the fiend and put him away come off a lot more heroic than those who let the guy walk. There weren't too many parades thrown for the Simpson jurors . . . not that there should have been.

So it's a crapshoot anyway, but an even more difficult one in this case. We're looking for open-minded people, should some happen to exist on this planet. We're also looking for people smart enough to embrace alternative theories, should we stumble on one.

Unfortunately, it doesn't seem as if these potential panelists were chosen from a list of Rhodes scholars, and we are having to settle for people who seem less than ideal for our purpose. My guess is that Dylan is feeling the same way, but that doesn't cheer me up to any great degree.

It's almost three o'clock before we have our panel in place, and Judge De Luca sends them home with the admonition to be back bright and early tomorrow morning.

He also reads a long, prepared speech about how the jurors are to avoid media coverage of the trial at all costs.

Yeah, right.

I'm assuming that they are normal human beings, and that they will therefore be channel-surfing tonight to find every bit of trial coverage that is available. And if they do, they will be seeing a lot of me.

I'm going on three cable news shows tonight, and all were eager to have me. It's a sign that the 24/7 cable news networks have enough real programming to fill up maybe 14/4, if that.

We timed my proposed appearances to come on the night before opening statements. I'm doing them all from a single studio on West Forty-eighth Street in Manhattan, and they're being beamed by satellite to the various networks. It's not exactly a long beaming, since they're all located right here in New York, but it certainly cuts down on cab fare.

I'm not going on alone; I'm doing so with Alexander Downey, Willie Miller's publisher. When I called and told him what I wanted him to do, he jumped at the opportunity.

The first show is the most serious. Douglas Burns has just gotten his own legal show on CNN, and unlike some of his colleagues, he examines issues from an intelligent, legally savvy point of view.

Burns is a former federal prosecutor, turned defense attorney, turned TV personality. He's done it all, and knows what he's talking about, so it's a little dangerous for me to go on his show. But if I can get by him, the rest will be easy.

Burns starts off the segment by summing up the issues in the case, utilizing all the evidence that has made its way into the public domain. It's a thorough, compelling presentation, and if I could get him to slant it in our direction, I could use it as my opening statement.

But I'm not here to discuss the evidence, or our strategy at trial. For one thing, the

257

evidence is stacked against us, and we haven't formulated a coherent defense, at least not for our case in chief.

I'm here to plant some things in the minds of the people that shouldn't be watching, the seven men, five women, and six alternates who are on our jury. But more importantly, I'm here to scare a bunch of people who aren't.

I'm easily able to deflect questions about the evidence and our strategy by claiming that we can't reveal too much, lest the other side gain an advantage. Burns understands that and backs off, and opens the door for me to discuss what I'm interested in.

I decide to be direct, and say, "To be honest, Doug, my hope is to use your show to send a message."

He smiles, spreads out his arms, and says, "That's what we're here for." He probably senses that this has the potential to be a big story, and besides, we're live on television. He's not going to throw me out; he's got air time to fill.

"There's a man named Ray Camby; he's a two-time ex-con who has been available for hire. From the moment I took on the Galloway case, he started following me."

"Why was he doing that?"

"Because there are people who are trying

to stop this trial, because they are afraid of what will come out. They are the people who killed Danny Butler." The audience will know who Butler is, because he was in Burns's setup piece.

"Do you know who these people are?" Burns asks.

"Not yet. But we're getting close."

"Is Ray Camby still following you?" He smiles, peers into the lights, shielding his eyes, and says, "Ray, are you out there?"

"You'll have to talk louder than that," I say. "Ray Camby was murdered last week, to prevent my investigators from questioning him. But we did manage to get a great deal of valuable information, and we've traced back Camby's connections."

"Who are those connections?"

"They are people in very prominent positions, in business and in government."

"You have names?"

I smile. "I do, but I'm not going to reveal them here, at least not tonight. My investigators are going to be approaching these people, starting tomorrow. They will be given an opportunity to cooperate, to discuss with us in confidence what they know about this situation. If they refuse, their names will be made public, and I will invite the working press to start digging."

"You're making a very serious threat," Burns points out.

"I understand that. But twenty-six people died in that fire, and two more have been killed in recent weeks. In addition, an innocent man faces the possibility of life in prison. I think it's time we played some hardball, and I'm not only willing to make these threats, but I'm very prepared to back them up. And that's where Mr. Downey comes in."

Burns then takes the cue and starts asking Downey how he is involved in this process. Downey announces that his company has accepted my proposal to publish a book I will be writing, mainly about the Galloway case, but also about others in my career.

"It will be after the conclusion of the case," Downey says, "so there will be no reason to hold anything back. Andy has promised to name names, most notably of those who have not cooperated with the defense."

Downey fends off Burns's questions about details, mainly because he doesn't have any. He doesn't even have a contract with me, not even an agreement that I will write the book. He certainly hopes I will, but the publicity this will generate for his company is payment enough for the moment.

We go through the drill twice more, on two other shows, and head home. The trial starts tomorrow, so I've got quite a bit of work ahead of me tonight.

I'm tired, but pleased with how it went. Hopefully I've made some people very nervous. I know I am.

"I thought I had seen it all," is how Dylan begins his opening statement. "I've been in this job a long time, and I thought I'd seen it all." He shakes his head, sadly, at the realization that in fact he hadn't seen it all.

"It's my job to deal with terrible things, and I've seen a lot of them. Every time someone gets robbed, or embezzled, or assaulted, or murdered, it comes through my office. And I have to admit my colleagues and myself get a little hardened to it; I suppose that's human nature.

"But every once in a while we're presented with something so terrible and so tragic that it stuns us all, and makes us recoil in horror. But someone in my job doesn't get to make it go away by turning off the TV, or not buying the newspaper. I need to face it head-on, as distasteful as it might be.

"And now, today, so do you. You are going to see things during the course of this trial that I wish you didn't have to see. You are going to hear things I wish you didn't have to hear.

"But it all comes with my job, and now it comes with yours. Because you and I need to do whatever we can to make sure that something as horrible as this does not happen again.

"Twenty-six people died a horrible death one night six years ago. Most of them were completely innocent, a few weren't. But none of them deserved the fate that they got. None of them deserved to suffer as they suffered . . . no one does.

"It took six years to identify the perpetrator of this horrible crime. There was certainly no rush to judgment here. Finally, when it looked as if it might go unsolved, someone came along and provided a key piece of information. After that, through diligent and dedicated investigation by the Federal Bureau of Investigation, all the pieces fell into place.

"Noah Galloway committed this crime. This is not the time for me to convince you of that fact; the evidence will do that. You will be left without a reasonable doubt, which is what our system properly demands.

"You will see Noah Galloway for what he is, and what he has done, and you will do your job. As unpleasant as all of this will be, I have no doubt you will do your job.

"So I thank you for your service."

Dylan has done an effective job of bringing the jurors on to his team, the team that is dedicated to protecting society from the horribly evil people on my team. It no doubt fits the narrative they came in with, so I'm sure it landed on receptive ears.

As I stand I glance at Noah, who is staring straight ahead and betraying no emotion, as I have counseled him to do. But I can't help wondering what's going through his mind. Before I met him, he was resigned to his fate, and comfortable with it. He felt he deserved whatever the system decreed, and that would be that.

But he's a smart guy, and though he isn't quite willing to admit it, he must be coming to believe in at least the possibility of his own innocence. That automatically gives him something major at stake, and also gives him a reason to be frightened, and bitter, and angry, and very, very anxious.

He's not showing it, and that's good, but he's got to be feeling it.

I pat him on the shoulder, as much for the jury's sake as his own, and stand. "I've been in my job a lot of years as well," I say, "but I've already had a relatively new experience this time. Very often I can go an entire trial without agreeing with anything the prosecutor says, but this time we are on the same page on a major issue.

"What happened that night six years ago is horrible . . . no doubt about it. And I would like the person who did it to go away for the rest of his life, and I would be fine if that life wasn't a long one.

"But your job is not to punish the person that the prosecutor says is guilty. You are not punishers, you are finders of fact. It is your job to decide whether Noah Galloway is guilty, not to protect society. Society is not protected by an innocent man going to prison; it suffers for it.

"Noah Galloway had a disease; it's called drug addiction. It is a horrible disease, and one that is terribly difficult to overcome. But he's done just that; he's turned his life around and become a model citizen. He's been recognized for his accomplishments and his good works by many, many people, a group that happens to include the President of the United States.

"But his achievements in the last six years don't make him innocent; nor do his troubles before that make him guilty. When you come to know him then and now, when you know who Noah Galloway is and what makes him tick, then you will know he is incapable of this kind of act.

"The evidence is convenient, rather than compelling. It suddenly appeared as if by magic, and it came in torrents. The case was handed to the prosecutor on a silver platter, and he ran with it. I don't know about you, but when I'm handed something on a silver platter for no reason at all, I check to see if it's real silver.

"Well, you will soon see that none of this is real, and that Noah Galloway is a victim. So, like Mr. Campbell, I ask you to do your job, based solely on the facts. Then maybe the police and prosecutors can focus on finding the real fiend, who is out there laughing at us.

"Thank you."

Noah whispers a thank-you to me when I sit down, and even Hike nods that he feels it went well. A positive nod from Hike is the equivalent of a ticker-tape parade from a normal person, so I'm feeling good about things.

That feeling is wiped away by one sentence spoken to Dylan, by De Luca. "Call your first witness."

I guess I was hoping the judge would forget about the witness part, and go right to the verdict.

It was one of the more unpleasant phone calls in Loney's recent memory.

Carmine Ricci had called at three A.M. and he was not happy. The hour of the call was not a surprise; Carmine was on Vegas time, so it was only midnight, and he never slept anyway. He also was not particularly concerned about waking Loney; in fact, based on the tone of his voice, he would have been happy to kill Loney.

"You been watching television?" Carmine asked, instead of "hello."

"Now?" Loney asked. "I've been sleeping for . . . what time is it?" He looked at his watch, and then continued, "Three hours."

"The lawyer was on television tonight."

"What lawyer? Carpenter?" Loney asked. "What did he say?"

"Find out yourself, and then call me to explain. If he calls me before you do, you've got yourself a problem."

267

"Okay . . . just tell me . . . what show was he on?"

"How the hell do I know? You think I watch that shit? I heard it was one of those lawyer shows."

Click.

Loney set about trying to find out what the hell Carmine was talking about, a task which proved easier than he expected. The cable news and talk shows are repeated frequently in the early-morning hours, and he was able to catch the appearance on the Doug Burns show at four A.M.

It confirmed his worst fears; Carpenter had traced the calls that Camby made, which would not have been that difficult. But then he had somehow managed to delve into Loney's phone records, and find out who he had called.

This would have been a disaster waiting to happen, if it hadn't already happened. He would have to call everyone on the list, and explain what had taken place. He would not mention Camby's death, though they would learn about it from Carpenter's TV appearances.

Actually, the circumstances of Camby's death might help him convince them not to talk to Carpenter. They would not want to share Camby's fate, and even though public disclosure by Carpenter could prove some-what embarrassing, a bullet in the head would be even more problematic.

His bosses would be upset, though that would quickly turn to anger. Loney knew that they saw him as a necessary evil, a conduit to use to accomplish their goals. Conduits are supposed to handle problems, not cause them, and his bosses were going to see this as a very big problem.

But the worst part was Carmine, because at the end of the day, Carmine was the only player here who was of any real importance. So if Carmine was pissed off, nothing else mattered. And Carmine was pissed off.

Loney called him back, but didn't bother to apologize. Carmine never wanted to hear apologies; he considered them unnecessary. He already knew that someone who dis-pleased him would by definition be sorry that they had done so, since they would want to stay alive.

All Carmine was interested in was that the situation be rectified, and Loney prom-ised that the process would begin, effective immediately. He didn't say how he would do that, since another thing Carmine was not interested in was details. He was a results-oriented guy.

In the morning, Loney set out to make

calls to everyone that could be on Carpenter's list. He started with Fowler, asking him if he was aware of what Carpenter had said on television.

"I saw it," Fowler said. "I'm still trying to figure out how you could have let that happen."

"It was a mistake," Loney admitted. "I'm dealing with it."

"You'd better. Your boss is as unhappy about it as we are."

"I've talked to him. Carpenter is in the dark on this, he's groping. If his people get in touch with you, your position should be that you don't know what they're talking about."

Fowler's voice sounded coldly amused. "Now you're telling me my position?"

"I'm telling everyone the same thing," Loney said.

"Just make sure they listen to you."

It was a ridiculous comment for Fowler to make, since there was no question the people on that list would listen to Loney. Their fear of Loney, and in some cases their dependence on him, is what made the entire operation run in the first place.

By noon, Loney had made all the calls. He knew these people, he knew what made them tick, and he could have anticipated each of their reactions.

Some were nervous and afraid, which for the most part they tried to conceal. A few were less concerned, and two even relished the danger. But all promised to stonewall anyone who contacted them. They would not be intimidated; if Carpenter made their names public they were prepared to take him to court for defamation of character.

It was the reaction Loney wanted, though he was not sure each of them could be trusted. He would have to monitor things vigilantly, and perform whatever corrective actions might be needed.

Corrective action was a Loney specialty.

Assistant Chief Peter Hayes is Dylan's first witness.

Chief Hayes comes from Passaic County Fire Department royalty; his family has been in the department since the early 1900s. Three of his ancestors have been chiefs, including his father, and there is no doubt that Hayes will ascend to the top spot as soon as the current chief reaches retirement age.

Hayes has an imperial attitude about him, as if his title should be "Emperor" rather than "Assistant Chief." Dylan treats him with a nauseating reverence, so much so that I'm surprised he doesn't spread rose petals in front of him as he heads for the witness stand.

Dylan starts by taking him through his career path. Hayes has been a firefighter for twenty-four years, and based on this endless testimony, he has received pretty much every commendation and award it is possible to receive, except for maybe a Grammy.

Finally I can't take it anymore, and I object. "Your Honor, the witness's service has certainly been admirable, but he's not here applying for sainthood. He's presenting evidence of a specific incident."

De Luca nods. "Sustained. Let's move it along, Mr. Campbell."

Dylan turns Hayes's attention to the night of the fire. "Were you the first one on the scene, Chief Hayes?"

"No, I wasn't. I got there seven minutes after the alarm was received, but three units were already deployed and on the scene."

"So you were not the first person to enter the burning building?" Dylan asks.

"No firefighter entered that building," Hayes answers, uttering the words as if they are momentous. "The intensity of the fire would not permit it. And within six minutes of my arrival, there was no longer any building at all. It had completely disintegrated."

"How many fire scenes have you visited, Chief?"

"I couldn't say. Thousands."

"Was this one unusual?" Dylan asks.

"You mean for reasons other than the toll in human lives?"

"Yes, I'm talking about the qualities of the fire itself."

"It was the hottest, most intense fire I have ever witnessed, or investigated."

Dylan pretends to be surprised by the answer. "Why is that?"

"The chemical mixture that was used, and the way it was distributed throughout the structure."

Dylan takes Hayes through a long presentation on the chemical compound that investigators determined was used to start and spread the fire. It was a combination of benzene and polystyrene. There was some gasoline added, which Hayes says made it easier to ignite.

"Is there a name for this mixture that we would all be familiar with?" Dylan asks.

Hayes nods. "It's a form of napalm."

Dylan is positively shocked to hear this. "Napalm? You mean the weapon used to incinerate jungles in Vietnam?"

"Yes," Hayes says, and goes on to describe the different types of napalm, and its devastating properties.

The description is impressive in its detail, and will be very damaging when the jury learns that Noah has the training and education to have concocted it.

Dylan is not going to wait for that to happen. He hands Hayes a piece of paper, and asks him questions about it. It is a copy of Noah's course studies in college and graduate school, and lists his Ph.D. in chemical engineering. I question the document's admissibility and Hayes's standing to testify about it, but De Luca shoots me down, as I knew he would.

"Does this background suggest to you that the defendant would know how to make this mixture of chemicals?"

I object on the grounds that Hayes could not be aware of Noah's base of knowledge. De Luca sustains the objection and asks Dylan to rephrase.

Finally, Hayes is allowed to say that people with Noah's background should certainly have the capability of concocting it.

Dylan does not ask Hayes anything about the incinerated bodies that were left in the rubble; he will call the coroner later to describe that in horrible detail. But Hayes has done a very effective job, and by the time Dylan turns him over to me, we already have a steep hill to climb.

"Good morning, Mr. Hayes." I'm not going to call him "Chief"; at the very least that gives him the upper hand and an added credibility in the jurors' minds. It's a small thing, but trials are made up of many small things.

"Good morning, Mr. Carpenter."

"You talked about the elaborate way in which the fire was started, how the mixture was carefully spread out and placed, and how igniting it would have been difficult."

"Yes."

"The person doing it would have to have been intelligent, or at least very familiar with this type of thing?"

"Absolutely."

"And he or she would have to have been patient in the process? It needed to be carefully thought out and executed?"

"Certainly."

"And clearheaded and alert?"

There's a flash of worry on Hayes's face; he knows that the prosecution's theory is of a drug-desperate Noah exacting revenge on the people denying him those drugs.

"I'm not sure I can speak to that."

"If you'd like to ask Mr. Campbell's permission, we can wait."

Dylan explodes out of his chair to object, and De Luca admonishes me.

"Mr. Hayes, you've already stated that the perpetrator had to be knowledgeable in these matters, patient and careful. You think someone could have done all this while not clearheaded and alert?"

"I suppose that would have been the case, at least for a short while," Hayes concedes.

"Good. Now this clearheaded, intelligent, careful, patient, alert arsonist would have to have had a knowledge of the chemicals in napalm?"

"Yes."

"Because you can't just walk into Home Depot and say, give me a jugful of napalm, can you? There are no Napalm R Us stores around, right?"

"That is correct. It is illegal to possess it, or purchase it."

"And it requires a chemical engineering degree to create it?"

"Certainly doesn't hurt," he says.

I introduce four pieces of paper and have them marked as defense evidence exhibits. I then hand the first one to Hayes, and I give copies of all four to Dylan.

"Mr. Hayes, I have just handed you a copy of a Google search page, have I not?"

Hayes holds it away from him, as if it might be contagious. "Yes, I believe so."

"You're not sure?"

"That's what it is," he says.

"Please read the subject line at the top."

" 'How to make napalm.' "

"And near the top it mentions how many

hits there were on that subject. Please read that as well."

He mutters the answer. "Two hundred and sixty-four thousand."

I tell him that neither I nor the jury could hear his response, and I get him to say it louder.

"Mr. Hayes, I think we can assume that these two hundred and sixty-four thousand napalm teachers think the reader has a place to do it, like a napalm office or something. In case they don't, can you read the subject line and the number of hits on this search page?"

I hand him the next piece of paper, which he sneers at. " 'How to make napalm at home,' " he says.

"And how many hits?"

"One hundred and ninety-five thousand."

"Now we're getting somewhere," I say. "But there's always a catch. For instance, what if the person wanting to make napalm can't read? Then he must be out of luck, right? Or maybe you can read this subject line." I give him paper number three.

" 'Making napalm videos,' " he says.

"And the hits?" I feel like I'm dragging him to the edge of a cliff.

"One thousand six hundred and ten hits."

"So I guess illiteracy wouldn't be a deterrent after all. Live and learn. My bad." I walk toward him with paper number four. "One more," I say, and hand it to him. "What's the subject line?"

" 'Need a chemical engineering degree to make napalm,' " he says.

"And the hits?" I ask.

"No results found."

I've only partially succeeded in my cross of Chief Hayes.

I've won what I classify as "debating" points, rather than "verdict" points. Debating points are part of a "gotcha" cross-examination, in which the witness might look bad, or get caught in a mistake. But those kinds of points don't accomplish much in real life; they don't win over the jury and help them make up their minds. Only verdict points do that.

I showed how silly it was to assume that it takes a chemical engineering degree to know how to mix the chemicals necessary to make napalm. I'm sure the jury gets that intellectually, and I even think they will give me credit for a smooth piece of lawyering.

But ultimately they will dismiss it as a debating point. At the end of the day they will think that if an arsonist went to the trouble of mixing such a concoction, then it is more likely than not that he had a knowledge of chemicals. And there, sitting at the defense table sits the accused, a chemical engineer.

It will all seem to fit for the jury. It won't be the deciding factor; it will be a contributing one. And unfortunately Dylan is not nearly finished making evidentiary contributions.

His next witness is Detective Sue Pyles of the Paterson Police Department. She's one of the lead detectives in the drug enforcement division. Pyles has been fighting the thankless, mostly losing battle against drugs for almost twenty-two years.

Dylan asks her about the occupants of the two ground-floor apartments in the destroyed building, and Pyles prefaces her testimony by saying that there are things she cannot say, and names she cannot mention, because it could prejudice an ongoing investigation.

What that means is that the department is still trying to make a case against Double J, who will be playing checkers at the Sunset Rest Home for Retired Drug Dealers by the time the cops get to him.

"But at the time of the fire, these two apartments were part of an active drug distribution center?" Dylan asks.

"They were selling drugs illegally, yes."

"How do you know that?"

"We had them under part-time surveillance. We were building a case."

"Were they being watched that night?"

Pyles shakes her head. "Unfortunately, no."

"So drug users would come to that building to buy their drugs?"

"Some would," Pyles says. "But in other cases the sale would be made elsewhere. Customers who were good enough might get theirs delivered, or the purchase would take place at a prearranged meeting place, perhaps a park."

"Back around the time of the fire, were you familiar with Noah Galloway?"

Pyles nods. "Yes."

"What did you know about him?" Dylan asks.

"He was an addict, and one of the customers of the people we are talking about."

"A good customer?"

A shrug from Pyles. "Depends on your definition of 'good.' He was certainly a frequent buyer, but there were times he was cut off because he had no money. They did not consider him a good credit risk."

"How did you know this?"

"Audio surveillance."

"If you had all this information, why had you not made any arrests?"

Pyles frowns, her frustration evident. "We were about to."

Dylan turns Pyles over to me. She hasn't done us much damage, merely set up some facts that we would have admitted to anyway.

Pyles's statement that Noah was a drug addict was something we acknowledged in my opening statement, and was widely known anyway. Noah had received much publicity when he got the presidential appointment, and his overcoming his addiction was a heroic aspect to it.

The fact that Noah was a customer of the people in that building was something that was going to come out anyway. Slightly damaging was the testimony that he sometimes couldn't afford his habit, and it is there where I will focus my cross-examination.

"Detective Pyles, you said you had audio surveillance of Mr. Galloway dealing with these people."

"Yes."

"Tapes?"

"Yes."

"Would you play them for us, please?"

"We couldn't find them," she says, appear-

283

ing uncomfortable.

I knew this from the discovery, but I wanted the jury to hear it. "Is that unusual?"

"It happens."

"Obviously. My question was whether or not its happening could be considered unusual."

"Yes, I would say it's unusual. But in this case the fire seemed to end our investigation, so perhaps not enough care was paid."

"You said the investigation is ongoing, and that's why you couldn't reveal certain names."

Pyles nods; to her credit she tackles the issue head-on. "Because of the intensity of the fire, many of the bodies could not be identified. We believed the ringleader of the operation to be one of the dead, but we learned quite a while later he was not."

I'm surprised by this; Double J must have gone undercover after the incident, perhaps considering himself still a target.

"So your recounting of what Mr. Galloway might have said on the tapes is by memory only?"

"Yes."

"How many people were on these tapes?" I ask. "How many customers did they have?"

"Maybe a few hundred."

"You have quite a memory. Do you re-member if a lot of the customers for these drugs were CEOs of large corporations, heiresses, members of royal families, people like that?"

"What do you mean?" she asks, though I'm sure she knows where I'm going.

"I mean, were they wealthy people? Titans of industry?"

"You'd be surprised how many wealthy people use recreational drugs," she says.

"That they were buying from this house, in this neighborhood in Paterson?"

She finally allows as how the clientele for this particular establishment were not particularly well-to-do.

"In fact, Detective, in your experience haven't you seen many people for whom drug use is financially devastating, and it becomes a constant struggle for many of these people to secure enough money to feed their habit?"

"I have seen that many times, yes."

"So if your six-year-old memory is cor-rect, and Mr. Galloway was having difficulty supporting his habit, he would have been one of many in that situation?"

"That's likely. Yes."

"And people who are desperate for drugs will usually do almost anything to get them, is that correct?"

Out of the corner of my eye I can see Dylan look up; he's pleased by my question. He wants Noah to be seen as desperate and willing to do anything.

"In my experience, yes," Pyles says.

"In their desperation to get the drugs, do you often find that they set fire to them?"

Pyles is obviously taken aback by the question, and all she can mutter is, "Every situation is different."

"But in this situation, the drugs that Mr. Galloway was desperate to get were destroyed by the fire he is accused of setting?"

"That is true. Yes."

"Thank you, no further questions."

Tonight is our anniversary.

Since Laurie and I are not actually married, assigning an anniversary date can be tricky. Obvious possibilities were the date we met, or when we started going out, or when we moved in together.

We rejected all those, and chose as our anniversary the day she moved back from Wisconsin to be with me. That seemed to be the date that our commitment became explicit, at least as far as she was concerned. I was hooked long before that.

We're not really the fancy-dinner, candlelight types, especially during a trial, when every minute counts. We also wouldn't think of going out on a significant occasion like this without Tara, since she is an integral part of our family. And as the largest, albeit temporary, member of our family, Bailey's company is welcome as well.

So we head to the Fireplace on Route 17.

They've got terrific burgers, roast beef sandwiches, and the like, and their hot dogs are among Tara's favorites. It is also one of the few places that takes me seriously when I say I want my french fries burned beyond recognition.

During the warmer months, we sit outside and eat, but that certainly is not an option tonight. They will let any human inside to eat, no matter how big a loser he or she might be, but dogs are not allowed in. Tara is cleaner than at least half the patrons, and probably smarter than ninety percent, but she and Bailey can't come in, so we eat in the car.

I have to make two trips from the restaurant to the car, because if I try and carry all of Bailey's food I could hurt myself. She's actually a fairly dainty eater, doesn't make a mess and licks her lips clean. She finishes four hot dogs before Tara has one, and eyes Tara's remaining food hungrily. But she doesn't go after it.

Laurie and I resolve not to talk about the case during dinner, but we break that particular resolution within five minutes. We have a lot to go over, and since we'd have to do it when we got home anyway, we decide to get a head start on it.

Laurie's report is depressing. She has

spent the last two days attempting to contact every person on our list of cell phone calls. She has been successful in reaching more than half of them, but unsuccessful in getting anyone to reveal anything of consequence.

"It feels like they're all reading from the same script," she says. "They all say they don't know what I'm talking about, and that while they'd like to help, they really need more information about what we're looking for."

"No unusual reactions at all?"

She shakes her head. "Not really. One of them actually laughed at me. A D.C. political consultant named Brett Fowler. He sometimes goes on those cable news shows. He had seen you on TV . . . thought it was a riot that he was on your list."

It's not an unexpected development, but nonetheless disappointing. The truth is that my threat to publicly expose anyone who didn't cooperate was basically an empty one. We know far too little to do any damage; we don't even know what it is we don't know.

I describe what happened in court today, as accurately as I can, and Laurie says, "It sounds like you did very well."

I launch into my "debating points" versus

"verdict points" theory, but she's heard it maybe a thousand times, so she cuts me short. "The key thing is you're not getting steamrolled," she says. "You'll have time to make your verdict points when you present your case."

There's no sense mentioning that we don't have a case, so I don't. But I'm also not about to fake being upbeat about our chances. "The emotional side of this is always going to be against us," I say.

"You mean the way the people died?"

"Yes. Every person on that jury has got an image in their mind of what it was like for the victims, and that's only going to get stronger. Dylan is going to sift through every human ash in the building."

"I wonder why they did it that way," she says. "I mean, regardless of who the target was, why not just come in and shoot them in the head?"

I nod. "I know; that's bothered me from the beginning. This was so much more difficult to pull off, and not as sure a thing. One person got out; others could have. Maybe even the targets."

It's weird how certain things happen, and how they can trigger thoughts. I wouldn't leave a Fireplace french fry uneaten if there was a tsunami bearing down on me, I'm almost finished with these, and the last few are just burned ash; if you saw one in a different context you would never know it was once a proud french fry.

But looking at it somehow gives me an insight. "The purpose was the obliteration," I say.

"What does that mean?"

"They didn't shoot their targets because killing them wasn't the only goal. They were trying to remove all traces of something."

"Any idea what that could be?"

I shake my head. "Not really. It could have been anything."

"Maybe it was identity," Laurie says. "There were people in there that have still not been identified, and never will be. The fire could have been set to hide who was in there."

"And even who wasn't," I say. "There was no real way to identify most of those people; it was based on secondhand reports. People believed their friends and family were in there, and that was confirmed by the fact that they were missing afterward. We could think somebody died that night who wasn't even there. That's why they used napalm; they wanted it to burn so hot that there'd be nothing left. Gasoline and a match wouldn't have accomplished it."

"They could have used the napalm to help point the finger at Noah," Laurie says. "Because of his background."

I shake my head. "I don't think so. We haven't even come up with a reason why anybody would want to do this to Noah. I think he may have just come in handy, as someone to blame it on."

"Which they waited six years to do?" she asks.

"That's been the key question all along, and I finally think I may know how to get to the answer. But it's going to have to wait until tomorrow."

"Why?"

I look at my watch. "Two reasons. One, if I call Pete this late, he'll kill me. And two, it's time to go home to celebrate our anniversary."

"You mean sex?" she asks.

"That's exactly what I mean."

Laurie feigns a yawn; at least I hope she's feigning. Feign detection has never been one of my strengths, and females have been yawning at my advances since high school. "Been there, done that," she says.

"Good," I say. "Then you'll know exactly what to do. I'm tired of having to teach you."

"Or we could not celebrate at all," she says.

"A night without sex?" I ask, and then shake my head. "Nope . . . been there, done that."

I call Pete at eight-thirty in the morning, on my way to court.

"What took you so long?" is the way he starts the conversation, dispensing with "hello."

"What does that mean?" I ask.

"You're calling because you've got some questions, and you think I have the answers."

"You got that right."

"So what took you so long?" he asks. "I was going to call you if I had to."

"So why didn't you?"

"Not my style," he says. "What are you doing now?"

"Going to court."

"Can you meet me at Stiff City at seven o'clock? I'll try and get Nancy to hang around."

"You want to give me a preview?" I ask.

"No."

The conversation with Pete has been intriguing, which is more than I can say for what is going to happen in court today. Dylan is planning a parade of witnesses who are going to say that Noah was a frequent presence in the area near the fire, and that he was known to be purchasing drugs from the "businessmen" on the first floor.

The first witness is Lawrence Cahill, known to residents of the neighborhood as Larry, showing if nothing else he believes in really clever nicknames. Laurie's investigation of Larry shows a person of less than the highest character, but he is dressed up today like he's heading straight for the senior prom after court.

Larry's tale is as advertised based on the discovery documents. He had seen Noah on a number of occasions in the neighborhood, at least a dozen by his recollection. Noah had been visiting the ill-fated house to buy drugs, and Larry and the other neighbors considered the activities a scourge on the community.

I'm not sure why Larry is here today, though it's probably to bask in the publicity limelight of the moment, and look good doing it. He doesn't get many chances to do so, and it probably was irresistible.

I could ask a few perfunctory questions

and let him go; that's probably what I should do. His testimony is not particularly damaging, since we are not contesting that Noah was a drug user, and that he bought from the occupants of the house. I should probably just let Larry have his pathetic moment in the sun, and let him go.

But I won't.

"Mr. Cahill," I begin, "how did you recognize the defendant here today?"

"What do you mean? I used to see the guy all the time in the neighborhood; he hasn't changed that much."

"So the fact that he no longer has the beard didn't throw you off?"

Larry seems a little worried about how to respond to this, so he goes with the relatively safe, "No, it didn't."

"What kind of beard did he have? Do you remember?"

Larry puts his hand to his chin, in a demonstration. "Just a regular one . . . you know, around the chin."

"Yes, that's where beards grow, around the chin. So you remember the beard, but you can't picture exactly what it looked like?" I ask.

"Right."

"What if I were to tell you that Noah Galloway didn't have a beard then, and never had one in his life? And that he had a moustache instead?"

A flash of panic on the good citizen's face, and then, "That's what I meant, a moustache. I'm a little nervous; I got the words confused."

"You meant to say he had a moustache on his chin? Where was the beard, on his big toe?"

The jury and gallery are laughing, which causes Dylan to come out of his stupor and object that this is irrelevant. De Luca overrules him and the fun continues.

"Noah Galloway never had a moustache either, Mr. Cahill. I could show you a picture, if you'd like. Are you sure it wasn't Abe Lincoln you saw in the neighborhood? Or maybe Adolf Hitler?"

Dylan objects again, and De Luca suggests I move on.

"You testified that Mr. Galloway was coming to the neighborhood to purchase drugs. Were you a witness to those purchases? Were you in the room when they took place?"

"No." Larry has decided to switch to the "fewer words is better" approach.

"How did you know which apartment he went to? Were you standing in the corridor at the time he entered the building?"

"Everybody knew," he says.

"So you heard this from other people?"

"I knew it also."

"Okay, let's assume you somehow knew which apartment Mr. Galloway entered," I say. "How did you know they sold drugs in there?"

"Everybody knew that too."

"Did this all-knowing everybody buy drugs from them as well? Or were you the only one?"

He shakes his head emphatically. "No way. Not me."

"Who did you buy your drugs from?"

"I never bought drugs," he lies.

"You have two convictions for possession, for which you served ninety days in prison. You were innocent of those crimes?"

"Yes."

"You pleaded guilty to throw the authorities off the track?"

Dylan objects, and De Luca sustains.

Time for me to wrap this up. "Mr. Cahill, one of those convictions was two weeks after the fire. Is it possible that in the weeks before that, your mind was impaired by drugs? And that instead of seeing Mr. Galloway, you saw some facial-haired person and got them mixed up?"

"No," he says.

"No further questions," I say.

298

I enjoyed that, but all I did was add debating points to my increasing total. Dylan is going to bring more witnesses to say basically the same thing that Cahill said. It was a stupid move on Dylan's part to have Cahill testify at all, and especially first.

Dylan calls four more witnesses in succession that place Noah in the neighborhood, having dealings with the drug guys on the first floor. These witnesses are not convicted drug users, nor are they lying. For that reason I barely lay a glove on them, and don't try too hard to do so.

There's no reason to make witnesses like this look bad. The jury will like and believe them, and they are testifying to facts that are really not in dispute.

It has basically been an uneventful day, and barely a diversion from my meeting with Pete tonight, which I hope will be the main event.

Alex Bauer knew the call was coming.

He had known since the moment he saw Carpenter on television. He hadn't needed Loney to call and alert him, but Loney had done so the next morning.

Bauer had been upset at the turn of events, and had let Loney know it in no uncertain terms. He didn't believe that Loney had cared one way or the other about his level of concern; Loney was not the type to be bothered by anything.

Bauer considered himself a cool customer as well, and he had no doubt that he would handle the call when it came. But he had been assured that there would be no slipups, and now all of a sudden there was a major one.

Bauer avoided the call twice. They came on his cell phone, as he knew they would, so there was no one to answer the call for him and make an excuse. He knew who it was because it was from a number he did not recognize, with a New Jersey area code.

The third time he answered it, if only to get it over with, and to find out how much they knew. It was a woman, which for some reason surprised him, but she sounded professional and self-assured. She introduced herself as Laurie Collins, an investigator working for Andy Carpenter.

She was probing, but it soon became obvious that she knew very little. She talked about his having received phone calls from a particular number, and wanted to know who the caller was and what the nature of his relationship with that caller was.

"Why are you asking me these questions?" he asked.

"It has come up as evidence in a major trial being conducted right now," she said. "Perhaps you're aware of the Noah Galloway trial?"

"The guy who set the fire?" Bauer asked.

"The jury hasn't made a decision on that question either way as yet. But it's a very public trial, and since you're the head of a public company, I would assume you'd want to stay as far away from it as possible. One way to insure that would be to answer my questions without the need for depositions or testimony."

It was a threat, not a very veiled one at that, and matched what Carpenter had said on television. In any event, Bauer was certainly not cowed by it, and he said what Loney had suggested he say.

"I'm sorry, Ms. Collins, I really have no idea what you're talking about. And if I have to testify to that, I'll find the time to do so."

"So you're saying you never received such a phone call?" she asked.

"I'm saying I receive many phone calls. As you pointed out, I am the head of a company. I have no idea which phone call you are referring to, and you don't seem to be in possession of much information to help enlighten me. So while I would very much like to help you, I'm afraid I cannot."

That effectively ended the call, though Collins said that he would be hearing from her again. She had no idea how close Bauer had come to telling her what she wanted to know, and he knew that there might well come a point when he would.

It was really up to Loney, and the judge in Delaware.

I meet Pete at the coroner's office at seven.

He's waiting for me in the lobby, and from there I can see that Nancy Adams's office is dark. Since we're there to meet with her, that strikes me as somewhat surprising.

"Nancy's out to dinner," Pete says. "She'll be back at seven-thirty."

"So why are we here at seven?"

"So we can talk."

"Good," I say. "You start."

He shakes his head. "No, let's start by you telling me what you think."

"Okay. I think that there had to be a reason Butler was sent in now to implicate Noah, rather than six years ago. The only thing I can think of is that whoever did set the fire was trying to hide something. And if all of a sudden they needed to hide something, it meant that somebody was out there looking." Pete isn't saying anything, so I add, "Jump in whenever you want."

"Go on."

"Two people have told me that they were interviewed by the police recently. They didn't say the FBI, though that's the kind of thing people remember and mention. The interviews were not in the discovery documents, because Dylan made his case from the FBI investigation."

Still nothing from Pete, so I go on. "You are in charge of the department's investigation of the fire, and have been since the beginning. That's why I called you."

"Not bad," Pete says. "You are not nearly as dumb as you look. You may not believe this, but there are people in the department who like me. They've known how this case has bothered me, and in their downtime, they sometimes work the case."

"You assign things to them?" I ask.

He shakes his head. "No. Most times I'm probably not even aware that they're doing it. It's only if they find out anything that could be significant that they come to me with it. And that rarely happens, believe me."

"But somebody was on to something this time," I say.

"I think so, although I don't know what it was. But I do know who it was."

"Kyle Holmes," I say. He was the young

officer who was killed along with his partner when they responded to that domestic dispute. Those killings took place three weeks before Noah's arrest.

Pete nods. "Kyle Holmes. Maybe there was more to his death than we thought."

Pete goes on to tell me that Kyle had mentioned to him that he was looking at the case from a new angle, but didn't say what that was. He was young and eager, and had a tendency to jump to conclusions, so Pete had told him to update him when he had something concrete to report. The next day he was shot and killed, and Pete of course had no reason to connect it to the fire investigation.

"So for the last week I've been trying to find out what he was doing," Pete says. "He usually took notes when he was out on a case, but there were none found on his body. No one thought anything of it at the time, but now it seems that maybe the killer took them."

"What have you learned?" I ask.

"Let's wait for Nancy."

Nancy Adams will be worth waiting for. She is absolutely beautiful, with long jet-black hair, a magnetic smile, and legs that would reach the floor no matter how low that floor happened to be. Looks-wise, she's in Laurie's class, which is an honors class all the way.

Whenever I see her I'm reminded of that old quiz show, *What's My Line?* If panelists had to guess what Nancy did, spending her time cutting up dead bodies would rank last on the list of possibilities, except for maybe sumo wrestler.

There's one other thing I want to talk to Pete about, while he is in a relatively helpful mood. "I need a big favor," I say.

"That's a real news event."

"I need a list of missing persons reports, starting a week before the fire up through a month afterward."

"Just for Paterson?" he asks.

"No, I need to cast a slightly wider net than that."

"New York, New Jersey?"

"I was thinking the United States. Continental would be fine."

"You're insane," he says.

"Okay, I'll make it easier for you. Do you get notified when a person reported missing is subsequently found?"

"We're supposed to, but I'm sure it doesn't always happen."

"Anybody that was found, you can leave them off the list," I say.

"What's this about?"

"The people that were unidentified in the fire. I want to find out if any of them could have been the target," I say. "I admit I'm grasping at straws here."

"I'd like to help, but there's very little I can do," he says, surprising me once again with his cooperative attitude.

"Why?"

"Because there are thousands of localities; I can't contact every one. You need to attack this nationally."

"I will," I say. "But for now, whatever you can do would be great."

He nods. "I'll do what I can."

"You can give the information to me as it comes in; then I can get my people started on it."

"Thanks a lot." He sneers. "You have people now?"

"I've got plenty of people. If you work really hard, one day you could be one of them."

Nancy shows up precisely at seven-thirty and we go into her office. I haven't seen her in a while, so we make small talk for a few minutes, until Pete grunts his displeasure.

"Tell Andy about your talk with Kyle Holmes," Pete says.

She nods. "Kyle came to see me, a few days before he died. He wanted to talk

307

about the Hamilton Village case, so I had the file in front of me. Not that I needed it; there are some things you don't forget."

"Were you here at that time?" Nancy had moved here from Boston a while back, but I don't remember if it was before or after the fire.

"It was one of my first cases when I took over the office," she says. "Not a great way to start."

"What did Kyle want?" I ask.

"First a little background, though I'm sure this is in the discovery documents," she said. "The fire was unbelievably intense, and it caused the second and third floors to cave inward. So the bodies were incinerated, not cremated but not too far off either. And because the building caved in on itself, the remains, such as they were, were mixed together. It was a horrible, horrible scene, by any standards."

I don't say anything; the information she's providing was in the discovery documents in excruciating detail. Reading them once was painful, and I was obligated to go over them a bunch of times.

She continues. "I'm embarrassed to say that there was very little science involved. We could independently identify very few of the bodies; it was really guesswork based on

308

secondary evidence, like testimony of people who claimed they knew who was in there."

"But some of the bones were intact," I say.

She nods. "Yes, but keep in mind we never had DNA samples of these people to start with, so even if we were able to extract some from the remains, there was nothing to compare it to."

"Okay, I understand the situation you faced."

"Good, because I never tried to hide it. It's in all my reports. And those reports are what Kyle came to talk to me about."

"Something specific?" I ask.

"Yes. He was interested in one of the victims. Roger Briggs."

I'm familiar with the name; he was the grandson of Jesse Briggs, whom Laurie and I interviewed. The child's mother, Jesse's daughter, was killed as well. "What about him?"

"Well, keep in mind that we did not attempt to put too much information about the victims in our report. We just couldn't do so from the remains alone, and the rest would be more of an investigative effort, which is not really what we're geared to do. We basically just listed each victim that we knew about by name, sex, and age."

"Roger Briggs was on the list," I say.

She nods. "Yes, but there was a mistake, and information was not transcribed correctly. It said Roger Briggs, male, eight. The fact that he was eight months old was not clear; it appeared from the list that he was eight years old."

"So?"

"So nothing about the remains listed in the report corresponded to the size of a victim of that age. Kyle was asking me about that."

"What did you tell him?" I ask.

"Well, I spent some time studying the report, and my backup notes from the examinations. It confirmed what I thought; there was nothing intact that corresponded to an eight-month-old. Of course, that isn't necessarily conclusive; those remains could have been burned too badly."

Pete speaks for the first time since Nancy started relating the story. "So bottom line, what do you think?"

Nancy pauses for a moment, seeming to weigh her words. "I don't think there was a baby in that fire."

It seemed significant when Nancy said it, but the possibility that there might not have been a baby in the fire is not exactly a case solver. First of all, we can't be sure it's true. Second of all, if it were true, we don't know where the baby is, or what he or she has to do with anything.

What is important is the knowledge that Kyle Holmes was working the case, and that he thought he was on to something. What might be more important is that someone else thought he was on to something, and killed him for it. Then, if my theory is correct, the frame of Noah that was kept in reserve was finally unveiled, to stop anyone else from following up on what Kyle was learning.

At this point, the threat to Becky, which was clearly a way to stop the trial, might even be logical. The perpetrators might have been banking on the case being so strong that Noah would have pled it out, and not gone to trial.

Once I convinced him to do so, and the trial date came so quickly, the entire matter would automatically be subject to intense scrutiny, which the bad guys clearly would not want.

So now, in addition to having no idea who the significant adults are in this case, we have added a baby to be in the dark about. But at least it's starting to make a little sense, and at this pace we should have the whole thing nailed by Noah's thirtieth parole hearing.

I ask Laurie to focus as much time as possible on learning whatever she can about Natasha and Roger Briggs. Roger was the only baby listed among the victims of the fire, and they lived on the third floor, which I have always considered worthy of special investigation. The fire would have consumed the entire house from the first floor up, yet special attention was given to spreading the mixture on the third floor.

Today is going to be another depressing day in court, watching Dylan parade his witnesses in front of the jury, questioning them in excruciating detail. It's like getting a legal colonoscopy.

Before I leave I take Tara and Bailey for

our daily morning walk, during which I get my monthly idea. With Bailey with us the walks are much slower; I think she would prefer that we push her in an enormous stroller.

Along the way we run into a neighbor walking her beautiful golden, Callaway. She's one of Tara's favorite dogs to interact with, they can spend all day sniffing and chatting. This time is a little different, as Callaway can't take her eyes off Bailey. It's like she wants to pull Tara aside and ask, "What the hell is that?"

When I get home I call Sam and ask him if he can recruit at least five people, with significant computer skills, who can work on the case under his direction.

"What about my computer class?" he asks.

"You take a computer class?"

"I teach one. A night course. I'm sure some of my students would love to do it."

"Can you bring them to my house to-night?" I ask. "Around eight?"

"That's pretty late," he says. "How about six? Does that work?"

"Sure," I say. "I'll move some stuff around."

I wish I could move the trial around, like around to August, but that's not going to happen. Dylan surprises me by telling the court he wants to call FBI Special Agent Neil Mulcahy. I knew Mulcahy would eventually testify, I just thought Dylan might hold him off until later.

Mulcahy is not going to have much to say, at least not on his own. He was the agent to whom Danny Butler spoke when he claimed that Noah had confessed setting the fire, and he will basically be reading the transcript of that interview.

I let Hike argue on our behalf that the testimony should not be admitted, since Butler is not here to be cross-examined. De Luca overrules our objection, as we knew he would. I consider it a bad law, but it's not De Luca's job to make those judgments. He has to implement the law as it is, not as he thinks it should be.

Dylan asks very few questions, just a handful to set the scene. He's correct in that approach; Butler's words, even when spoken by Mulcahy, are powerful and speak for themselves.

In fact, the words are much more powerful than if Butler were here. Mulcahy is an impressive guy, and as an FBI agent he commands the kind of respect that a slimeball like Butler never could. The words have more credibility coming out of Mulcahy's mouth than they would dripping out of

Butler's.

The original version of the interview took about two hours and fifteen minutes, and that's how long the reenactment takes. Dylan actually plays the part of Mulcahy in asking the questions, and Mulcahy plays Butler.

I watch the jury as they watch the performance, and they are paying rapt attention. I'm surprised they haven't asked for a playbill.

We take a break before my cross begins, and I call Cindy Spodek on my cell phone. Cindy is an FBI agent, recently promoted to assistant bureau chief in Boston. She is a very good friend to Laurie and me, which I constantly take advantage of to get information when I need it.

"What do you need now?" she asks, when she gets on the line, which is not exactly warm "friend" talk.

"What I need is to find out how my friend Cindy is doing, to find out what is going on in her life, because I care deeply about her. That is my whole reason for calling. It is my whole reason for being."

"You're full of shit," she says.

"What tipped you off?"

"You only call when you're on a case. This is about Galloway."

"Actually, now that I have you . . ."

I go on to request the same missing persons information that I asked Pete for, since Cindy would have much better access. It takes some cajoling, but she basically likes to be helpful, and she's not the type to let down a friend. Those are the kind of people I can take advantage of.

"This will take a while," she says.

"I don't have a while; the trial is almost over."

"Good-bye, Andy."

I head back to court for the Mulcahy cross-examination. I have little ammunition with which to challenge him, since he really was not the witness against Noah; he was only channeling Butler. But I have to give it a shot.

"Agent Mulcahy, did Danny Butler have a criminal record?"

"He did."

"Did he have three convictions for drug possession, and two for breaking and entering?"

"Yes."

"Was he arrested but not convicted on three other occasions?"

"Yes."

"Was he himself addicted to drugs?" I ask.

"Enough so that he was in rehab on four

separate occasions?"

"Yes."

"Did you believe his story?"

"I did."

"Because of his status as an upstanding citizen?"

"We take information and judge it no matter where it comes from. It's not always upstanding citizens that have information about a crime."

"What would Butler's background have to have been for you to doubt what he said? Maybe time as a Taliban commander? Or a Nazi SS officer?"

Dylan objects and De Luca admonishes me to cut it out. Business as usual.

"Did you check into Butler's background after you talked to him?"

"I did."

"Did he graduate high school?" I ask.

"He did not."

I introduce Butler's high school records, which include a PSAT combined score of 614, and I point out that in those days one got 400 for signing one's name.

"In the interview, Butler said that his conscience had been bothering him all these years, and when he saw Mr. Galloway on television as a representative of the U.S. government, it pushed him over the edge.

Made sense to you?"

"I had my doubts," Mulcahy says, surprising me. "But when I checked it all out, I was convinced."

Mulcahy has opened a door for me, that I was planning to open myself. "Checked it out how?"

"I compared it to the evidence of the fire. Everything Butler said was accurate, and it was information that was not publicly available."

I introduce as evidence Butler's records from one of his drug rehabs, and refer Mulcahy to the date on the report. "Is that two weeks after he says Mr. Galloway confided in him?"

"Sixteen days, yes," Mulcahy says.

I then get him to read a paragraph from the initial statement Butler made to the rehab facility, admitting to heavy drug usage for the two months previously. "So by his own admission, Mr. Butler was using drugs during the period that he claims Mr. Galloway confessed to him?"

"Yes, but not necessarily that day."

"Maybe it was a drug holiday," I say. "Or maybe it was Thanksgiving, and he was going cold turkey for the day. But in any event, his recounting of the details of the fire, how it was set, et cetera, all of that proved to be

318

accurate?"

"Definitely."

"Down to the last detail?"

"Yes."

"So let's recap. A man with five felony convictions and extraordinarily low intelligence recounted almost verbatim technical details of a conversation he had six years earlier, when he was taking so many illegal drugs that he would soon be forced into rehab? And all because he was suddenly conscience-stricken. Is that about right?"

"That's your description," Mulcahy says.

"Which part of it is inaccurate?" I say.

"You left out the fact that there was no other way he could have gotten the information."

"There was no other way that you could find," I say. "Now, you said that Butler was subsequently killed in Las Vegas, and that Mr. Galloway is said to know people there."

"That's correct."

"I also know people there. Are you going to cuff me?"

Mulcahy surprises me with a smile. "I'm tempted," he says, and the jury laughs.

"Where did he get the money to go to Vegas in the first place? Did he have a job?"

"I don't know."

"Maybe he suddenly came into money?

Perhaps for performing a service?"

"If he did, I'm not aware of it."

"Maybe he just needed a vacation; conscience clearing can be exhausting."

Mulcahy just smiles, as if these barbs are to be expected from a defense attorney who doesn't have the evidence on his side. He's an experienced, excellent witness because of his confidence and lack of fear; the jury thinks that means he's telling the truth and hiding nothing.

I let him off the stand, having accomplished as much as I could, which is not nearly enough.

"Mr. Mandlebaum, I think you'll be more comfortable in this chair."

That's what I hear Laurie say as I walk into the house. What I see is Laurie, Sam, Tara, Bailey, and five very old people, four of them men.

"Andy, I've got some people I want you to meet," Sam says. "This is Morris Fishman, Leon Goldberg, Stanley Rubinstein, Hilda Mandlebaum, and her husband Eli."

"Nice to meet you all," I say. "You're Sam's students?"

They all nod their confirmation of my question.

"At what school might that be?" I ask.

"The YMHA in Wayne."

He's talking about the Jewish version of the YMCA, meaning it's the Young Men's Hebrew Association. Except they aren't "young" and Hilda isn't one of the "men." Perhaps it should just be called the HA.

321

I ask Sam if I could talk to him in the kitchen before we get started. Once we're in there, I ask, "Does their age have anything to do with why you wanted to make the meeting early?"

He shrugs. "They're sharper earlier in the day," he says. "They usually have dinner around fourish, and then to bed by eight."

"I'm not sure this is going to work, Sam."

"They're up at five in the morning, Andy, so we'll have a full day. And you should see them on a computer; they're as good as any students I've ever had."

"How many classes have you taught?" I ask.

"This is my first."

"Sam . . ."

"It will be fine; trust me."

I actually do trust Sam, especially when it's in the area of computers, so we go back into the other room. Morris Fishman is in the process of telling Laurie she looks just like Esther Fleischmann, his high school sweetheart who cheated on him in 1947 when he went to Rutgers and she stayed home.

"Morris," Laurie says, "you deserved better."

Eli Mandlebaum is petting Tara, and Leon is petting Bailey, and they seem quite content about it. Based on their relative sizes, Leon could be Bailey's jockey. Tara has always been an equal opportunity petting receiver; she is unconcerned about race, religion, sex, or age. Clearly she's teaching Bailey her open-mindedness.

Sam turns the meeting over to me. I can tell I need to get it over with quickly; it's getting close to six-thirty, and I think Hilda is starting to nod off.

I explain where we are on the case, as it relates to the cell phone records. "We have all these people that were called. They live in different places and have quite different occupations. The only common thread that we know about is that they were all called at some point by the owner of that particular cell phone."

"So you want to find out if there are any other connections?" Stanley asks.

"Exactly. We need to dig as deeply as we can into each of their lives, and find out if they are connected in any other way. No matter how insignificant the link might be, I want to know about it."

"How do we do it?" Leon asks.

"I have no idea," I say. "Sam is in charge of that. He'll instruct you on what to do. Right, Sam?"

"No problem."

323

"I'm also going to be getting a list of missing persons from around the time of the fire. We're going to need to track them down as well."

"We're on it," Sam says, and then turns to his team. "We start bright and early at six? The computer room at the Y?"

Everyone nods their agreement, and Hilda says that she and Eli will pick up bagels and lox on the way in. With that, Sam leads the "over the hill gang" out the door.

When they leave, Laurie says, "I hope I'm just like them if I get to be their age. And I hope we're just like Hilda and Eli."

"What do you mean?"

"Didn't you see them holding hands? Hilda told me they've been married sixty-one years. And they're still holding hands."

I hadn't seen them holding hands, but I don't say that. The truth is, I see the possibility of turning this situation to my own sexual advantage. The trick is to appear sensitive. "I'll hold your hand as long as you let me," I say, and take her hand.

"You think you're going to use Hilda and Eli's love for each other to get me into bed?" she says.

"It was worth a shot," I say.

"Okay, here's the deal," she says. "There's a definite chance you're going to get lucky tonight, but you need to understand that it has nothing whatsoever to do with the Mandlebaums. You got that?"

"Yes, ma'am. The Mandlebaums are a nonfactor."

"Okay, let's go," she says, and starts leading me up the steps to the bedroom.

"I just hope that I don't scream out Hilda's name," I say.

Today's testimony is going to be both dry and terribly damaging.

The witness is Special Agent William Rouse, the assistant head of the FBI crime lab located in Baltimore. He supervised the bureau's testing on the metal can found three blocks from the scene.

It's a large can, standard make, capable of holding almost four gallons, and Dylan proudly holds it up before introducing it as evidence and showing it to the witness. I've seen pictures of it from the discovery, and learned that it's available at Home Depot and pretty much everywhere else.

"Is this the can you were given to test?" Dylan asks.

Rouse nods. "It is."

"What types of tests did you run?"

"Fingerprint analysis, blood typing, and DNA."

"Were you able to get satisfactory results

in all three areas?"

"We managed to retrieve DNA and blood type results. There were no fingerprints."

"These tests that you conducted, were the same ones done by the local police at the time the can was found?"

"Yes, I was subsequently shown those reports after we conducted our tests."

"Were your results consistent with theirs?" Dylan asks.

"Identical."

Dylan takes him through the results, which are of course a match for Noah's DNA and blood type. Rouse says that there is a one in four billion chance that the DNA results are inaccurate. Based on the media reports I read before coming to court this morning, that matches our chances of getting an acquittal.

Dylan then addresses the question that the jurors must certainly be wondering. "If the police had these DNA results six years ago, why wasn't an arrest made back then?"

"Because Mr. Galloway's DNA was not in the database at the time. Recently he attempted to gain clearance because of a federal job he was taking, and a DNA sample was required. That's the reason we got a hit when we ran it this time, acting on Mr. Butler's information."

327

"Your witness," Dylan says to me, in a tone that doesn't seem to contain much worry.

I start by opening a package under the defense table, and I take out a can that is identical to the one that Rouse tested. "Is this the can you were given to test?" I ask, mimicking Dylan's question.

Rouse looks confused, and points to the previously introduced can, now resting on a side table. "No, that one is."

"How do you know that?" I ask. "Don't they look identical?"

"I assumed Mr. Campbell was showing me the correct can."

I nod as if this makes perfect sense. "So you said you were certain that was the can, even though it just looked like it, because you just believed whatever Mr. Campbell said?"

"I tested the can that he gave me," Rouse says, finding apparent refuge in a non sequitur.

"Good for you. How long was Mr. Galloway's DNA on that can?"

"At least six years," he says.

"You can tell that from your tests?"

"No. But as I said, my results matched the police tests."

"The results that Mr. Campbell showed

you, and you accepted at face value."

"Yes." He manages to sound slightly indignant at my inference.

"Agent Rouse, you are here as a supposedly independent expert witness. The court members and I would appreciate it if you would limit your answers to what you know independent of what Mr. Campbell or the police told you. Can you do that?"

Dylan objects, but De Luca overrules him, and Rouse agrees to my request.

"Thank you," I say, acting as if I have triumphed, when in fact I haven't. Rouse's test results are still staring me in the face, and the jury will believe them.

In situations like this, I feel it's important that I do more than just attack the witness; I need to present an at least somewhat plausible theory of my own. It's tough in this case, because I truly have no idea how Noah's burned skin got on that can.

"So, based on your own tests, that DNA could have been left on that can three years ago?"

"It's possible."

"Three months ago?" I ask.

"Possibly."

"Was he conscious when he touched the can?" I ask.

"I can't say that from my testing."

"Did he touch it willingly?" I ask.

"I don't know. That is not within the scope of my work."

"Was his skin on the other cans as well?"

"I only tested the one can. I was told that it was the only can recovered."

I show Rouse a page of the report by the fire department, which estimated that seventeen gallons of the napalmlike substance was used. "This can couldn't hold seventeen gallons, could it?"

"No."

"It would take five such cans to hold that much, would it not?" I ask.

He nods. "It would."

"So the theory is that Mr. Galloway fled the scene, but for some reason decided to leave one can to be found, while taking the others with him?"

"That is not part of my testing." I knew that, but I don't really care what he says. I'm doing the testifying now; I'm just using Rouse as a foil to get my words out.

"You'd have to ask someone else that."

"Thank you, Agent Rouse. You can be sure I will."

The birth certificate of Roger Briggs is on file in the Paterson Hall of Records.

It shows that he was born to Natasha Briggs at Paterson General Hospital. There is no father listed on the certificate, and no explanation for the omission.

Tragically, the death certificate for Roger Briggs is also on file, and it is dated slightly more than eight months after his birth. Cause of death is asphyxiation by fire; which is standard procedure in cases of these types, though an incinerated body can yield no such evidence. Even the bureaucracy can't seem to stomach the concept of a human being, in this case a baby, being consumed by flames while alive.

There is good reason to doubt that Roger Briggs died in that fire, and it is not just that the coroner found no traces of a body that small. My doubt more strongly stems from the fact that a young officer named

331

Kyle Holmes seems to have had the same doubt, and I believe he died because of it. And if he was in fact murdered by someone threatened by those doubts, then they move up a step toward certainty.

Our investigation outside of the trial is moving very slowly, and at this point is mostly dependent on Sam Willis and the "over the hill gang." I'm also anxiously waiting for Pete and especially Cindy to come through with missing persons information, but that is pretty much a shot in the dark.

Our situation within the trial is considerably more dire, and unfortunately moving at a faster pace. Dylan has maybe four days' worth of witnesses still to call, and then it's our turn to present our case, such as it is.

I believe in being completely honest with my clients, except when I think it is in their best interest to conceal things or flat-out lie to them. My moral compass pretty much always points south.

But in Noah's case there's no reason not to be straight, so in our daily meeting before court I lay things out as best I can. As he always does, he listens respectfully, with no apparent emotion, and then asks intelligent questions when I finish.

Once I've answered everything completely, if not to either of our satisfactions, he says,

"It's funny in a way; the longer this has gone on, the more I've believed in my own innocence. And the more I've wanted to win."

"That's only natural," I say.

He nods. "I suppose. But there was something very comforting in not caring. The worst had happened; that was as bad as it was going to get."

I know exactly what he's saying, and I'm feeling very guilty about it. I gave him a reason to hope, I gave him actual hope, and to this point I'm not delivering on it. I've built him up for a fall, and we both know it.

But he's going to try and let me down easy. "On the other hand, Andy, the relief that I feel that I didn't kill those people makes anything that happens worthwhile. I had to live with that horror for a long time, but it's gone. When I wake up in the morning, I don't hate myself."

I just nod my understanding.

"Instead I hate you," he says, and laughs to let me know he's kidding.

Before we head into court, Noah tells me that he heard from Becky and Adam this morning, and that they're doing well.

"She wanted me to ask you if she can come back to attend any of the trial," he says. "She wants to support me, and she wants the jury to see her supporting me."

It's actually a good point, and one I've thought about. The jury may be wondering why she's not here, and I'm going to answer that question for them in our case.

"But I told her no," Noah says. "I want her where it's safe, and I sure don't want her here when the jury tells us their verdict."

The truth is, I'm not that anxious to be here for that either.

Dylan doesn't have much more to say, so he's going to keep saying it.

His first witness today is Randall Henderson, a forensic scientist with the New Jersey State Police. He is the person who did the original testing on the paint can in the days after the fire, and whose work has since been confirmed by the FBI's lab.

If I play my cards right, he will be the only witness today. One of the jurors has a doctor's appointment that has been deemed necessary, so court will not be in session this afternoon. Since it's Friday, that will give me two and half days out of this courtroom, which will feel like a three-month world cruise.

Henderson is a very competent professional, and there is little doubt that his testing was done correctly. Though I made the FBI scientist look bad on cross-examination, the fact that the test results of both labs were identical makes it impossible to effectively challenge the results. They know that, Dylan and I know that, and the jury sure as hell knows it.

Dylan does me a favor by dragging out his testimony for two hours. I just have to keep Henderson on the stand for a few more minutes, and it's hello, weekend.

"Mr. Henderson, in examining the can, did you weigh it?"

"No, there was no reason to, not for my purposes."

I take the can and ask De Luca if I can hand it to him. When he says that I can, I ask Henderson to hold it and guess its weight. "Maybe six pounds," he says.

"And it's empty?"

"Yes."

I walk back to the defense table, and Hike hands me the second can, which I give to him. "What about this one, which is now two-thirds filled with liquid?"

Henderson is a pretty big guy, maybe six feet, a hundred and eighty pounds, and he has no trouble lifting it. "I don't know . . . fifteen pounds."

"I weighed it earlier, and it totaled thirteen and a half pounds. Does that seem about right?"

"I would think so," he says.

"There was earlier testimony that the amount of flammable liquid used would have required between four and five of those cans. That would mean between fifty-four and sixty-seven pounds, correct?"

"Yes."

"Would it not be incredibly difficult to carry four or five of these rather unwieldy cans, weighing sixty or so pounds?"

"I really couldn't say."

I receive permission from De Luca to ask him to step down from the witness stand. Hike reaches under the table and starts handing me additional cans, one at a time. I pretend that I'm having a little difficulty carrying them, and I make four trips over to Henderson, each time carrying one can.

"Mr. Henderson, each of these cans is identical to the original, wouldn't you say?"

"They look the same," is his grudging reply.

"And they all are filled with fluid, and each weighs thirteen and a half pounds. You don't have a bad back, or anything like that, do you?"

"No," he says.

"Great. Then would you please carry them to the back of the courtroom? All at once, please."

Dylan stands. "Your Honor, please . . ."

De Luca stares him down. "Your Honor, please?" he mimics. "Is that an official objection?"

De Luca instructs Henderson to carry the cans as I asked, providing he is not afraid he will injure himself. It's a fairly impossible task, because there is no way two hands can grip all the various handles at the same time.

Henderson gives it his best try, and much to my delight drops one of the cans after walking only a few feet.

"Pretty tough, huh?" I ask. "And remember, this fire was set on the third floor, so these cans were carried up the steps."

"It's difficult, but not impossible," Henderson says.

"You want to try it again? We've got time."

He doesn't want to, so I let him get back onto the stand.

"Mr. Henderson, let's say for argument's sake, all evidence to the contrary, that one person could do what you just failed to do. If you saw someone doing it, just walking down the street, do you think you would notice him?"

"I suppose I would, depending on what I was doing at the time."

"Yet no one reported seeing Mr. Galloway doing that."

Dylan finally makes the correct objection that these questions have nothing to do with Henderson's lab work, and De Luca sustains.

"When you were testing this can in your lab, did you ever have trouble finding it?" I ask.

"What do you mean?"

"Ever misplace it?"

He shakes his head. "Of course not."

"It stands out, doesn't it? Be pretty tough to lose."

"I certainly would not lose it, or misplace it."

"Yet no other cans were found, not in Mr. Galloway's apartment or anywhere else. Does it seem strange to you that he would leave the can with his charred skin on it right out on the street, but would hide the other cans so carefully that an entire police department could not find them?"

Before he can answer, Dylan objects, and De Luca tells him not to answer the question.

I try another one. "Did you have occasion to test any items from the actual house itself?"

He nods. "I did."

"Any significant results?"

"Depends what you mean by significant,"

he says. "But basically no. Everything in that house was pretty much incinerated."

"Do you think that was the plan, and that's why napalm was used?"

"What do you mean?" he asks.

"Well, would whoever used the napalm have been likely to know that incineration would be the result?"

He nods. "I would certainly think so."

"Then why not leave the cans behind to be incinerated along with everything else?" I ask. "Why take one can that he burned himself on, and carry it three blocks?"

"I can't say."

"That's too bad."

"We got something, Andy. Hilda found it."

It's the first message on my answering machine when I get home, and as I'm listening to it, Laurie walks into the room.

"Sam found something," I say.

"I know; I spoke to him. They're on the way over."

"They?"

She laughs. "Apparently they travel as a group." When I grimace, she adds, "They're nice people, Andy. This is an adventure for them."

"Do you know what they found?"

"No, Sam wouldn't say; he wants Hilda to have the honor."

"The State of New Jersey, the prosecutor's office, and the FBI versus Hilda Mandlebaum. It's a steel cage fight to the finish."

"My money's on Hilda."

Before they arrive, Marcus shows up. Laurie had called him in case whatever it was that Sam's gang came up with needed following up.

Tara practically lights up when she sees Marcus, who never fails to pet her. She follows him as he heads straight for the kitchen and the refrigerator, giving me time to ask Laurie, "How many of Sam's five interns are going to have a coronary when they see Marcus? I would make the over-under number three."

"I think they're probably tougher than you think," she says.

Sam and his gang walk in about fifteen minutes later, four hundred and twenty-seven years of hard-nosed investigators, not including Sam. Each of them carries a briefcase; they look like an army of aged accountants.

If they are intimidated by Marcus, they don't show it, and Morris Fishman mentions that Marcus looks like somebody he knew in Korea.

"You fought in Korea?" I ask.

He shakes his head. "I bought fabric there. I was in the dress business . . . shmatas."

Marcus nods knowingly, as if he's spent the weekend shmata-shopping with Hilda. I feel like I'm on the planet Goofball.

"Let's get started, shall we?" I ask.

Sam nods. "Sure. Hilda?"

Hilda shrugs and says, "You go ahead, Sammy. You can tell it better than I can."

Sam opens his briefcase and takes out some pieces of paper. He hands a copy of the first one to Laurie, Marcus, and me. Each of the "gang" also takes out their own copy to refer to it. It's a photograph of a distinguished-looking man, about forty-five years old.

"This is Walter Holland. He's the presiding judge in the Delaware Chancery Court. Undergraduate at Princeton and then went to Virginia Law, top of his class. Clerked for a justice in the Fourth Circuit Court of Appeals. Married to the former Alice Simmons for three years; they have one adopted child, Benji, and they live a mile from the courthouse. Very well respected, and considered to be the leading jurist on business law in the country. We've listed the rest of his bio and some of his most important cases at the bottom of the page."

I don't have to ask why I should care about Judge Holland or his background, since he was on the cell phone list. Laurie had tried repeatedly to reach him, but was unable to. What I am now waiting for is what Sam has learned about Holland that has caused him to single him out.

Sam takes out more paper from his briefcase, again handing a copy to the three of us. Again, the "gang" does the same. Another man is pictured in this photo, a little younger than Holland, and a little harder. Even in this photo, it's clear that this man does not suffer fools gladly, and is used to getting his way.

"This is Alex Bauer," Sam says. "He is the CEO of Entech Industries, a relatively small energy company, with holdings in the South and Midwest. He's a former marine, former amateur boxing champ, reputation for being tough."

"I spoke with him," Laurie says. "He gave me the party line, that he had no idea what I was talking about, and I should call him back when I had more specifics."

"Well, you're about to have some. For the last five and a half years, Entech Industries has been trying to acquire Milgram Oil and Gas, a publicly owned company with a market capitalization that makes it maybe thirty percent larger than Entech."

"So Entech is borrowing the money to buy it?" I ask.

"That's not clear," Sam says. "Either that, or they have other investors behind them, or they'll sell off pieces of the acquired company. One way or the other, Bauer and Entech do not seem concerned, and they're offering a forty percent premium on the stock, up from an initial offer of a twenty percent premium."

"Why isn't Milgram accepting the offer?" I ask.

"Two reasons. One, it's a mostly family-owned company, been one for generations. Between five siblings they have more than thirty percent, and just don't want to give up the business. The second reason is that they have been pioneers in wind technology, and have invested heavily in it. There's a school of thought that as a country we are headed in that direction, and that the government is going to make a huge investment in it. They'd be on the ground floor."

"Is that why Entech wants it?" Laurie asks.

"Probably, but they haven't commented on it. Milgram also has land holdings that it is drilling for oil on, and a lot that it has the rights to but hasn't gotten started on yet."

"Why haven't the other seventy percent of the stockholders taken the offer?"

"Because the board is controlled by the Milgram family, and they've adopted a poison pill. Stanley used to be a stockbroker . . . Stanley?"

Stanley says, "Companies that don't want to be taken over, but think, oy, it could happen, make a poison pill. There are different types, but this one says that if any outsider buys more than twenty percent of the shares, the current shareholders can buy more shares at a reduced price. It dilutes the value of the newcomer's shares. The more he buys, the less they're worth."

"Oy," Laurie says, and I look at Marcus. If he says "Oy," I'm out of here.

"But how do the two tie together?" I ask.

"Bauer and Entech are suing Milgram, claiming the poison pill is illegal," Sam says. "If they win, they get the company. Milgram's been fighting it, and draining their assets in the process. It's considered very unlikely that they'd have the resources to appeal and have this drag on further in the courts."

"Let me guess. The suit is being heard in Delaware, with Judge Holland presiding."

Hilda points at me and says to Sam, "He's very good."

"Hilda, if I was that good, I'd know what to do with this."

I tell Laurie I'll work on Judge Holland, while she deals with Bauer.

The problem is that I have no idea how to do that. It's pretty tough to get hold of big-time judges, though the fact that Holland doesn't know me is a plus. Judges who know me have a tendency not to be too fond of me.

It's also not the smartest thing in the world to accuse judges of doing bad things, especially when the accuser has no evidence and doesn't know what the bad things are.

So basically, I need to figure out a way to reach him, and then figure out what to say if I do.

"Judge Holland's office," is how the woman answers the phone when I call. I'm surprised anyone answered the phone, since it's Saturday. But he's apparently preparing an opinion, so I thought I'd take a shot.

"I'd like to speak to the judge, please," I

say. "My name is Andy Carpenter."

"May I ask what it is in reference to?"

"It's a personal matter between Judge Holland, Alex Bauer, and myself. Mr. Bauer suggested that I call."

"Just a moment, please."

Waiting for her to come back on the phone, I figure there is about a two percent chance that Holland will get on the phone. Maybe less.

"I'm afraid Judge Holland is unable to speak with you, Mr. Carpenter."

"Unable or unwilling?"

"I assume you are aware that Judge Holland is currently presiding over a case in which Mr. Bauer is an interested party?"

"I am."

"Then you should know that all contact must go through the court. Good day, sir."

As my mother would have said about my attempt to reach Holland, "Nothing ventured, nothing gained." I always found the saying annoying, but it crystallized a clear difference in attitude between us. To her, the "ventured" part was important; while all I ever really cared about was whether something was "gained."

With nothing better to do, I plunge into as much information as I have been able to accumulate about the case before Judge

Holland in Delaware.

Financial litigation has never been a specialty or interest of mine, and this case, if nothing else, confirms that attitude. It is deadly dry, lawyers arguing in arcane legalese about issues which do not seem terribly consequential. Regardless of which company prevails, the world will not be a better, or even appreciably different, place.

But there is something in here, something that relates to Noah Galloway's trial, and to the murder of twenty-six people six years ago. At least I hope that's true, because it's the only hope I have.

The phone rings, and it's Pete, telling me that he has the list of missing persons from that period six years ago. It's a very, very incomplete list, he says. "If it helps you, I'll be surprised."

I ask him to e-mail it to me, and then I call Sam and tell him I'm forwarding it to him. It's Saturday, probably a day that most of his gang rests, but he promises to get right on it.

He asks what I specifically want. "Actually, hold off until I get you the rest of the names," I say, thinking of the list that Cindy Spodek is working on. "Meanwhile, any other connections between people on the cell phone call list?"

"No, but we're still rechecking it," he says, and I let him off the phone to do his work.

I take Tara and Bailey for a walk, and when we get back, Laurie comes out on the porch to greet us. "I reached Bauer," she says.

"And?"

"He did a one-eighty; now he wants to talk. He says he has a lot he needs to say."

"Needs?" I ask.

She nods. "Needs. It sounds like he wants to get something off his chest."

"Sounds good to me. Does he have a specific time and place for the unburdening?"

"He's going to call me back; he said this must be done in absolute secrecy. Made me promise that I would never reveal that he talked to us."

"Did you promise?" I ask.

"Of course."

"I'm glad I didn't."

"Andy . . ."

"Let's see what he says, okay? Maybe he'll admit to setting the fire. Either way, let's see if keeping your promise justifies Noah spending the rest of his life in jail."

"Carpenter called me. He said he was calling on behalf of Alex Bauer."

If it wasn't panic in Judge Holland's voice, it was something close to it.

"Did you talk to him?" Loney asked.

"Of course not. I had my assistant tell him it was inappropriate for me to do so, because of Bauer's involvement in the case."

"Good," Loney said. "You handled it perfectly."

"You don't seem to understand; he obviously knows what's going on. You think he's going to stop because my assistant said I wouldn't come to the phone?"

Loney was tired of babysitting these people. They were all leaders in their fields, accomplished people, yet they turned to mush when the going got difficult. "He's not calling you because he knows . . . he's calling you because he's trying to find out."

"How do you know that?"

"Because if he knew what was happening, you wouldn't be the judge that he would go to," Loney said. "His focus is on his trial, and getting Galloway off."

"Galloway should get off."

"Get a grip, Judge. Your part in this is almost over."

"It doesn't feel like that. It feels like it will never end," Holland said.

"Have you finished writing your opinion?"

"Almost."

"Good. Issue the damn thing already and you're done."

"Why does Bauer want the company?" Holland asked. He'd been curious about that since the suit was filed; Milgram was a struggling company, and the legal process had been steadily draining them, to the point where they would not be able to afford a lengthy appeal if they lost.

The wind turbines were promising, but overall the company should not be a ripe takeover target. In fact, noticeably absent these last few years was any other bidder for it; Bauer was the only one.

"There is no need for you to know, and you don't want to know," Loney said. "Your sole function here is to make sure he gets it."

"I'll post the opinion to the court Web site

on Tuesday, after which I will never hear from you again."

Loney laughs off the threat. "Hey, you called me this time."

"I mean it, Loney. This is the end of it. I swear, I'll tell everything I know and go to jail. I might even be able to live with myself."

"You going to take your wife and child with you? Maybe get adjoining cells?" The threat was very clear, and Loney had made it multiple times before. If Holland did not do as he was told, exposure of his wrong-doing would not be the only retribution.

So for the moment Holland did the only thing he could do. He hung up.

"There's a motel on Route 46 in Clifton called the Parker Court. I'm in room 216."

Bauer is saying that to Laurie, and I'm listening on the speakerphone. He has driven up from his home in Cherry Hill, from where he commutes to his office in Philadelphia.

I've passed by the motel he's talking about many times; it is not where you'd expect to find the CEO of a big corporation, unless he was meeting a hooker.

"When should we be there?" Laurie asks.

"We?"

"Andy Carpenter and myself."

"Oh," he says, and then is silent for a few moments while he considers that this secret is expanding. "That'll be okay. Now would be good; the less time I spend in this dump the better."

"We'll be there in thirty minutes," Laurie says, and hangs up.

She starts heading for the car, and I say, "Might make sense to bring Marcus. We don't know whose side this guy is on."

She shakes her head. "No time, and I don't want to scare him off. I've got a gun, in case you decide we should shoot him."

We are at the motel with five minutes to spare. It's one of those places where you enter the individual rooms from the outside, so we head for 216 and knock. Alex Bauer opens the door in ten seconds.

"I'm Alex Bauer," he says. "Come in."

We enter the drab, nondescript room and introduce ourselves, and he says, "Sorry I can't offer you anything. I would have ordered from room service, if not for the fact that they don't have any."

"No problem," Laurie says.

"I'd like to get right to this," Bauer says. "I'm a little nervous, and I don't want to change my mind. But I need your promise this will go no further. If it does, I believe I will be killed."

Laurie and I both make the promise; I might even keep it.

There are two beds in the room and a chair. Laurie and I sit on one of the beds, but Bauer paces rather than sitting down. "I'm being blackmailed," he says. "It's been going on for almost six years."

There is no limit to the number of questions that this surprising admission raises, but I start with, "Who is doing the blackmailing?"

"The person I deal with, or rather the person who deals with me, I guess you'd call him my handler, is named Loney. His first name is Alan, but he never uses it, at least with me. He works for a man named Carmine Ricci, who is a mob boss in Las Vegas. But I'm not supposed to know that."

The mention of Vegas is particularly interesting to me, since that is where Danny Butler was killed. "How do you know it?"

"I've hired some private investigators to find out. They didn't dig too deep, because I didn't want to have them caught in the process."

"What are they forcing you to do?" Laurie asks.

"I have tendered an offer to purchase a company called Milgram Oil and Gas. It's been very contentious, and the case is in a Delaware court right now. A decision is expected at any time."

"What do they have to gain from that?" I ask.

"I don't know. It is not a move I would have made without their intervention. It won't hurt my company either way, but as they say, the juice has not been worth the squeeze."

"What happens after you get the company?"

"There will be further instructions, which they assure me will be painless." His smile has no humor in it. "Painless is not how I would describe this situation."

"And what if you don't get the company?" Laurie asks.

"They don't seem to be concerned about that. My analysis is that it's a close legal call, but if Loney is worried, he certainly hides it well."

There is no doubt in my mind that this is where Judge Holland comes in, and less doubt that he will rule in favor of Bauer and Entech Industries. Alex Bauer is not the only one they have something on.

"Why are you cooperating with them?" Laurie asks.

"That I can't reveal, to you or anyone else. Suffice it to say that they have knowledge of something that, if revealed, would destroy my career, and most of my life. But I will tell you that it has absolutely nothing to do with the fire, or the Galloway trial."

"How did they get that knowledge?"

"That is something I've never been able to uncover. It may seem a little cryptic for me to say this, but they may have been responsible for facilitating the situation in the first place."

"They set you up?" Laurie asks.

"It's possible, but ultimately I am to blame."

"Why did you come to us with this?" I ask.

He shrugs. "Probably because you were coming to me, and I figured you'd find it all out anyway. But I also would like to nail them, and I'm hoping that you'll be able to do that." He pauses, and then says, "While leaving me out of it."

"That would be nice," I say.

"Where the hell have you been?"

Vince Sanders is referring to the fact that I haven't been to Charlie's to watch football for a couple of weeks. He's yelling, so I hold the phone a few inches from my ear, which is the position it's usually in when I'm talking to Vince.

"I'm in the middle of a trial, Vince. It's on the front page of your paper every day."

"So you're in a trial, and I have to buy my own beer?"

"Vince, it was completely inconsiderate of me, and I apologize. From now on, just put everything on my tab."

"You don't have a tab," he points out.

"Damn. If I get one, put everything on it."

"What do you want?"

"What makes you think I want something?" I ask.

"When people ask me for a favor I get a

rash. I've been scratching ever since the phone rang."

"What about when the favor could result in a big story, which you would get the exclusive on?"

"That, my dumb, annoying friend, is like a soothing balm. What are we talking about here?"

"I need to talk to Dominic Petrone right away." Petrone is the head of the largest organized-crime family in New Jersey, and he is one of the four or five billion people that Vince has access to.

"Why don't you 'friend' him on Facebook?"

"Vince . . ."

"What should I tell him this is about?"

"The Galloway trial."

"Let me have your credit card number," he says.

"Why?"

"Because if Petrone puts you under Giants Stadium, I don't want to have to buy my own beer."

"Why do you say that?" I ask, but realize the answer as I ask him.

"Because they tried to pin the fire on him when it happened. The theory was that the drug guys in the house were moving on his territory. He was all over the papers, including mine, and he wasn't happy about it."

"But he got cleared of it," I point out.

"I still wouldn't go around accusing him if I were you."

"I'm not accusing him; tell him it's about Carmine Ricci."

"Stay by the phone."

"For how long?"

"Until it rings."

Click.

Vince never says "hello" or "good-bye." It's part of his charm. But he does have the significant trait of always coming through, and the phone rings ten minutes later.

It's Vince. "Be outside your house at nine P.M."

"At night?" I'm nervous enough about meeting Petrone, since all he would have to do is nod for someone to kill me. It just seems somewhat safer during daylight hours.

"Wow, you don't miss a thing."

Click.

Meeting with Dominic Petrone is one of those things that seems right when you plan it, but then dread when the actual time approaches. In this case the dread starts as soon as Vince hangs up the phone.

"Let me go with you," Laurie says.

I shake my head. "No. This is me and

361

Dominic, one on one, mano a mano."

"Mano a mano?"

I nod. "Right. Law of the jungle."

"You're a wonderful, talented man, Andy, but the jungle is not your thing."

"What does that mean?"

"Well, you're afraid of wild animals, bugs, snakes, lizards, spiders, scary-looking plants, and not having indoor plumbing. I have a feeling you wouldn't sleep that comfortably in your tent if you knew that Mafia dons were lurking around either."

"While all of that may be true, I told Vince that I wanted to talk to Petrone. I didn't mention anyone else, and I don't want to pull any surprises."

I go outside at a quarter to nine, and exactly fifteen minutes later a black sedan pulls up. One of Petrone's very large people gets out of the backseat, and holds the front door open for me. I get in the passenger seat and see that two other goon clones are in the car, one obviously driving.

"Hey, guys," I say, and none of them answer. That sets the tone for the rest of the ride, as they don't speak a single word the entire way. It makes me uncomfortable, but I'd prefer the silence to somebody saying "Sonny says we're going to the mattresses," or "Leave the gun and take the cannolis."

362

We get on Route 80, which surprises me because I know from previous visits that Petrone lives in the Riverside section of Paterson. Then we get on the lower level of the George Washington Bridge, but the driver does not execute the amazing U-turn that they did in *The Godfather.*

My keen intuition tells me I'm seeing Petrone in New York.

We head down to lower Manhattan, and park in a lot in the West Village. We get out of the car, and I follow them down the street. They stop at a building on the street, with no sign, though there is a flag flying above the door. It's not a flag I recognize.

The driver knocks on the door, and within fifteen seconds it opens. The person who opens it looks at us and opens the door wider, so we all go in. Still not a word has been spoken.

It seems to be some kind of restaurant/ club that we're in, but certainly a private one. I follow my escorts to a back room, which is an ornate bar. Petrone is having drinks with four other men.

They all turn to see us as we enter, and the four men start to get up in unison, obviously preparing to leave us alone. Petrone slightly shakes his head, and raises his hand, as if telling them to stay, and they sit back down.

Petrone gets up and walks into an adjacent room, and I am led into it as well. My three escorts, whom I've really grown close to, stand with their backs to the wall, while I sit at a table with Petrone.

I'm very nervous, but not quite as much so as in previous meetings with Petrone. I assume that is because in each of those meetings he hasn't killed me, so therefore my chance of survival this time seems good. Had he killed me one of those other times, I would not be so optimistic now.

"Hello, Andy," Petrone says. "To what do I owe this unexpected visit?" Petrone can be quite gracious, a refined gentleman, probably in his mid-fifties, who seems the type that might have some mixed emotions when he orders people executed.

"There is something going on that I thought you might not know about."

He smiles. "There's always a first time."

"Carmine Ricci from Las Vegas; I assume you know him?"

"I prefer you to make statements, rather than asking questions."

I nod. "Gotcha. Anyway, it seems that Mr. Ricci is involved, at least peripherally, in a case I'm working on. And his involvement consists, among other things, of having a man in his employ do some rather illegal things. Right here in North Jersey." My assumption and hope is that Petrone will not like a counterpart from across the country operating in his territory.

"Interesting," Petrone says. "And the name of this man?"

"Loney. If I'm right, he's already committed a murder, blackmailed a bunch of people, and threatened a woman. And that's just before lunch."

"Do you have any reason to believe that Mr. Ricci is an interested party in this, other than providing access to one of his employees?"

"I don't know that either way," I say.

"What would you have me do about all this, on the off chance that I believed you?"

"Well, in a perfect world, first you would call Mr. Ricci and get him to withdraw his troops, so to speak."

"You think he and I are part of one large club?" Petrone asks.

"I think he might respect you enough to see your point."

"You said 'first.' Is there a second?"

I nod. "Yes. I'd like to go talk to Mr. Ricci, perhaps make him a proposition. Under your protection."

"What might be in this for me?"

"Well, the fact that I've alerted you to this situation is something I would hope you'd appreciate. And then there is the help I provided on Quintana." I'm referencing my providing Petrone with a way to get rid of a former rival, who in terms of viciousness made Petrone look like Mary Poppins. It also benefited me on a case, but there's no reason to mention that now.

"I'll call you at noon tomorrow," Petrone says.

"Great. I'll look forward to it. How's the food here?"

"The best in the city; I'm looking forward to dinner right now. Good-bye, Andy."

I've got a hunch I'm not eating here. Maybe my three buddies and I can stop at a Taco Bell on the way home, where we can eat quesadillas and chat the night away.

Hike comes over at eight o'clock in the morning.

He does so for two reasons, probably of equal importance in his mind. The first is that he knows Laurie makes French toast on Sundays, and there is no better French toast on planet Earth. The second is that I pay him by the hour, and if it meant getting paid, Hike would eat asbestos toast.

He's already there when I come back from my walk with Tara and Bailey, hovering around the kitchen while Laurie cooks. When I enter he looks at his watch, and says, "You're late. We've got a lot of work to do."

"Sorry. Maybe we should skip breakfast."

He laughs. "Not in this lifetime."

During breakfast we talk about our next steps in the investigative, nontrial area of our efforts. More accurately put, Laurie and I talk, while Hike mostly chews. When it comes to eating, Hike is a mini-Marcus.

"No matter what Petrone sets up, I don't think you should go to Vegas," Laurie says.

"Why not?"

"It's not obvious? Ricci is the head of an organized-crime family. If he's been behind all this, then you have set yourself up as, if not his enemy, then at least a pain in his ass. He could decide to remove the pain."

"But maybe he's not, maybe he's just providing the muscle. That's what Petrone implied might be happening. In that case, he has no overriding interest, and he might pull the plug."

"You're dreaming."

"I'm not."

"I'm going with you."

"You're not."

We argue about this for a while, and we finally settle on a compromise, which is mostly in my favor. If I go to Vegas, Marcus comes with me.

"What about the judge in Delaware?" Hike asks.

"What about him?"

"He seems to be a key part of this. Maybe we can pressure him to cave."

"He won't even take my call," I say.

"Maybe we can find out who he's called. That might lead us to Loney."

"How would we do that?" Laurie asks. I think I know what Hike is thinking, but I hope I'm wrong.

I'm not.

"We have his cell number from Loney's original phone, right? So we find out who he has called. If Loney was calling him, the reverse is probably true, and we can get Loney's new number."

I put down my fork. "You're going to try and illegally obtain the private phone records of a prominent judge?"

Hike shakes his head. "Who said anything about me? I'm a law-abiding citizen and, I might add, an officer of the court. Sam can get it."

"Let's assume for a second that Sam would be crazy enough to do it . . ."

"A likely assumption," Laurie says.

I nod. "True. But what does it really do for us? We already know who Loney is, and that he has been in contact with the judge. Do we really need more confirmation of that? What we need to do is find Loney."

"That's what I'm talking about," he said. "Call Sam; let's make sure my idea will work."

I call Sam and put him on the speakerphone. After hearing Hike's plan, he confirms that it is very feasible, and blames himself for not thinking of it earlier. If we can get Loney's number off the judge's records, Sam could hack into the phone company's computers, something that is for him about as difficult as breathing.

Once in the computer, he could trace the GPS signal that is within every cell phone. In that way we could locate Loney's phone, and very likely Loney.

"And you are willing to illegally invade a prominent judge's records?"

"A crooked prominent judge," Sam points out.

"You can mention that at your sentencing hearing," I say.

"I'm not going to jail," Sam says. "Not with you as my lawyer."

I try to talk him out of it, but of course I'm not sure if I really want to. Hike's idea, while risky, is a good one, and could lead us to Loney. Of course, I have no idea what the hell I would do with Loney if we found him, but suffice it to say Marcus would be involved.

"I've got to get off the phone," I say to Sam. "I'm waiting for a call from a Mafia don."

"Now that's cool," Sam says.

Among the more admirable qualities of ruthless crime bosses is their punctuality.

The phone rings at noon, though it is not Petrone who calls. It's his first lieutenant, Joseph Russo, which doesn't make me any less nervous. It's a sign of how uncomfortable these people make me that I'd rather deal with lawyers.

"Mr. Ricci will see you in Suite 36575 of the Mandalay Bay Thursday afternoon at three P.M."

"Thursday is Thanksgiving Day," I point out.

"Tell me something I give a shit about."

"Is Ricci aware that I am under Dominic Petrone's umbrella of protection?"

Russo laughs. "We'll find out soon enough, huh?"

"I'm going to bring one of my investigators, Marcus Clark."

"I don't care who you bring."

Click.

Nobody says good-bye anymore.

Court is closed on Wednesday because of personal business Judge De Luca has to attend to, and it's obviously closed for the four-day Thanksgiving weekend. Which means I only have to get through two court days, stretching it so that I don't have to start presenting the defense case this week. The way Dylan is dragging this out, that shouldn't be a problem.

Once the call is behind me, and I can breathe normally again, Hike and I settle in to go over the witness list and make our preparations. There is nothing in it that we haven't gone over ten times before, but total familiarity with everything is absolutely necessary, and there's no other way to get it.

At one o'clock I turn on the Giants game as background noise, though the truth is I pay more attention to that than the case files.

Cindy Spodek calls at halftime, which is probably a coincidence, since she is not generally that considerate.

"Is your fax number still the same?" she asks. "I have a list to send you."

"These are people that were reported missing during that period and never found?"

"Right," she says. "Six hundred and forty-one names."

"That many?"

"And I'm sure there are quite a few that never made it to us. I believe this is the part of the conversation where you say, 'Thank you, Cindy. I don't know what I would do without you.' "

"No, this is the part where I ask if you've ever dealt with Carmine Ricci, and you say, 'Sure, he's a pussycat.' "

"You're dealing with Ricci?"

"I'm meeting with him next week," I say.

"I've got a better idea. Don't."

"Can't be helped, Cindy. Any tips?"

"Besides getting your affairs in order? Andy, seriously, this is not a wise idea."

"Did I mention it can't be helped?"

"An hour before you see him, call my number here at the bureau on your cell phone. If you feel things are getting dangerous, show him that you made the call, and tell him that we know where you are."

"Good idea. I will," I say. "Thank you, Cindy. I don't know what I would do without you."

"Very well put," she says. "Now let me talk to Laurie."

I give the phone over to Laurie, and she

373

and Cindy chat for about an hour. Most of Lauric's side of the conversation consists of her saying things like, "I can't stop him. Believe me, I've tried."

I call Sam and tell him that I'm going to be faxing him Cindy's list of names of missing persons from around the time of the fire. He can add it to Pete's list and get started.

"What am I supposed to do with it?" he asks, a perfectly logical question.

"Find out whatever you can about these people. I know you don't have time to dig too deep into each one; the public records should be enough. I want to know if they were connected to any of the people involved in this case, any of the people you've already found in the phone records. Pay particular attention to the various players in the Delaware trial."

"Got it," he says.

"How is it going on getting the judge's phone records?"

"Should have it very soon. And then we use it to find Loney."

"Yes, but that part is going to have to wait until I get back from Vegas. If we're going to deal with Loney in person, I want Marcus there."

"Okay, whatever you say. Meanwhile we'll

get started on this list."

"Can you get more help?"

"Don't need it. We're fine."

"Sam, your staff does not consist of people we want to overwork, you know?"

"Andy, they're amazing. I tell them to go home and take the rest of the day off, they say no. I hope I'm that energetic when I'm their age."

"I was never that energetic at any age," I say.

As I hoped, Dylan's big mouth works in my favor.

He spends the next two days putting on witnesses of little consequence, and then questions them as if they were crucial to his case.

None of the witnesses present direct evidence about Noah. They either talk about the extent of Noah's addiction, or his expertise in chemical engineering.

I question each of them, and make points which show the jurors our side is still alive and feisty. But all I'm really doing is biding time until Vegas.

We have to fly out on Wednesday, since I don't want to risk a flight cancellation that would leave me unable to make the meeting with Ricci.

I haven't been to Vegas in twenty years, and I have no idea where to stay. When I mention that to Marcus, he says, "Mandalay Bay."

I'm surprised that he even knows the name of a hotel there; Marcus does not seem like the Vegas type. "Why?" I ask.

"Sushi bar."

Marcus eats sushi; this truly is a global society. Mandalay Bay is where I'm meeting with Ricci, so staying there may not be a positive. If his goons chase me out of the room with guns blazing, I don't want to run next door to my room.

But ultimately I make the reservation there, telling the reservations clerk that I want to be as far as possible from suite 36575, which is where the meeting is. The clerk says that it's no problem, and at the end of the call tells me to "have a lucky day."

I'd better.

When we are leaving for the airport, Laurie hugs me very hard and long. It feels good, but less so when I realize that she is doing it because it may be the last time. Tara licks my face when I kneel down to pet her; and I whisper to her that Laurie should be her go-to person for biscuits and stomach-scratching if I don't come back. I pet and say good-bye to Bailey, nearly waking her in the process.

I bought first-class tickets for Marcus and me from Newark to Vegas. Marcus gets through security without incident, which means he's not carrying a gun, and he's not actually made of steel.

The other passengers in the waiting area all seem to be staring at Marcus; he is someone you stare at until he stares back at you, and then you pretend you weren't staring and walk away.

I can't imagine they're pleased that they're going to be on the same flight as Marcus. If it's overbooked, and the airline looks for volunteers to give up their seats, there will likely be a stampede.

Conversations with Marcus do not come easy for me, since he says almost nothing, and what he does say I can't understand. I actually prepare a few things to say, which I figure I'll spread out throughout the trip, and hopefully get by.

Marcus sits at the window, and I sit next to him. I turn to say something to him when the plane starts to leave the gate, but he's sleeping. He sleeps the entire way, and I have to wake him at the gate in Vegas. This works out well, since I can now save my planned conversational tidbits for the trip home, should he happen to be awake, and should I happen to be alive.

Vegas looks nothing at all like it did the last time I was here. The cab driver takes us on the scenic, longer route, since that is the best way for him to drive up the cost on the meter.

The hotels are simultaneously remarkable and ludicrous. There is one meant to look like the skyline of New York, one of Paris, and one of Venice. They are cleverly and respectively called New York, New York, the Paris, and the Venetian.

Strangely, I don't see any hotel designed to replicate Paterson. Perhaps "the Patersonian" is on the other side of the strip.

Marcus and I enter the hotel. Between that moment and the moment we go up to our rooms, four different hotel employees say things like, "Welcome back, Mr. Clark," and "Good to see you, Mr. Clark." Marcus just grunts in response, but no one seems put off by it.

Marcus has a life, and I don't.

I meet Marcus for dinner and drinks at the sushi bar, because that's where he wants to go. As we walk up to the person behind the desk, she lights up and starts talking a mile a minute in Japanese.

I'm about to tell her that I don't understand what she's saying, until I realize that she's talking to Marcus, and "Clark" is sprinkled through the diatribe, though it sounds like "Clock."

Marcus is smiling and nodding, hanging on every word. He even grunts in Japanese, though his normal "yuh" sounds more like "yih."

The maître d' comes over and joins in, and they're laughing and chattering away, still in Japanese, which means it takes a long time to get our table. Which is fine, since I don't like sushi anyway. Fortunately, Marcus makes up for that by eating enough for me and half the guests in the hotel.

Once he's finished, and before the enormous check arrives, he grunts and leaves. I head up to my room, where I order room service, call Laurie, turn on the TV, and fall asleep.

I sleep maybe four hours; I'm way too stressed to relax. Marcus and I meet in the morning at the buffet, which has an unbelievable array of very appealing food. For me it represents a potentially fitting last meal; for Marcus it is a chance to provide onlookers with a lasting memory and bragging rights. They will forever be able to say that they were there the day Marcus Clark defeated the Mandalay Bay's all-you-can-eat buffet.

Two o'clock rolls around all too fast, and five minutes before the appointed hour Marcus and I go up to Ricci's suite. I don't

380

think there is any chance that Marcus will be allowed in the meeting with me; I'm sure that my being alone will be the only way I'll get in. But I like having Marcus with me, and I want them to know he's here.

I knock on the double doors to the suite.

It's showtime.

"We need to meet with the judge."

Brett Fowler had said it, and it immediately pissed Loney off.

"No, we don't," Loney replied, trying to remain calm. Loney always had anger issues, which was generally not a good thing for the person he was angry at.

"Yes, we do. Carpenter called him."

"I know. I spoke to him." Then, pointedly, "He's my contact."

"Then you know he's freaking out. Look, Loney, I'm sure you think I'm stepping on your toes here, but I don't really give a shit. This guy is about to issue his ruling. We've been waiting six years for this, and we're going to make damn sure he doesn't change his mind, or jump off a building."

As annoyed as Loney was, he knew that Fowler was right. "Okay, I'll set it up."

"I already did," Fowler said.

"You're crossing the line."

"I know," Fowler said. "And I'll cross back as soon as he issues his ruling. So for now let's not argue about this, okay? You're not the one calling the shots here."

Loney also knew that was true; he was essentially a hired gun. For now. "Where's the meeting?"

"In Delaware, about a mile from where he lives. It's a place I have set up there." He gave Loney the address, and told him it was a warehouse. "The last thing we want is for the judge to be seen with us, especially me." Since Fowler was a professional political operative, such a sighting would cast any judge in a negative light.

"He'll be there at ten tonight," Fowler said. "Can you make it?"

"I'll be there."

Fowler liked the action; he always had. That's why he'd spent seven years in the Marines, and that's why he became a political operative in Washington. War, Fowler understood as well as anyone, is war. No matter what the battlefield looked like.

On the drive to Delaware he reflected on the progress that had been made. The only thing he had not anticipated was the speed at which the events would take place. The precipitating factor in that was the implication of Galloway. It sent things a little more out of control than Fowler would have liked, and Carpenter had proven to be something of a wild card.

But ultimately the result would have been the same; all that Carpenter had really changed were the tactics and the timing.

The big picture was intact and moving along beautifully. Holland would stay in line and rule in Entech's favor, which was the key all along. Everything would flow from that, and quickly, since there would be nothing to impede the progress.

Galloway would probably be convicted, at least that's what the media had been saying. Fowler really had not been paying much attention. Even though he was mostly responsible for Galloway being on trial in the first place, the end result of that trial was not particularly important.

People were going to die; there was no getting around that. Anyone who knew what was really happening, who had helped in making it happen, was going to have to die. Just like those twenty-six people had died at his hands. The secret had to be preserved, or there would be no place on the planet to hide.

That was coming soon, and Brett was gearing up, getting ready for the action, for the war.

Damned if he wasn't looking forward to it.

He got to the warehouse at nine-thirty. Loney drove down from New York, and was there ten minutes later. It was formerly a medical supplies storage facility, but was now mostly empty. The FOR LEASE sign looked weather-beaten and the place was old and in terrible shape; it seemed likely that the medical supplies it housed must have included whiskey and bullets to bite on for pain.

They briefly went over the plan for the meeting. Loney would do the talking, since the judge knew him, and was aware of the danger he represented. Fowler was just there to be a calming influence, should one be needed.

Loney was to tell the judge that it was almost over; that once he issued his ruling this would all be behind him. Providing the judge kept his silence on the matter, neither Loney nor anyone else would ever call or visit him again.

It's a message that had been delivered repeatedly ever since the trial date was established. Loney doubted the judge ever believed it, or that he would believe it now.

The fact was that it wasn't true. The judge knew too much, and was too unstable emotionally to be trusted. It wouldn't happen the next day, or the next week, or even the next month, but the judge would soon take his secrets to his grave.

It wasn't until ten after ten that Fowler looked at his watch and said, "I don't like this."

"He'll be here," Loney said. "If I have to drag him out of bed."

"He should have been here by now. This is not a guy who's out drinking beers and forgot the appointment. To him this meeting is one of the most important of his life."

"Then let's go find him," Loney said.

"Where?"

"His house."

Fowler shook his head. "No, we don't want his wife and kid to see us. That just complicates things."

"So let's grab the wife and kid. Then the judge will do exactly what he's told."

"No. Let's call him first. I think you should be the one to do that. Tell him that not coming here is unacceptable."

Loney nodded, and took out his phone. Just as he was about to dial, Fowler said, "Hold it. I think I hear a car."

He walked to the window, which was behind Loney. He had to wipe away the dust to look outside, then stared out there for about ten seconds.

"You see him?" Loney asked.

"No. You'd better call him."

Loney turned back to his phone. It was set up exactly the way Fowler wanted it. Loney was concentrating on dialing, his hands occupied, and his back to Fowler.

It was therefore the easiest thing in the world for Fowler to take his handgun from his pocket and shoot Loney three times in the back.

Loney fell forward, landing on the floor just before his cell phone did the same. He was already dead by that time, but Fowler felt for a pulse to make sure. "Damn," Fowler said to Loney's body. "Now that I think of it, I forgot to tell the judge about the meeting."

Fowler wasn't terribly worried about the body. It would be a long time before anyone entered this warehouse, and the discovery of a dead gangster could not in any way come back to him. He had been careful not to leave fingerprints or any other evidence that could implicate him.

But he didn't want to just leave the body where it was, so he took one of the large, empty drums that was in the warehouse, and laid it on its side. Then he half pushed and half rolled the very large Loney into it.

He put the top on, but could not lift the drum upright. Which was fine.

Fowler locked the place and left. It had been a while since he had personally killed anyone, and as a marine in Kuwait that had been done more anonymously.

But this didn't bother him at all. Not a bit. Which was good, because Loney would not be the last person he would have to kill.

The door opens and two men step out.

They're not particularly large, maybe an inch taller than me and not much heavier. One of them looks at me, then Marcus, then back at me. "Not him," he says. "Just you."

I nod and ask Marcus to wait outside the door. He doesn't seem happy about it, but it's been prearranged, so he goes along with it. I let the two men lead me into the room, realizing with horror as they do that I forgot to make the call to Cindy at the FBI, so I could show it to Ricci on my phone.

I thought they were leading me into a hotel room, but that's not what this is at all. It's an apartment, as nice as any I've ever seen. It is amazingly elegant, and the main room is an atrium with a glass ceiling and a spiral staircase up to the second floor.

The furniture seems clearly very expensive and perfectly designed to complement the room, though I don't have the slightest knowledge of furniture, designs, or even rooms. In the center of the room is a grand piano.

The room is set down a few feet, and one has to go down two stairs to get to it. I wonder if the people in the rooms below it have to duck down, because their ceilings are lower than everybody else's.

Making the place somewhat less appealing to the eye are three very large men, none of whom are smiling. One of them comes over to me and frisks me, very carefully and intimately. If the TSA people frisked people at airport security like this, everybody would take trains.

I'm assuming that none of these people are Ricci, since they all seem to have basically the same level of authority. Once it's determined that I'm not armed, they lead me into another room off the main one. Only one of the goons goes in with me, but he leaves moments later, leaving me alone in what seems to be a den.

The room has a desk and three chairs, all recliners, all facing a wall with eight televisions. There is one large one in the middle, probably sixty inches or so, and then a bank of seven others, each maybe thirty-two inches.

The one in the center has the Lions-

Packers game on; it's a measure of how scared I've been that I had forgotten that Thanksgiving is a big NFL football day.

I watch the game for about five minutes, still all alone. If I'm being kidnapped and held, I can think of worse rooms to do it in. There's also a full bar, but I resist the temptation to make myself a drink.

I could really use a drink.

Finally, a door opens and a man comes in. I assume it's Carmine Ricci. He's dressed casually, tan slacks and a green pullover shirt, and seems to be in pretty good shape. He doesn't have the sophisticated air of Dominic Petrone, and is at least twenty years younger. Ricci looks like he's earned his stripes the hard way.

"You a football fan, Carpenter?"

I nod. "Big Giants fan. Huge."

"I have a large bet on the Cowboys to win the NFC."

"I hope they wipe the floor with the Giants."

"Dominic Petrone says you're a wiseass, but that I shouldn't kill you unless you really piss me off."

"Trust me, my goal is not to piss you off."

"Then talk," he says.

I ask him if he knows about the Galloway case and he says that he does, from reading the papers.

"Galloway is innocent," I say. "He's been set up; he didn't set the fire."

"Why should I care about that?"

I decide to go head-on. "Because your man Loney has been doing all the dirty work. Among other things, he threatened Galloway's wife, he killed Danny Butler, and he has blackmailed a number of people, including a judge."

I'm not sure if all the things I said are true, but I'm also not sure Ricci would know if I'm wrong.

He doesn't say anything, so I continue. "There's a lot more that I suspect, but which I'm not sure of. But rest assured I'm in the process of finding out."

"Get to the part that will make me give a shit," he says. I don't think I've cowed him yet.

"This is all going to come out in the trial; I have an obligation to do it on behalf of my client." I pointedly add, "If I were suddenly unavailable, my associates would do it. But I can leave your name out of it; Loney will be my target. But I need you to call him off."

He thinks for a moment. "So you're threatening me that if I don't call Loney off, assuming I know who the hell Loney is, that you'll drag my name through the trial?"

"I wouldn't call it a threat," I say.

"What would you call it?"

I think for a moment, but come up with nothing. "I don't really have a name for it," I say. "But I definitely wouldn't use 'threat.' "

"If my name comes up in that trial, you are a dead man," he says.

"Will you call Loney off?"

"If my name comes up in that trial, you are a dead man."

The door opens, and the guy who led me in comes in to lead me out. I don't know if Ricci pressed some kind of button or the guy was listening on an intercom, but he knew when to show up.

Thirty seconds later I'm in the hall with Marcus.

"Okay?" he says.

"I'm okay."

He nods and says, "Sushi."

Six hours later we board the redeye, and Marcus shows that the trip out was no fluke; he simply spends every moment he is on a plane asleep.

It gives me time to think about how the meeting with Ricci went. Other than the fact that he didn't kill me, it's hard to know if I accomplished anything. Certainly he didn't say anything to make me think I had, but I wouldn't have expected him to openly agree to anything. The real answer will come from his actions, from what he does with Loney.

Although the fact is that I may never find out what Ricci does. Loney and Ricci operate in the shadows, and I haven't come close to penetrating their world. Ricci could have him killed, or appoint him Emperor of Crimedom, and I probably wouldn't know it.

And whatever I don't learn, the jury doesn't learn.

Carmine Ricci got the phone call about an hour after his meeting with Carpenter.

He was having lunch, or maybe even breakfast, though it was four P.M. Carmine rarely slept, and when he did it was almost never at night, so assigning names to meals based on the time he ate them was not something he bothered to do.

It was a call he expected, and no time was wasted on chitchat. "It's done," Fowler said.

"Without incident?" Carmine asked.

"Without incident."

The fact that Fowler was able to dispatch Loney so easily impressed Carmine, though he would never admit it. Loney had been tough and smart, not Carmine's most talented employee, but right up there.

"This puts you out of it," Fowler said. "It's been a pleasure doing business with you."

"Not quite," Carmine said. "There is a large amount of money outstanding."

"I understand. We've discussed and agreed to the timing of that. Thirty days from the conclusion of the operation."

"Where does that stand?" Carmine asked.

"It will be very soon. I can't say exactly."

Carmine didn't want to ask too many questions about the operation, but he was pretty sure that he knew the basic points. The firestorm that it would create would be too hot for anyone, even Carmine, so he wanted no connection to the actual events whatsoever.

Carmine had simply provided the muscle, and much of the financing. Substantial, secret collateral had been provided, but all parties knew that debts to Carmine were always paid in full, or the debtor did not live to borrow again.

"Carpenter was here to see me," Carmine said. "He knew all about Loney."

"That's not a problem, seeing as how Loney no longer exists."

"The next time I hear from you, you will be calling to arrange payment."

Fowler smiled. "I look forward to it."

Sam Willis finally got what he was after.

Actually, he didn't personally get it; Hilda Mandlebaum once again had that honor. But they were a team, and their triumphs were joint ones.

The first step was getting Judge Holland's phone records, supposedly safely tucked away in the phone company's computer system. Once they had that to examine, Sam was sure that he identified the number that the judge called that belonged to Loney.

Andy Carpenter had provided the idea. He told Sam the date and time he had tried to reach the judge, mentioning Bauer's name to the assistant. Andy figured that the judge might get worried and quickly call people related to the case, hopefully Loney.

Sure enough, a call was made from the judge to a cell phone just two minutes after Andy had called him. The call lasted four minutes. And when Sam obtained the phone

397

records for that number, it was registered under a fake name.

It had to be Loney's.

The next step was equally easy; they retrieved Loney's phone records. But that was not the big prize, and they just printed out a copy of the records to show Andy. The big prize was delivering on Hike's suggestion. Hilda, under Sam's able direction, was able to use the phone company's computers to track the GPS signal to learn where Loney was. They had the street address in Dover, Delaware. The significance of that was not lost on Sam. He knew that Judge Holland lived in the same city, and MapQuest quickly told him the two addresses were less than a mile away.

Andy was in Vegas, and when Sam tried to call him it went straight to voice mail. Marcus was with him, so he wasn't an option. Sam considered calling Laurie, but she would just tell him to wait until Andy got back.

Sam didn't want to wait.

Leaving his elderly crew behind to continue work on the list of missing persons from the time of the fire, Sam made the three-hour drive to Delaware. It was Hilda's responsibility to keep track of Loney's GPS signal, in case Loney was on the move. She would be able to redirect Sam to where Loney had moved to.

But Hilda kept reporting in that the signal had not changed, which Sam was pleased about. He used the drive to figure out what he would do when he got there.

He had no intention of being a hero; he was not going to go in, guns blazing. He had brought his gun, but only for protection, in case things were to go wrong. His goals were modest. He would confirm that Loney was there, and perhaps follow him if necessary to learn where he lived.

Perhaps more importantly, he would try and get a look at Loney. Loney was a mystery man so far, and Sam was sure that Andy would appreciate his getting a cell phone picture of him.

When Sam arrived at the GPS address, he was surprised to see that it was an abandoned warehouse. He had expected it to be a hotel or apartment building, and the fact that it was not caused him to rethink his plan. There was no real way to approach the building without being seen, and Sam had no desire at all to be seen.

So he sat in his car for two hours, a half block from the warehouse. It was a fairly deserted area, so there was a danger that Sam could be noticed by anyone inclined to care, but no one around seemed to pay any attention. And no one went anywhere near the warehouse; the abandoned building certainly seemed abandoned.

But Hilda was certain that the GPS signal still showed that the phone was in there, which meant that Loney very well might be in there as well.

It was not in Sam's DNA to turn around and go home, so he got out of his car and walked down the street, toward the warehouse. He did so nonchalantly, as if he had not a care in the world, but his hand was in his jacket pocket, clutching his gun.

When he neared the warehouse, Sam walked around to the back and looked in the window. It was dusty and hard to see through, but Sam saw no signs of life. He checked some other windows to give himself a different vantage point, but again, there was no apparent activity at all.

Feeling more emboldened but fearing that this entire episode was a waste of time, Sam checked each window until he found one that was unlocked. He climbed through the window, not the easiest maneuver in the world for the unathletic accountant.

But before long he found himself in the very large warehouse, and he certainly seemed to be alone. Sam took out his own cell phone, and dialed Loney's number. He nearly jumped out of his skin when he heard it ring; the GPS signal was right after all. The phone was there.

Sam headed for the sound, but it stopped ringing before he could find it. He had to call it twice more before he had enough time to locate it, but eventually did so.

What attracted his attention, more than the cell phone itself, were the obvious bloodstains just a few feet away. And it didn't take a forensic scientist to follow the smeared blood to the large drum lying on its side.

Sam was scared to death, but determined to take the top off the drum and see what was inside. It came off easily, and Sam realized it had only recently been placed there.

There was no reason to empty or explore the drum, the body was obvious as soon as the top came off. And Sam was not about to examine it, or stick around; he made a beeline for the same window he came in, and ran to the street.

Sam had no idea what to do, but he knew who to ask. He called Laurie and told her the entire story. He had to stop a few times to catch his breath; he was that scared.

"Laurie, I'm sure I left my prints all over the place . . . on the window, the drum, I don't know where else."

"That's okay, Sam, because you're not going to deny you were in there. You're going to report what you found to the police, and answer any questions they have."

"They'll ask me why I was in there in the first place."

"Right. And you'll tell them the truth; you are there because it's part of an investigation being run by Andy for the Galloway trial. You were looking for Loney, but you really don't know anything more specific than that. They really need to ask Andy why he sent you there."

"Okay. Should I just call 911?"

The question made Laurie think of another way. "No. Just stay where you are; I'll take care of it. Give me the exact address."

He did so, and Laurie got off the phone and called Cindy Spodek. This had been an FBI investigation from the start, and she would rather Cindy take the lead, at least for the moment. Cindy knew Sam, and the people she was directing would therefore be less inclined to think Sam committed the murder.

So Laurie called Cindy, explained the situation, and Cindy promised to get agents there immediately.

Laurie hung up and waited for Andy's

plane to land. She would have quite a story for him.

Laurie calls me five minutes after I get off the plane.

I can't talk to her, because I'm on the phone with Cindy Spodek, who called me one minute after I got off the plane. It would have been four minutes after I got off, but I spent three minutes waking up Marcus.

I tell Laurie I'll call her back and that I'm on with Cindy. Based on the start of the conversation, I'd rather talk to Laurie.

"Andy, what the hell was Sam Willis doing in a Delaware warehouse with a dead body?" Cindy asks.

"I don't know what you are talking about," I say.

"You don't know anything about this?"

"I know Sam Willis, but that's it."

"He found the dead body of one Alan Loney in a drum in a Delaware warehouse. He claims that you sent him there as part of

404

an investigation."

"Oh, that Delaware warehouse. I wasn't sure which one you meant. The state is full of them."

"Andy, unless you want to spend eight hours in a room with four agents who have no sense of humor and look exactly alike, tell me what you know about this."

She doesn't sound in a bantering mood. I'm not either, but I don't know what the hell is going on, and I don't want to say anything stupid. "Cindy, Sam is working on the investigation. We are trying to find Loney, and I gave him some leads to follow, all of which are protected by attorney-client privilege. I assume one of them took him to this warehouse, but it sounds like he got there too late."

She asks me a bunch of additional questions, some of which I evade because I really don't know the answers, and the others I evade because I want to evade them. The entire time we're talking, I'm wondering if crazy Sam actually shot the guy.

"Do you know the time of death?" I ask.

"Why? You trying to come up with an alibi?"

"No, I'm covered on that score. I was with Marcus in Vegas; believe me, people noticed us."

"You saw Ricci?" she asks.

"I did. Charming gentleman."

"Let's see how charming he is when he finds out that his top man was stuffed in a drum in Delaware."

"You were about to tell me the time of death," I say.

She tells me the coroner's estimate, which is soon after my meeting with Ricci. Could he have reacted to our talk by immediately having Loney killed?

I promise Cindy I'll fill her in as I get more details, which we both know is an out-and-out lie. As soon as she lets me off the phone, I call Laurie, who gives me the version of events according to Sam.

"Do you think Ricci could have had Loney hit because of my threat?" I ask.

"I don't think so," she says.

"Why not?"

"Well, for one thing, you're not really that intimidating. For another, I can't believe that what you said was news to Ricci. Loney couldn't have been doing all this behind his boss's back; so if Ricci wanted him to stop, he wouldn't have had to kill him to do it."

Neither of us has any other explanation for Loney's murder; we can just add it to the list of things we are bewildered by.

"How is Sam doing?" I ask.

"He's on cloud nine," she says. "Except for a high-noon shootout, this is the most fun thing that could have happened to him."

When I get home we talk some more about it, and I call Sam to hear it fresh from his perspective. It's a rather lengthy perspective, and he so obviously relishes the telling that I think the recounting takes longer than the actual event. For example, it takes a good five minutes for him to describe how he followed the bloodstains to the drum; unless the trail was half a mile long, that seems like a bit much.

I admonish Sam for doing what he did; it was dangerous and not an area he should be involving himself in. My gentle reprimand clearly has no effect; Sam has now tasted the "action" and will want nothing more than to jump back in the fray.

I call Hike and ask him to come over. We have developed quite a bit of evidence in our investigation, though it's hard to be sure just what it is evidence of.

The problem is that the jury knows nothing about it. We've got to get it in front of them, which is not going to be an easy thing to do. Dylan will say that it's not relevant, and Judge De Luca will be hard-pressed not to agree with him.

The problem is that Dylan can argue that

none of the material we have is necessarily related to the Galloway trial. It all began, for instance, with someone following Laurie and me. We assumed that it was related to this case, but we have no proof of that.

If we can't convince De Luca that Camby was following me because I was representing Noah, then everything that followed is legally meaningless, and certainly inadmissible.

The reasoning that we will have to employ is something Hike is particularly good at, and he helps me focus in on the key points to present to De Luca. If the judge doesn't buy them, we are nowhere.

I contact the court clerk, who is available even on weekends, and tell her that I need a special session in chambers before court on Monday. I describe it as urgent, and I have no doubt that it will be granted.

I then call and leave a message for Dylan, telling him what I've requested of the court. I say that I'm doing it as a courtesy, but I'm not. What I'm really doing is giving Dylan something to worry about.

Alex Bauer saw the story about Loney's murder in the newspaper.

It was buried on page six, and he almost didn't notice it. There was nothing that significant about it to warrant more attention; no connection was known between Loney and the Galloway case.

But for Bauer, it just about jumped off the page, and he quickly went online to see if he could find more coverage. A couple of outlets mentioned Loney's suspected mob ties, but that was basically it.

Bauer immediately picked up the phone and called Andy's office. Andy was in court, but Laurie took the call, and she could tell immediately that he sounded scared.

"Loney is dead," Bauer said. "He was murdered."

"Yes, I know that."

"Was it Ricci? Did he have it done?"

"I don't think the police have any leads

yet, but we're not privy to their investigation."

Bauer yelled at her. "I don't care what the police think!" Then he lowered his voice, trying to remain calm. "I want to know what you think."

"I don't know," she said. "But it's certainly possible."

"Does Ricci know that I talked about Loney? Could that be why he was killed? Because his involvement in all this was revealed by me?"

"I have no reason to believe he knows about anything you said. If he does, he didn't learn it from us."

He was trying to read between her words, to pick up any information he could. "Did you talk to Ricci? Did Carpenter?"

Laurie was not having any of it. "Mr. Bauer, we really can't talk about what is going on in our investigation. But believe me, your name has never been mentioned by Andy or me, in any context. That I can guarantee."

"All right," he said, calming somewhat. "It's just that soon after we spoke, I saw this about Loney."

"I understand your concern, and you were right to call," she said. "Have you been approached by anyone else? Anyone stepping in for Loney?"

"No. You think I will?"

"Yes, you need to expect that." For a CEO and no doubt an educated, sophisticated man, he wasn't thinking very clearly. Fear will do that to you. "Whatever Loney had on you, whatever he wanted, he was just the front man."

"God, I wish this were over," he said.

"Please let me know when you are contacted," she said. "I'll try to help and —"

She didn't finish the sentence, because she realized he had already hung up.

Less than an hour later, Bauer received a call, and the caller ID showed the number was blocked.

"Hello, Alex," said Brett Fowler, a smile on his face as he talked. "This is your new contact."

"Your Honor, next he'll be talking about Colombian death squads."

Dylan is referring to the attempt by the original Simpson lawyers to claim that Nicole Brown Simpson and Ronald Goldman were killed by mysterious, vicious Colombians in some kind of drug vendetta.

They had absolutely no evidence to support their theory, and Dylan is saying that my presentation regarding Loney et al. is similarly without relevance to this trial. If I were in his shoes, I'd be saying the same things, and I'd be confident in my position.

"These people make the Colombian death squads look like Donny and Marie," I say. "People are dying all over the place, and my client is sitting in jail. The jury has a right to know that."

Dylan thinks he's playing a winning hand here, and he will not let anything go unanswered. "The fact that there are murders being committed in large metropolitan areas is not exactly unusual," he says. "If that were simply the standard for admission, trials would never end. Mr. Carpenter has to establish a connection, and he has not come close to doing that."

It's my serve. "Your Honor, Mr. Camby was following me, and was killed before I could question him. I firmly believe that his interest in me related to this case, since Mr. Galloway is my only client at the moment. However, the fact that we have phone records connecting Mr. Camby to Mr. Butler would push the possibility of co-incidence way beyond logical."

"Camby never called Butler," Dylan points out.

De Luca is sitting back and letting us fight this out. "Loney is the connection," I say. "Camby called Loney repeatedly, and Loney called Butler. And now Loney is dead as well."

"The phone calls could have had nothing whatsoever to do with this case."

I see an opening, and I try to pounce on it. "You know what, Your Honor? Mr. Campbell is right. The phone calls could somehow be unrelated to this case, and just an extraordinarily bizarre coincidence. And maybe the jury would decide that's exactly what it is. But we gain nothing except a few days by not giving them that chance."

Dylan is vigorously shaking his head. "That could be said about anything. Why not let the jury hear it and decide? But that is why we have standards of admissibility, and why it is clearly within the province of Your Honor to rule it out."

Dylan also raises the issue of the accuracy of the phone records, and questions where they came from. I don't answer that directly, but instead I ask Judge De Luca to allow us to issue a subpoena for the same records, so that there will be no question of their authenticity should they ultimately be ruled admissible. He agrees, which gives me some confidence in what his ruling will be.

I have one significant advantage over Dylan in this situation, and that advantage could be called unfair. Most judges, when faced with a decision like this, are more inclined to side with the defense than the prosecution.

The reason for that bias is that if the defendant is convicted, the defense can appeal the verdict. If the verdict is for acquittal, the case is over with no appeal possible. That would be double jeopardy, and is absolutely prohibited.

So to side with the prosecution is to invite

a future appeal, and if there is anything a judge hates more than annoying lawyers like me, it is being overturned on appeal. Siding with the defense, at least on matters that could go either way, is a way to avoid that embarrassment. No judge would ever admit that this is a factor, and no lawyer would ever doubt that it's often the determining one.

There is also the more human side. To send someone away for the rest of his life is a very serious matter, and compassionate judges would certainly try to avoid doing that unjustly. It just seems easier and more decent to let the jury decide what they believe, rather than preventing them from hearing it at all.

But even with all this on our side, I am still very concerned about our ability to prevail in this argument. The link between our evidence and the case is tenuous at best, and De Luca must know that it would lead the jury down a convoluted and lengthy road. He would not want to do that; I'm just hoping he feels he has to.

"I need to consider these facts," De Luca says, then to me specifically, "call your witnesses unrelated to these matters today, and I will rule before court convenes tomorrow morning."

It's a victory of sorts for our side that De Luca didn't rule against us out of hand, but I suppose Dylan might feel the same way. All we can do now is wait.

Once we move back into court, I call Tony Cotner as my first witness. Now in his mid-sixties, Cotner has run a homeless shelter in Clifton, for the last thirty years. The major difference between Tony and me is that he has spent his life helping people, while I have spent mine hanging out with them.

Tony's shelter is the one at which Danny Butler claims Noah made the confession to him about starting the fire. Reading about it in the paper prompted Tony to call me and offer his help.

"You must have a lot of people go through there over the years," I say, after we set the scene for the jury.

He nods. "Too many; there is simply not a sufficient safety net for the most unfortunate in our society. When economic times are bad, the people on the bottom of the ladder suffer the most."

"Yet with all those people, you remember Mr. Galloway?"

"Very well," he says. "I was impressed with him, and considered him a friend."

"Why is that?"

"Well, he was obviously well educated,

and his decency shined through in the way he dealt with others."

"Yet he had a drug problem in those days?" I ask.

"Most definitely. It was very sad to see, but not unusual. Addiction can strike all kinds of people at all different times for all different reasons."

"But you and Mr. Galloway talked frequently?"

"Yes, we did."

"Did he ever talk about the fire at Hamilton Village?"

"Not that I can recall," he says.

"If he had told you he set it, would you be likely to recall that?"

"Absolutely."

"Do you monitor conversations that your visitors have, but that you are not a party to?"

"In a way, yes."

I ask him what he means, and he tells me that he encourages people to come forward if they are aware of drugs being used on the premises, or if they become aware of criminal conduct. Certainly, he says, any confessions about setting a fire that killed twenty-six people would have been reported to him.

"So you feel confident that Mr. Galloway did not make such a confession?" I ask.

"You mean beyond the fact that I would never consider Noah capable of such an act?" he asks, a response that I am delighted with.

"Yes, beyond that."

"I believe I would have heard about it, especially if it was said to more than one person."

"Do you remember Mr. Butler?" I ask.

"I do not. He could not have been there very often."

"So you would be surprised to hear that he and Mr. Galloway had a significant friendship with your facility as their home base?"

He nods. "I would be shocked by that."

I turn him over to Dylan, who makes it clear he considers the testimony to be of little significance. After having Cotner admit that there are usually between seventy and a hundred people in the shelter for every meal, he asks if he is privy to every conversation that goes on there.

"Of course not," Cotner says. "That would be impossible."

"How many conversations that took place there yesterday, that you were not directly involved in, can you relate to us today?"

"None."

"Thank you."

I usually have lunch at a coffee shop near the courthouse.

I often take Hike with me, more for self-discipline than anything else. His conversation makes me not want to linger over lunch, and gets me back to our courthouse office to bone up on the next witnesses.

This time Hike is talking about the local rodent population, and how they have infiltrated every restaurant in the area, including and especially the one we're in.

"They're out of control," he says. "Fortunately they're not very bright as far as animals go. There are so many of them that if they ever organized and got their act together, we'd be on the menu instead of them."

I try not to respond to his ramblings, but this time I can't help it. "What the hell does that mean? I don't see any 'rodent' on the menu."

"Just don't ask the waiter what today's specials really are."

"So you think they serve baked rat?" I ask.

"I can't prove anything, but did you notice I only order salads?"

I decide to drop it, mainly because the hamburger I'm eating is growing "chewier" by the moment. But I would have dropped it anyway, because just then Sam walks in the door. He never comes to court, so this must be something pretty important.

It is.

"Morris Fishman found something," he says. "I figured you'd want to hear it right away."

"What is it?"

"There's a guy on the missing persons report, the one from your friend at the FBI, named Steven Lockman. Young guy, thirty-four years old . . . married . . . his wife was five months pregnant when he disappeared. He was reported missing two days after the fire, to his local police department."

"Where?"

"East Brunswick. Lived there for three years; nobody in the community had any idea where he went, and the police never found anything. Never been heard from since."

It's just like Sam to dramatically hold back

the reason we should be interested in Lockman until after he tells us the details. Even though I'm dying to know, I can't help having some fun with him.

"Okay, Sam, thanks. That's helpful."

"What's helpful?" Sam asks, knowing he hasn't gotten to the key point yet.

"Lockman's information. Tell Morris he did good."

"Don't you want to know why Lockman is important?"

I open my mouth and cover it with my hand, as if I'm shocked. "You mean there's more?"

Sam finally gets it and smiles. "You're busting my chops, right?"

"Right," I say. "Tell me the rest about Lockman."

"You know that company Bauer is trying to take over? Milgram Oil and Gas? Well, Lockman worked for them."

"Whoa, that is important, Sam." If anything, I'm understating the case; this is way too big to chalk up to coincidence. "You digging into this guy's life?"

"I've got Hilda and Morris working full-time on it."

I tell Hike that I'll handle court by myself this afternoon; I want him to hang out with Sam and the gang and keep me posted on all developments. We need to focus on this as much as we can.

The afternoon court session is relatively uneventful. I introduce a series of witnesses, all of whom knew Noah in the weeks before and after the fire. They all claim to be unfamiliar with Danny Butler, and quite sure that Noah would not have confided in him.

All also say that Noah never talked to them about the fire. Dylan has some success on cross, but basically I've used the day to make it seem unlikely that Noah would have confessed a mass murder to Butler.

If Butler's statement was the only evidence Dylan had, our success today might even mean something.

Gail Lockman doesn't want to talk to me, but feels she has to.

She has suffered these past six years from the loss of her husband. He didn't die, or at least if he did she doesn't know it. He rather just disappeared, without a trace, or a hint of explanation.

She has never really entertained the possibility that he left willingly, not even in her most private thoughts. They were happy, in fact had never been happier. Their baby was soon to be born, and it is inconceivable to her that Steven could have voluntarily spent all this time without any contact with either of them.

So she is sure he must have lost his life, somehow, yet not a day goes by that she doesn't remain alert, looking everywhere for a sign of him.

That's where I come in. I had Laurie call her, because to have her talk to Hike would have been the icing on her Depression Cake. Laurie asked if she would see me tonight, to talk about something that has come up regarding Steven. I'm sure she would rather do anything other than talk to a stranger about Steven, but there is always that hope . . .

Gail works in the admissions office at Rutgers University, and wants to meet me in the student center coffee shop. Laurie and I drive down, park, and walk across campus to meet her. I watch as one male student after another stares at Laurie. If any co-eds eyed me, they did it without my knowledge.

Gail is waiting for us, sitting at a table and looking at her watch impatiently. We're not late, so she's either counting the minutes until this is over, or hoping that we will be late so she can leave. When we introduce ourselves, I can't tell if the look on her face is disappointment, anxiety, or hopefulness.

In any event, it's soon replaced by a practiced smile, if not a desire to chitchat. "I understand you want to talk about Steven," she says.

"Yes. His name has come up in connection with a case we're working on. It may have nothing to do with him, but I felt it important to follow up."

"The Galloway case?"

She obviously and not surprisingly has done some homework on me since getting the call. "Yes. Your husband disappeared around the time of the fire, and the company he worked for, Milgram, has become part of the investigation."

"Milgram? In what way?"

"I'm afraid I can't say," I lie. "It's covered by attorney-client privilege."

I need to start asking questions rather than answering them, and Laurie picks up on this. "Have you at any time considered that Steven's disappearance could in some way have been connected to his work?"

"As you can imagine, I've analyzed it from every angle, including that one, but I haven't come up with anything. Steven seemed mostly happy with what he was doing. In fact, in the days before he left . . ."

She pauses for a moment. She used the word "left," but it seems as if she has never really come up with a word that she is comfortable with, or that seems to fit. She continues. "He was particularly upbeat. That's one of the things that has always seemed so strange . . ."

"So nothing about his work was bothering him in any way?" I ask. "You said 'mostly happy.' "

She shrugs. "He wasn't making as much

425

money as he thought he should, but he felt that was going to change. We were about to have the baby, and earning money had become very important to him."

"What exactly did he do for Milgram?"

"He was what they call an assayer. He had a master's in quarrying and extraction, and he went to land that Milgram owned and estimated how much oil and gas, or other resources, were there. You know, so they'd know whether to drill or not, I guess." She smiles. "Truth is, I never really understood it myself."

"Is that why he traveled so much?" Laurie asks.

She nods. "It wasn't so much, just more than I would have liked. I wanted him home as much as possible." She shakes her head and smiles sadly, "Look how that worked out."

"Would you have any way of knowing where he traveled in, say, the two months before he disappeared?"

She nods. "Absolutely. I gave the police all of that information, his records, his calendar . . . and they gave them back about a year later. When they gave up looking."

"You still have them?" I ask, knowing there is not a chance in hell she threw them out.

"Yes, in case the police ever found a lead. But I want to keep them. I could copy them for you."

"We would appreciate that," I say, and Laurie arranges to pick them up tomorrow.

On the way home, Laurie says, "It's pretty hard to imagine anything worse than someone you love like that just disappearing. And to never find out what happened . . ."

"I think we're going to be able to tell her what happened."

"You think he was in the fire?" she asks.

"Probably. But even more than that, I think he might have been the reason for the fire."

427

Judge De Luca calls Dylan and me into chambers prior to the start of court.

He has the court reporter in there to record everything, something he doesn't always do.

"I've decided to grant the defense's request and admit the evidence as proffered," he says. Once he does, Dylan formally objects again, for the record, but he knows it's a lost cause, and De Luca confirms that for him.

De Luca then launches into a speech which, if listened to out of context, would lead one to believe he had ruled against us. He goes on and on about how the ruling is a limited one, capable of being changed or curtailed at any time. He warns me not to take this too far afield, and not to allow witnesses to speculate.

I believe he is covering himself for the record, though the prosecution is unlikely to stop the trial in order to appeal it to a higher court. They also cannot appeal it after the fact, should Noah be acquitted. But if the transcript is later scrutinized for any reason, De Luca wants to look as unbiased and evenhanded as possible.

I've given a lot of thought as to how I can introduce the evidence that De Luca has now ruled admissible. Part of it, Camby's shooting, involves Marcus, but there is no way I'm going to call him to testify.

The jury, not knowing better, would look at Marcus and definitely not consider him one of the "good guys," and since he is on our side that would not cut to our benefit. It also would not be fair to the court reporter; Marcus is tough enough to listen to; to have to accurately transcribe what he says is covered under the Constitution as "cruel and unusual" punishment.

Instead I call Laurie. She was enough of a participant to get by, or at least I hope so. And it's something of an understatement to say that the jury will find her more appealing than Marcus.

Laurie describes for the jury how she and I had just come from interviewing a witness, and she noticed that we were being followed. "So we pulled into a 7-Eleven parking lot, and while you went inside, I called one of our investigators, Marcus Clark."

"Why did you do that?"

"So that he could come and follow the man following us. We were confident it had to do with the Galloway case, since that was the only one we were working on. It was important to learn why someone thought they needed to monitor our movements."

She describes how she signaled me to stay in the store until Marcus was in place, and that when she was certain that he was, it was okay for me to come out. She throws in the information that I brought out a "bread and some bleach," which brings a few snickers from the jury, and more from the gallery.

"What happened next?" I ask.

"We went to your house and waited for Marcus to call, which he did. He had attempted to question the man, but before he could do so, a sniper fired through the window, killing him."

Laurie goes on to say that Marcus took the man's cell phone and that we found out later that it was Camby, and that we were able to trace the phone records, which eventually led us to Loney.

Dylan focuses his cross-examination on the shaky connection between Camby and

Galloway, claiming that there is no basis for us to assume that link.

"Mr. Carpenter has been a criminal attorney for a number of years, has he not?" he asks.

"He has."

"And you were a police officer here in Paterson? And then a police chief in Wisconsin?"

"Correct."

"Did you arrest a lot of people?" he asks.

"My share."

"So it's certainly possible that someone was following you, unrelated to this case?"

"It would have been possible, had not subsequent investigation confirmed our suspicions."

It was a great answer, nailing Dylan in his tracks, but he quickly recovers. He smiles condescendingly, and says, "We certainly look forward to hearing about that."

The decision was posted at noon on the Delaware Chancery Court Web site.

It was twenty-one pages, and filled with legalese and rationalizations. But the summary page was all that one needed to read to understand that it represented a sweeping victory for Entech Industries.

The poison pill that Milgram had attempted to adopt was considered by Judge Holland to be a "fraudulent attempt by the board of Milgram to thwart the purchase," and not in the best interests of the Milgram shareholders.

Savvy legal minds, were they inclined to read and analyze the full opinion, would note that Holland's ruling relied mostly on fact, rather than law, which would make it even less likely for an appeals court to overturn. Since it was widely known that Milgram did not have the resources nor appetite to mount an appeal, Holland's approach made such an attempt even less likely.

Sure enough, within an hour of the announcement of the ruling, Milgram's board indicated reluctant acceptance. Though they disagreed in principle with Judge Holland's decision, they pledged to work with Entech to insure that the purchase would move immediately to completion.

Alex Bauer on behalf of Entech followed in kind, releasing a statement praising the work of the court, and Milgram's acceptance of the decision. The statement indicated that the purchase of the outstanding shares would begin within twenty-four hours, and promised that the future of the combined company and its employees would be an outstanding one.

For Judge Holland, the issuing of the opinion brought a mixture of shame and relief. It was the first time in his career that he had ever been coerced into giving a particular ruling; it violated every principle he had ever lived by.

But he had known he was going to do it for a while; no other option presented itself as feasible. It was over now, it was well behind him, and he knew that he had done it masterfully, and that it would withstand whatever scrutiny might be applied to it.

He would go home, and spend some pre-
cious hours and days with his family.
And then he would say good-bye.

Sam is proving to be a surprisingly good witness.

I'm pleased and relieved about that, because even though we've rehearsed his testimony a few times, I was afraid that he would love the drama of it all and turn into a loose cannon on the stand.

I take him through the phone records, and the process by which we zeroed in on Loney, as well as the other various players. I avoid naming the important people on the list, including Bauer and Judge Holland. We may wind up going there, but I'm reluctant to do so. Once they are named, then the threat of doing so becomes an empty one.

Sam refers during his testimony to the subpoenaed phone records, which helps to avoid having to explain how we got the previous, hacked versions.

Finally, he describes finding Loney's body in the Delaware warehouse. "I called his cell phone, and it led me to the bloodstains, which led me to the body."

"What did you do then?"

He grins. "I climbed back through the window and ran across the street."

"How about after that?"

"I called Laurie . . . Ms. Collins, and she said to stay there, that she was going to call the FBI, and that I was to just tell the truth about what happened."

"And did you do that?" I ask.

"Yes."

"And did you tell the truth today?"

"Yes."

I turn him over to Dylan, who continues to take the same approach to what he considers tangential testimony. He doesn't want to get too far into the nitty-gritty of it, fearing that would give it credibility, and worse, relevance.

"Mr. Willis, that was quite an adventure you went on."

"I guess . . ."

"Discovering the body of a known mobster like that, it must have been frightening," Dylan says.

"It was, but I handled it."

"Obviously. Now that it's over, and you can look back on it, what does it have to do with the Paterson fire that was set six years ago?"

I had told Sam that Dylan would lead him down this path, trying to get Sam to give a tortured explanation of how Loney's death could possibly relate to Noah's guilt or innocence. But the quick flash of panic in Sam's eyes makes me fear that in the pressure of the moment he's going to forget the plan.

He doesn't.

"I'm afraid I haven't given that any thought," he says. "My job was to analyze the phone records, and try to track down Mr. Loney. I wasn't told to work on any theories. That's above my pay grade."

It stops Dylan in his tracks; he wants to attack the relevance but can't, since Sam didn't testify to it. He tries to come at it from a few other angles, but Sam is ready for him, and deflects it.

All in all, it's a tour de force performance, and I don't even have to ask any additional questions on redirect.

I am not at all happy with the quality of our defense, or where we stand in the trial as we reach the end. We've thrown a bunch of stuff on the jury wall, but at this point there is little chance that it stuck. I'm going to have to explain what it all means during my closing statement, and hope that we can get to that elusive reasonable doubt, at least in some jurors' minds.

Where I think we have been successful is in casting doubt on the Butler statement recounting Noah's "confession." It should be clear by now that Noah barely knew him, and would have been very unlikely to have confided such a monstrous secret.

Working against us, of course, is the fact that Butler's statement is corroborated by other evidence, most notably the DNA on the paint can. That is simply not something that we have been able to effectively rebut.

Closing statements will be tomorrow, and I head home to do some preparatory work. Laurie is not there; hopefully she's out either solving the case or, if not that, maybe getting some sexy lingerie to please her man.

I take Tara and Bailey for a walk and then settle in to read through the files for what seems like the five-millionth time. Laurie comes home at around nine o'clock. I don't see any Victoria's Secret bags, so hopefully she solved the case.

The look on her face says that she just might have.

"I've been at the hospital," she says. "Seeing Jesse Briggs."

"How is he?"

"Not good. He's not going to leave there, and he knows it. The doctors have stopped treatment."

"That's too bad," I say. "But why were you there?"

"I've been finding out as much as I can about his daughter and her baby, but I needed to know something else, and I knew he could tell me. She moved back to Paterson a few months before the baby was born."

I nod. "I know. Tony told us that when we were at Taco Bell."

"Good memory," she says. "But do you know where she moved from?"

"No."

She smiles. "Delaware. Dover, Delaware."

"Well, you've now heard all of the evidence," Dylan says.

"I know that it wasn't easy. Sometimes lawyers like me have a tendency to speak more than we should. My wife often says that I take five sentences to say something I shouldn't say in the first place."

He pauses to smile, so the jurors will know he's joking, and a few of them return the smile.

"And it wasn't just long and sometimes dull; some of it was difficult to watch and hear. I know that, but there was no way around it. You are the triers of fact, and you needed to know the facts.

"Now you do.

"Every fact in the case points to Noah Galloway as the arsonist, as the mass murderer. He bought drugs from the dealers in that building. They cut him off, and he became furious. He knew how to mix the chemicals. His DNA was on the murder weapon. He confessed the crime, in detail.

"It couldn't be clearer.

"And how does the defense respond? Not with evidence, because they have none. So they talk about other murders, which have nothing to do with this case. One of the murdered people called Danny Butler. That's it, yet they try to create an entire defense around it.

"You'll notice at no point did Mr. Carpenter offer a theory as to why these evil-doers framed Mr. Galloway, or why they planted all this evidence, but then waited six years to reveal. Or even who has been doing these killings, or what they have to do with this trial.

"So when I say that you've heard all the evidence, I mean that you've heard all that relates to this case, and a heck of a lot that doesn't.

"I thank you for your patience, and I especially thank you for your service. All I ask is that you continue to exercise your best judgment, and keep your eyes on the true facts. And then follow those facts to justice."

I stand even before Dylan sits down; I don't want to let his words sink in too deeply. "There is much that I don't know,"

I say. "I wish I knew more, so that I could tell it to you, and everything would be clear.

"Unfortunately, life doesn't usually work that way, and trials almost never do. So all we can do is go by what we know at the time, and what we think that could mean.

"The prosecution would have you believe that Noah Galloway, a man who never committed a violent act in his life, decided one day to ruthlessly burn twenty-six people to death. And why? Because he had a grudge against three people.

"They would have you believe that instead of killing those people, perhaps with a gun, Mr. Galloway somehow carried in a mixture of napalm, in so many cans that it would have been impossible for one person to hold. Then he went through the building, spreading out this mixture, risking detection at any point. And then he set fire to the building, in the process burning up all the drugs they say he was so desperate to have.

"And then what did he do with the cans? Leave them to be incinerated and destroyed in the fire? Not according to the prosecution's case. No, they think he carried at least one out and left it a few blocks away, with his burned skin on it.

"But if that wasn't a crazy enough thing for him to do, their theory is that he then

442

confessed the crime in minute detail to a relative stranger, for no apparent reason. And that stranger, drug-addicted himself and not very bright in the first place, remembered every single detail, so as to be able to repeat it six years later.

"And now, six years later, people are continuing to die. Noah Galloway sits in a prison cell, as airtight an alibi as one could imagine, while people involved in this case continue to die.

"Ladies and gentlemen, it makes no sense. What does make sense is that Noah Galloway has been made a fall guy. I can't tell you why right now; I expect that someday I'll be able to. But your job, and even my job, is not to find all the answers. It's to judge the guilt or innocence of one man.

"Noah Galloway is an exemplary citizen, who overcame a terrible problem and has helped countless others overcome theirs. His is a comeback and a story to be celebrated. He deserves our thanks, not our condemnation. And justice, true justice, demands that he be set free.

"Thank you."

When I finish, Noah shakes my hand, and even Hike nods his approval. I hear Judge De Luca say that court is concluded early for the day, and that he will issue jury instructions tomorrow.

But I'm only half listening, and I'm out the door as soon as he finishes talking.

I've got a long drive ahead of me.

Laurie got the call about an hour after Andy left.

It was from Alex Bauer, and the fear in his voice was evident. He was standing in his den, pacing as he talked.

"They're coming after me," he said. "Somebody has stepped in to replace Loney."

"Who is it?" she asked.

"His name is Brett Fowler. He's an ex-marine who has a consultant business in Washington."

"Did he say what they want?"

"They want me to sell the wind-turbine business," he said. "I don't know why; it might have to do with the land that it's on. I would do that, to keep them off my back. But I don't think that will be the end of it."

"Why not?"

"Because Ricci is calling the shots. Fowler even admitted it."

"So what are you going to do?"

"I don't know. But once I do what he wants, Ricci is going to get rid of me. I'll know too much."

"You need to talk to the FBI, Alex," Laurie said. "We can help you do that."

"You only care about your client."

"Ending this will help both you and Galloway. It's the only move for you to make, and I think you know that without my telling you."

"I've got to think about this," he said, desperation in his voice. "If what they know about me ever comes out, I'll be destroyed."

"You'll be alive."

"I've got to think."

Click.

Laurie got off the phone, called Andy, and relayed the conversation to him. "What do you think he'll do?" he asked.

"I don't know. He's scared, so it will be hard for him to think rationally."

"Fowler was on the call list. Tell Sam to dig deep on him."

"I will," she said.

She and Andy were of course unaware that the person they just decided to dig deep into was at that moment at the door of Alex Bauer's house.

"Aren't you going to invite me in?" Fowler asked.

"Come in."

He offered Fowler a drink, which he declined. "The judge has ruled. The ruling was perfect," Fowler said.

"I know. I issued a press release praising it."

"I saw it. Nicely done. Have you taken the other actions?"

Bauer nodded. "I have."

"Then do you know what time it is?" Fowler asked. He smiled, not waiting for an answer. "Time for you to die."

I'm surprised to see where Judge Holland lives.

It's strictly middle-class all the way, and has a real neighborhood feel. The houses are modest, and each is set on a piece of land that has to be less than a quarter of an acre. If someone here raises their voice in their living room, neighbors on both sides know what they're saying.

For some reason, even though judges do not make that much money, I always picture them as living in stately mansions with big white columns and long circular driveways. So far I've been wrong one hundred percent of the time.

I get there at around eight P.M., well past dark. My plan, such as it is, is to ring the bell and confront him. It's not that well thought-out, since for all I know he could be away on vacation. But I was never going to get through by calling, and I want to see his face when he hears what I have to say.

I pull up and am about to get out of the car when I see his front door open. Judge Holland is standing there, with his wife, Alice, and son, Benji. I've reread all of the background information on Holland that Sam had dug up, so I'm very familiar with his family situation. In fact, it's the reason I'm here.

Holland kisses Alice on the cheek, then picks Benji up and gives him a hug and kiss. Then he closes the door and leaves.

He heads for his car, in front of the house. I get out of my car across the street, and call to him just as he's opening his door. "Judge Holland," I say.

He looks up in surprise; I have no idea whether he recognizes me or not, but he doesn't say anything, just stares at me.

"I'm Andy Carpenter."

"Leave me alone," he says.

"I can't do that. I'm here to talk about Benji."

It was an educated guess, and it's only when I see him stiffen that I have confidence that I'm right.

He quickly recovers, gets in the car and drives away. I get back in my car and follow him, and we drive about twelve blocks. He's not going quickly, making no apparent effort to lose me, though it wouldn't be tough to do so. Car-following is not my specialty.

He turns into a small park, not at all well lit, and I follow him in. There are tennis courts near the rear of the park, and he pulls up and parks his car in a small parking lot adjacent to them.

I'm not at all comfortable with this. I'm not panic-stricken; following a judge to suburban tennis courts is not exactly like meeting Double J in his drug hideout. On the other hand, I don't have Marcus with me.

I don't see how he can be leading me into a trap; it's not like he knew that I would show up. On the other hand, he could have called from his car and told them where we were going. I think they have cell phones in Delaware.

My hope is that he is willing to talk with me, but wanted to lead me somewhere private. That seems the most logical explanation, so I get out of the car when he does, and I walk toward him.

"So, Mr. Carpenter, what do you know?"

Judges have been seeing through my bullshit for years, so I decide to be straight with this one. "I don't know much for sure, but I have very strong hunches, and they are hunches that can be verified. What I do

450

know is that you adopted Benji before you were married, not unheard of, but an unusual thing for a single man to do.

"I also know that the mother of Roger Briggs, the boy who was supposed to have died in that fire six years ago, moved to Paterson from here in Dover. What I believe is that Roger Briggs is Benji, and that you are his real father. I believe that after his mother left and gave birth, she wouldn't give you access to him. Maybe she was trying to extract money from you . . . I don't know. So you hired people to bring him to you, and they set the fire."

He nods slowly in a final confirmation that I'm right. "They were supposed to give her money, or scare her, or both. She was an addict, Mr. Carpenter. She couldn't take care of him; she couldn't give him any kind of life."

"Why did they burn the house down?"

"I don't know," he says. "Maybe to hide the fact that he was missing, but I've always thought there was much more to it. He would never tell me. But no one was supposed to get hurt; he had promised me that."

"Loney?"

"Yes."

"So they had you on tape, and they could

connect you to the fire. That's how they blackmailed you."

"Yes."

"They told you how to rule in the Milgram trial."

"Yes."

"Did they demand anything else?"

"No."

"You need to tell the truth now. You can't let Noah Galloway be convicted of this crime."

"They would take Benji; Alice is his mother, as surely as if she gave birth to him. He needs her, and she needs him."

"You don't understand," I say. "I know the truth. I'll reveal it with or without you."

"No one will believe you. I'm a respected judge." He laughs a short laugh, recognizing the irony.

"You're wrong about that," I say, even though I know he's probably right.

"No," he says, and in the dim light I can see him reach into his pocket and take out a gun. There is a glint of light off the barrel.

"Don't do it, Judge. People know where I am, and they know why." Even in my panic, the irony that a judge might shoot me is too obvious to miss. They'd probably never find another judge to convict him.

"I know something about guilt, Mr. Carpenter. I've lived with it for many years. You needn't suffer with it; I was coming here anyway."

I don't know what he's talking about, but it only takes a few seconds to find out.

"Don't take my son from his mother," he says, just before he puts the barrel of the gun to his temple and pulls the trigger. He says another word, but it is mostly drowned out by the sound of the shot. I think it was "please."

It was the most horrible thing I've ever seen, and nothing comes in second.

Judge Holland's head literally exploded, sending pieces of it in all directions.

It all happened too quickly for me to react. Of course, the truth is that my reaction time in moments of physical danger is such that he would have had time to load a Revolutionary War cannon and shoot himself with it.

I edge over to his fallen body, but I don't get too close. There is no way he could possibly be alive, and I wouldn't know what to do if he was. Instead I call 911 and report what has happened. I don't really know where I am, so it's hard to direct them to the scene. I do the best I can, and they seem to be confident that they will find me.

Before the police arrive, I call Cindy Spodek and tell her what has happened. "A judge, Andy?" she asks.

"Not just a judge. The presiding judge of the Delaware Chancery Court."

She tells me to hold while she notifies agents in the area, then gets back on the line. "Are you okay?" she says. "I've seen someone commit suicide before; it was probably ten years ago and I still can't get the image out of my mind."

"It's going to be a while," I say, as the police cars and an ambulance make their appearance. "Gotta go, the locals are here."

"Don't let them take you anywhere until our agents get there."

The police come out of their cars, guns drawn, as is appropriate for the situation. They have no way of being sure what really happened here; for all they know I could have been the shooter. They have me turn and put my hands against my car, and then frisk me.

They tell me to wait, and I hear one of the officers, who is looking at Holland's body, say, "I'm pretty sure it's him."

This is going to be a monster of a story. Anything unsavory involving a judge is automatically big news. Judges represent an occupation that people hold in very high regard.

That reverence is a little weird, because lawyers are scorned almost as much as politicians. Where do people think judges come from, the Judge Fairy? They're lawyers, and very often lawyers who've leveraged political connections to get where they are. For the most part the ones I know are decent people, but the truth is I would say the same about lawyers.

The story will be even bigger because of my presence. Not because I'm any kind of celebrity, but rather because the media will correctly jump to the conclusion that this is related to the Galloway case, which is already a huge media event.

The detectives start to ask me questions, initially focusing on what happened rather than why it happened. That suits me just fine, because it is the "why" questions that I'm not sure how to answer.

My first obligation is to Noah, so I want to try to manage developments to his benefit, if there is any benefit to be had. Secondly, and probably incorrectly, I have a concern for Judge Holland's son. He has no parents, and his grandfather is dying. At the moment he is apparently living with a loving woman he considers his mother, and I would hate to see him taken from her and put into the public system.

Also, not too many people have made a dying wish to me. Holland did so, asking that I protect his son and keep him with his mother. It would be nice if I could grant it.

After about ten minutes, two FBI agents show up, and there are quick, huddled conversations. Both sides obviously want and are claiming jurisdiction. There is as much chance of the local cops prevailing as there is if the mayor of Dover duked it out with the President of the United States.

The agents question me for three hours, and I limit what I tell them. Basically, I just say that I was investigating a lead in the Galloway case, and that Holland's name came up. When I approached him, he led me to the park and killed himself.

All of that is true, but I describe the conversation I had with the judge as minimal. I just don't see the upside to bringing Benji into all of this now, or maybe ever. He and his mother are about to have enough to deal with.

During the questioning one of the agents gets a call. He steps away to take it, but when he comes back he says, "Special Agent Mulcahy will have some questions for you when you get back to New York."

"Great. That will give me something to look forward to."

I finally leave at just after three in the morning. I have satellite radio, so I spend the first half of the three-hour drive listening to news about Judge Holland's suicide, without commercial interruption.

But there is another interruption, a news bulletin that reports that Alex Bauer was killed in an intense fire that consumed his Mercedes sedan, with him in the driver's seat. The car was virtually incinerated, burning out of control in a secluded rest stop near Camden.

They didn't waste any time.

I didn't know Bauer very well, but the news is still jarring. People are dying all around us, and I'm unable to figure out how to stop it. If I don't do so soon, Noah Galloway will be the next victim. His sentence won't be death, but a lifetime in prison for an innocent man might be even worse.

As I approach my house, I see that it is filled with media people and trucks, so I drive around the block and sneak in through my neighbor's backyard into mine. Laurie is up and waiting for me; we've talked on the phone, but she still has many more questions.

Most annoying is that I can't take Tara and Bailey for our morning walk; the media crush is just too great. So instead, they, Laurie, and I hang out in the backyard until it's time to go to court.

    I'm a little tired . . . it's been a long day.

Entech filed a barrage of paperwork with the federal government.

For the most part they were notifications that work was to begin developing previously undeveloped land just purchased as part of the Milgram takeover.

Very little of it was actually going to happen, and the multiple filings represented a cover-up so that no one could focus on the one piece of land that was in fact important.

Area TX43765 in Texas.

Once the filings were complete, the men who had prepared the mine under that land could move back in. Slowly, since there was no sense at this point creating any stir or attracting unnecessary attention.

In any event, no one would question them. Senator Ryan's amendment had made it possible to mine land without having to serve notice of intent to, or receive approval from, the government. It was allegedly designed to facilitate the development of energy resources, but that was not Ryan's motive at all. He put in the amendment because Fowler forced him to.

It would take no more than a week to put the material in canisters, and then load them on to a truck. The actual amount and weight of the materials was not daunting, but the nature of them made careful handling a must, especially because of the extraordinary depth of the mine.

Once they were ready, they would wait for the final word to come down, and for the truck to arrive. Then they would load the truck and collect their money.

It would be more money than any of them had ever seen.

Judge De Luca calls Dylan and me into chambers before the start of court.

When he sees me, he says, "Is there more than one of you?" He's referring to the fact that he watched coverage of me in Delaware just a few hours ago.

"At this point one feels like more than enough."

The banter part of our conversation is over, and De Luca gets down to business. I notice that this time there is no court reporter present, which means that De Luca the fair-minded judge is going to become De Luca the take-no-prisoners dictator.

"Here's how this is going to go, gentlemen," he says, and then turns to me. "I assume you are going to move for a judgment of acquittal?"

It's standard for defense attorneys to move for a judgment of acquittal, which in effect asks the judge to acquit without even turning it over to the jury. It almost never works, and certainly won't here. "Absolutely, Your Honor."

He nods. "Okay, I'll deny it."

Judgments of acquittal can be renewed within fourteen days of denial, but that's not something that fills me with hope either.

He continues. "Then I assume you'll want to reopen testimony so they can hear about your little Delaware adventure last night?"

"Yes, definitely," I say.

"I'll deny that as well. The jury has heard your theory. If they believe it connects to this case, that's fine. If they don't, one more incident won't change things."

"I strongly object, Your Honor," I say. "There is more than just Judge Holland's suicide. Alex Bauer was on the call list as well."

"That was quite a list," De Luca says. "The objection is nevertheless overruled. Once these motions are dispensed with, I will give my charge to the jury, and then we're out of here. Nice and quick. There's a lot of interest out there in the media, gentlemen, especially after what happened last night. I will not have my trial turned into a media circus."

I make another attempt, but there is no arguing with De Luca on this. I had very much hoped to get the Judge Holland suicide entered into evidence, and possibly even Bauer. Not only would it have been significant in and of itself, but the unusual step of restarting the trial would have likely had a great effect on the jury.

But that's not happening, and all we have left is the possibility of using the ruling as the basis of an appeal should Noah be convicted. That's not exactly a major consolation.

Hike and I meet with Noah for ten minutes before court is convened. As a prisoner in solitary confinement, he's one of the few people in America that hasn't heard about Judge Holland. I explain to him what it means in the context of the trial, which isn't much.

"How long do you think the jury will be out?" he asks.

"I have no idea."

"And the verdict?"

I'm not about to lie to him now. "I think we're going to lose," I say.

He nods. "Me too. I think you've done an amazing job, and Becky and I will be grateful to you for as long as we live. But if I were on the jury I would vote to convict."

"I think we're going to win," Hike says.

Hike, who at any given time expects the

world to come to an end within an hour, thinks we're going to win.

"There you go," I say to Noah. "The incurable optimist has spoken."

Noah laughs; he has gotten to know Hike quite well. "Why do you say that?" he asks.

Hike shrugs. "I've just got faith in human nature."

I've got to get out of here before he breaks out in a rendition of "Put on a Happy Face."

Once I leave I turn on my cell phone. There's a message from Laurie asking that I call her, which I do.

"I got the travel records from Gail Lockman for her husband."

"Anything interesting?"

"He made four trips in the six weeks before the fire. The first one was to Texas, then Georgia, Arkansas, and Texas again."

"If there's something revealing in there, I'm missing it."

"You'll find it eventually."

"Eventually isn't going to be nearly good enough."

When I get back to the office, Agent Mulcahy is waiting for me.

Which is good, because I was going to call him. We have a lot to talk about.

The fact that he has come to my office gives me a small advantage; usually in a case like this he would try to summon me to the bureau offices, and then intimidate me when I got there. Of course, that small advantage does not quite make up for the fact that he has the entire government of the United States behind him, while I have Hike and Edna.

But for now it's just him and me talking alone in my office, which is interesting in itself. Usually agents like Mulcahy travel in twos, and play "good cop/bad cop." In this case Mulcahy is playing "only cop," and that could mean he wants to trade.

"Nice place you got here," he says, looking around as if he stepped in shit.

"Thanks; I'll convey your appreciation to my decorator."

"You do that," he says. "So I read the transcript of your interview with our agents in Delaware. From what I gather, you and the judge were just chatting away, about nothing in particular, and he shot himself?"

"That pretty much sums it up," I say.

"Having heard you talk in court, it does make some sense," he says. "I took the bullets out of my own gun before coming here, just in case."

I nod. "Wise move."

"Other than you annoying him to death, why did he do it?"

"Mmmm, that's a tough one."

"Be careful, Carpenter."

"No, I don't think so. I've got a guy who's never hurt a soul probably going off to prison for the rest of his life. If I'm going to prevent that, the last thing I need to be is careful."

"Is that right?" He doesn't seem cowed, but I'm not in the mood to care.

"That's exactly right. And you know what else? I think you know he never set that fire, and you're sitting back and watching it happen."

"You should have presented a more effective case," he says.

467

"Okay, here's the way we're going to do it. You're going to tell me information you have that can help me, and then I'm going to tell you information that I have that will help you. And you're going to go first."

"Why would I go first?"

"Because I don't trust you, and because you're worried, and because my information is probably better than yours."

He smiles, as if he thinks that's amusing as hell, even though he doesn't. "What would possibly make you think I'm worried?"

"Because you're sitting here. Your agents already asked me every question there was to ask. If you're sitting here, it's because you have a different agenda."

"Okay," he says. "Deal."

"I'm not finished with the terms yet. You're going to go to the judge with me, on the record or off, and tell him to reopen the trial."

"You think I can tell De Luca what to do?"

"I think you can try. Now tell me something I don't know."

He pauses, as if trying to decide what to say. There's no doubt that he knew even before he got here what he could and could not say; he's probably under very specific orders about it. But his open pondering is to give the illusion that he is in charge.

"There has been a lot of chatter these last few months."

I interrupt. "Chatter?"

"That's spy talk meaning we hear stuff. A foreign entity has been very interested in the result of the Delaware trial."

"Which foreign entity?"

"You don't need to know that," he says. "Let's just say that it isn't Switzerland or Luxembourg. It's a country that we very much do not want to have WMDs."

"And is that what this is about? This chatter?"

"It's very possible," he says. "Which makes this a little bigger than Noah Galloway."

I shake my head. "That's not how the system works. I'm his lawyer; for me there's nothing bigger than Noah Galloway. How long have you known that this foreign stuff is tied to this case?"

"Not very long; in fact, we're still not positive that it does. But you're making a good case; we're more willing to see all possibilities than a jury is."

"Tell it to the judge."

He nods. "Now tell me what I don't know."

"There's a cottage blackmail industry

469

that's been thriving; Loney was one of the people behind it. They find things out about people, or they do them very illegal favors. Either way they've got them from that point on, and they extract favors from them. Judge Holland was one of those people; Alex Bauer was another."

"And they told Holland how to rule in that case?"

"I'm sure they did. Alex Bauer told me so." I feel as if I can break the confidentiality of what Bauer told me; being dead means he doesn't require protection.

"Give me a name besides Loney," Mulcahy says.

"Brett Fowler. He's a political consultant in D.C. He either killed Bauer or had it done."

Mulcahy doesn't take any notes; he either knows Fowler or has confidence in his own memory. "What else?"

I don't want to tell him about Judge Holland's son. I don't see how I could be risking national security in the process. It doesn't matter what they were blackmailing Holland with; the important point is that they were doing it.

"Steven Lockman was an assayer employed by Milgram. He disappeared around the time of the fire, and was never heard

470

from again."

"You think he was in the fire?"

"I do. I'm speculating here, but I think he found something important, maybe on Milgram land, and the wrong people found out about it before his management did. They killed him, and used Bauer to get the company. But it took a long time."

"The people we're dealing with are patient," he says. "We think in weeks; they think in decades."

"Lockman's last trip before he died was to Texas; he flew into Dallas. He went there twice, and Milgram has land in east Texas waiting to be drilled on."

"It can't be about oil," he says.

"What about something dangerous, like uranium?"

He shakes his head. "No. Uranium can be had; it's enriching it that's the tough part."

He doesn't wait for me to respond. "Thanks for this," he says. "Set up the meeting with De Luca."

I get a little anxious while waiting for a verdict.

At least that's how I would describe it. Laurie sees it a little differently; she says I get "totally psychotic" and "unbearable to be with."

I am not generally a superstitious person, but during a verdict-wait superstitions run my life. Everything I've ever done during this period on a case I've ultimately won becomes something I have to do each subsequent time. It's exhausting.

I'm always pessimistic while waiting for a jury; but this time I'm even more sure we're going to lose; I believe that if I were on the panel I'd vote to convict.

It's the ultimate defense attorney's nightmare. A client whom he likes and knows to be innocent gets convicted and spends year after year in jail. There is no question that a life sentence for Noah would mean one of my own as well.

Usually I have nothing to do other than wait, but this time is different. If we're going to lose this trial, then we need to develop evidence that can exonerate Noah, or at least earn him a new trial. Focusing on the investigation at least takes my mind off the verdict. A little bit, anyway.

I spend some time on a computer trying to figure out what could possibly be on that land that could be of consequence to a foreign power looking to develop WMDs.

One of the things I examine is the possibility that certain plants or bacteria could be growing there, perhaps a rare growth that could be used to make biological or chemical weapons. So I spend hours reading scientific stuff online, only to discover I have no idea what I'm reading, or what I'm talking about.

"Let's look at where we are," I say to Laurie. "We know from Mulcahy that there is the potential for a country to be helped in its WMD program from Entech buying Milgram. It can't be intellectual property; there's no secret formula in the Milgram safe, with Entech now having the combination."

Laurie nods. "So it has to be something substantive, something tangible."

"Right. Plus, I'm positive that Lockman's disappearance ties into this. And Lockman's profession was to analyze what materials are in the ground. I don't know what that material is that is so important, but it doesn't matter for our purposes. We just know it's there, and that Entech now owns it."

"This is the endgame for the bad guys," Laurie says. "All the other blackmails were small potatoes. Killing off Bauer, and especially Loney, means that they want to eliminate everyone who knows anything. The payoff from this is big enough that they are willing to dismantle the operation."

"What about the people physically taking the stuff out of the ground?" I ask, knowing the answer as I ask the question.

"I wouldn't want to be holding their life insurance policies."

"Ricci behind this?" I ask.

She shakes her head. "I could be wrong, but I don't think so. I think he provided the muscle, and maybe some financing, but that's it."

"Why didn't he get revenge for Loney?" I ask.

"Maybe he did. Or maybe Petrone got him to back off. That's still to be learned."

"So where are we?"

She thinks for a minute. "I'm not sure,
but I know where we should be. East Texas."

Laurie, Marcus, Hike, and Sam are on a flight to Dallas, when I get the call.

FBI lawyers have petitioned De Luca to grant status to address the court *in camera* this afternoon. That literally means "in a chamber," but in the non-Latin world means "in private." De Luca has granted the request, which was a formality. The meeting is called for two P.M.

We had no real strategy for sending the "east Texas delegation," even Laurie admitted that. We just felt that was where the real action was, so that's where they should be. I would have gone along, but I needed to be here to deal with the court.

They're going to drive around the land owned by Milgram, which is now owned by Entech. It's an enormous area to cover, and the chances of them actually hitting on something are minute. They'll ask people about unusual activity, but chances are what is going on does not seem unusual to anyone.

The plan is to split into pairs to cover more area, and I can just imagine the maneuvering going on to avoid being paired with Hike. I hope Marcus doesn't draw the straw, because Sam or Laurie would just throw Hike out of the car when he got annoying. Marcus would kill him.

Dylan, Mulcahy, and I assemble in De Luca's chambers at the appointed hour. De Luca has invited lead counsel only, which is just as well, since my "staff" is driving around Texas looking for bad guys. Mulcahy brings a bureau attorney with him.

"To what do I owe this interference in the workings of this court?" is how De Luca opens the session. I would have to say that as opening lines go, that one is not a particularly good sign.

"We have information which leads us to strongly believe that a conviction of Noah Galloway would represent a miscarriage of justice."

"Very well," De Luca says. "Let's hear it."

Mulcahy turns it over to the FBI attorney, who proceeds to give a dry recitation of facts, head down and reading every word. Worse yet, it's basically just a rehash of the case we've already presented. Since De

Luca turned down our request to reopen the trial, there is nothing here to make him reconsider, other than possibly the fact that the FBI is doing the talking, instead of me.

De Luca seems as unimpressed as I am. "That's it?" he asks.

"Not quite," Mulcahy says. "There are two more things. The fire that killed Bauer in his car was started with an almost identical mixture of chemicals as that of the house fire." This surprises me, and I assume it was left out of the media reports for investigative purposes.

"Second, and far more important, is the fact that there are serious national security implications to this case."

That gets De Luca's attention. "Are you officially telling me that the national security of the United States is threatened by the jury reaching a verdict in this trial?"

"No, that's not what I'm saying. But I am saying there are serious connections between this case and matters of national security."

De Luca considers this for a few moments, and then says, "Okay, gentlemen. Here's where I come out on this. Basically the information before me has not changed. What I am being told is that the FBI thinks Mr. Galloway is innocent."

Mulcahy nods. "We do, Your Honor."

"However, the reason this trial ever started, the reason Mr. Galloway was arrested in the first place, was because the FBI conducted an investigation and came to the conclusion he was guilty."

"The facts have changed," I point out.

De Luca nods. "Maybe, or maybe just the interpretation of those facts have changed. In any event, even though the FBI originally thought Mr. Galloway was guilty, our system decided in its infinite wisdom not to just accept that and convict him. It decided a jury was better equipped to make that decision."

This is heading south.

De Luca continues. "I'm going to side with the system, gentlemen, and let the jury make the call, without interruption."

The FBI lawyer starts packing up his briefcase. He couldn't have cared less which way De Luca was going to rule; it was simply his job to present the case and get out. Mulcahy looks at me with some sympathy; I think he wanted the right thing to happen here, and he knows it didn't.

Dylan hasn't said a word since "good afternoon," but I think he's never been more eloquent.

I leave the court, having accomplished

absolutely nothing. The only way the visit could have been worse was if I was there to hear the verdict.

When I leave I call Laurie, who sounds like she's had a worse day than I have.

"We've accomplished absolutely nothing," she says.

"Join the club," I say, and then update her on the meeting with De Luca.

After that's over, she says, "There's a lot of land out here, Andy, especially since we have no real idea where to look, or what we're looking for."

"And you're asking people that you see?"

"When we can find any. But of course they have no idea what we're talking about, because we have no idea what we're talking about. And that's not the worst part."

She hesitates for a moment, then. "Hike." Another pause. "He's driving me crazy."

I'm glad she can't see me smiling. Whenever I complain about Hike, she defends him and tells me I'm too hard on him. Now that she's spent time with him alone, it appears that the depressing tide has turned.

"Really? Hike?" I ask.

"Yes. I'm with Hike, and Marcus is with Sam. Everywhere we go the land is dry and desolate, and Hike says it reminds him of

480

the Dust Bowl during the Great Depression."

"Interesting historical reference," I say.

"Andy, Hike thinks of the Great Depression as the good old days. He says we're heading for much worse, that the way things are going, the United States is soon going to consist of two things, Wall Street and dust."

I try to stifle a laugh, but can't quite do so.

"Andy . . ."

"I'm sorry. Where is he now?"

"In a diner, possibly using the bathroom."

"Why possibly?"

"It's our fourth try. The last three weren't sanitary enough. He said something about dysentery, and lizards, or something. I'm losing track."

"What are you and Hike doing tomorrow?" I ask.

"We're going to drive around for a while, and then I'm going to strangle him and bury his body."

I've got nothing to do and nowhere to go.

I'd like to be in Texas with Laurie and the team, but I need to be here in case the jury has a question or, God forbid, a verdict. What I really should have done was keep Hike here, and gone down there in his place. I think Laurie would have been in favor of that.

So I'm tied to the phone, hoping Laurie will call with good news, and hoping the court will not call with bad news. Instead nobody calls, with the exception of Willie Miller, asking me if I'd read his book when it's finished, which is apparently going to be any day.

"You think I need to read it?" he asks.

"No, you already know the ending."

"Cool."

I head down to the jail to see Noah and brief him on what's going on. I've been a little lax in doing so, and he wasn't even aware that the meeting was taking place between the FBI and Judge De Luca.

Before I even relate the story, I tell him that the outcome was not positive. I don't want him to get his hopes up, even for a few minutes. He's the one with his freedom on the line, not me, and he needs to know the straight scoop.

"Becky thinks the jury is going to say I'm not guilty," he says. "At least that's what she tells me."

"Needless to say, I hope she's right."

"But you don't think she is."

I shake my head. "No, I don't. But I do think it's a good sign that they haven't come back yet. Maybe we've got some holdouts on our side."

"Maybe."

"Noah, if you get convicted, it's not over. I really mean that; we've got a lot going for us. This thing hasn't played out yet."

I don't think he believes me, and I can't say I blame him. I tell him that I'll let him know if anything happens, and I leave to go home.

I'll take Tara and Bailey for a walk, and then I'll look through the case files again, just in case I've missed something the other four hundred times I've read them.

But basically I'll do nothing.

Deep under the ground, the eight men were finished with their work.

The canisters had been taken up the elaborate system of pulleys, and loaded onto a waiting truck. It was the culmination of years of work, done in secret.

The men had been chosen well. They were extraordinary workers, loners without family or close friends. They could be trusted to keep the confidentiality of the mission, and would basically do anything for money. Investigators had been tracking them, without their knowledge, and all were judged to have kept silent.

They were, of course, very well paid, but what really motivated them was the promise of a huge bonus when the work was completed.

They had just gotten an apparently sincere thank-you speech from a man they had never met before, but who seemed as if he was in charge of the entire operation. More importantly, they had just received their bonus checks, and were delighted to see that each was twenty-five percent higher than promised.

The man also thanked them for their having kept the secret for so long, and impressed upon them the importance of continuing to do so. He also made a surprise promise that if, in five years, the operation was still a secret, each man in the group would receive another check.

Were any of them to move, the man gave them a number to contact, to inform him of their new address and contact information. That was to enable him to forward that supplementary bonus, but also to make it possible for them to be reached should another job like this one come up.

And with the kind of money that they'd earned, another job like this one would be very welcome.

The man went around and shook each of their hands, offering personal thanks. He then went up the pulley to the truck, asking them to wait at least a half hour to leave, and then to leave one at a time, so as not to call attention to themselves, should anyone be around.

Then the man went up to the truck, where

the driver was waiting for him. He signaled for the driver to come down out of the truck and help him load something, and when the driver did as instructed, the man shot him through the head.

The man dragged the driver's body a few feet to the open mine, and pushed it over the edge. He listened, until he could hear the body strike bottom, though the drop was so long that the sound was barely audible.

The man then climbed into the truck, drove half a mile, and then took out his cell phone, and dialed a number. It was a number that was prearranged six months ago, and it set off the explosives that had been planted at the same time.

The explosion was enormous, and the man could see and hear it from his distant vantage point. He knew that it had forced the mine to cave in on itself. Of the nine dead bodies that were in there, the driver was the only one not to have been buried alive.

And then the man drove away.

There is one report in the file that I haven't read multiple times.

It's not even a report, but rather the travel documents and records that Gail Lockman had provided to us. I had read it, and noted that it confirmed Laurie's report of where Gail's husband Steven had traveled in the period before the fire, just before he went missing.

I will never understand how people, me in particular, can see something one time and not another, when looking at the same thing each time. But it happens to me all the time, and I assume I'm not the only one.

Laurie and I had asked for the information for the purpose of learning where Steven Lockman had gone on his business trips before the fire. That made sense, and it led us to believe that Texas was the place to focus on. That may or may not prove to be a good decision.

But what we didn't notice were Steven Lockman's return flights. On the two non-Texas trips he flew back to Newark Airport, which was logical, since he lived not far from there. On the two Texas trips, however, he didn't fly to Newark.

He flew to Philadelphia.

I call Gail Lockman, and catch a break when she is there and answers the phone. I tell her I have just one more question about Steven, and I can hear the apprehension in her voice. It's a wound that I keep opening.

"In the weeks before Steven's death, he flew back to Philadelphia rather than New Jersey. Do you have any idea why?"

"That can't be right," she says.

"Why do you say that?"

"Because he would have told me. And we had a thing, call it a superstition, that I always picked him up at the airport. The company would have paid for a cab, but I picked him up every time."

"And never in Philadelphia?" I ask.

"Never."

"Did he know anyone there?"

"Not that I know of."

There seems to be a real possibility that Steven landed in Philadelphia, did whatever business he had there, and then drove to Newark and pretended to his wife that he had flown there. The chance of an affair comes to mind, but it was only twice, and apparently for very short stays.

I think I know the real reason.

"Did Steven have any business dealings with people or companies in Philadelphia?"

She's becoming annoyed with my questions. "Mr. Carpenter, Steven was an assayer. His job was to tell his company what was under the ground that they owned. There are sewers under Philadelphia."

I thank her and apologize for bothering her. I start to dial Mulcahy's number when I see that Laurie is calling me on the other line. I stop dialing and take her call.

"Andy, the world down here just exploded."

"What are you talking about?"

"There was a huge explosion, maybe five miles from here. We could see the cloud go up, and our car shook."

"What was it?"

"I can't be sure, but it happened out here in the middle of nowhere, and it was on Milgram land. I don't believe in coincidences; it might have been the place we're looking for."

"Okay, let me think for a minute," I say, but then only use up ten seconds of my requested time. "We have to assume that

489

they took whatever they needed to out of the ground, and the explosion was to destroy the mine and cover their tracks."

"So it's got to be on a truck," she says. "There are no train tracks out here, and I haven't seen any planes take off."

"Right, and it's got to be going south."

"Why?"

"Because there's a foreign connection here; that's what Mulcahy said. Assuming it's too large to get on a plane, then it's going to leave by boat, and the nearest water is south. You should at least start heading in that direction."

"Marcus and Sam are three hours south of us right now. They were driving around the Milgram land down there."

"Then call them and tell them to head south, and wait for further instructions, in case we figure something out."

Laurie promises to do so, and I call Mulcahy. He's not there, so I tell them to have him call me, that's it's a matter of life and death.

There's nothing I can do except wait for him to call, so I turn on the television and see that the first reports about the explosion are coming in. They are saying that a mine blew up, possibly from leaking natural gas, but that no people were believed to have been in the mine.

I have my doubts about the lack of casualties; starting with Loney, people with knowledge of the operation are being wiped out. But I have more than doubts about the "leaking natural gas." That is pure bullshit.

It takes forty of the longest minutes I've ever experienced until Mulcahy calls me, and I don't waste any time. "The mine explosion is what we were watching for. They've taken out what they need, and are covering up the evidence. Unless I'm wrong, they've covered up a bunch of people in the process."

"Shit," he says. "Do you have any idea where they're going with it?"

"No, but they've got to get it out of the country, and . . ." It hits me as I'm talking, and I'm immediately angry with myself for not seeing it earlier. "Hold on a minute. I've got an idea."

I put the phone down and grab the case files. I search for Sam's report on Loney's phone records, scanning down the list of files until I find what I'm looking for.

I grab the phone again and say, "Galveston. He's heading for Galveston."

"How do you know that?"

"One of the people on Loney's phone records is a guy named Jason Young. He's a

491

customs official in Galveston. It all fits; they must be blackmailing Young to get him to do something for them. And that something is to pave the way for this shipment to get on a boat and out of the country."

"I'm on it."

"You want to know who you're looking for?" I ask.

"Who's that?"

"Unless I'm wrong, it's Alex Bauer."

"He's dead," Mulcahy points out.

"He might not be as dead as we think."

I check the files again, and then call Sam to update him.

"We're only about a half hour from Galveston," he says. "But we're going to die before we get there. Marcus is driving about four hundred miles an hour."

"I'm pretty sure you're ahead of Bauer," I say. "And you both might be ahead of the FBI. Head for the port; I was there a bunch of years ago; I think there's one main road in."

"What are we looking for?"

"A large truck with Bauer in it."

"And if we see it?"

"Stop it."

"How the hell are we going to do that?" he asks.

"Marcus will figure it out."

I call Laurie and brief her on what's going on. She's heading in that direction as well, but is pretty far behind. Whatever is going to happen will take place well before she gets there.

"It'll be okay. They'll have agents all over that place."

"I know, but Bauer has been outsmarting everybody all along. Once he gets the material off the truck, there's no telling where it could go."

"Andy, what makes you think Bauer's alive?"

"Steven Lockman made two secret trips to Philadelphia on the way back from Texas. According to his wife, he had been worried about money, with a baby on the way, and felt he was underpaid. My guess is he felt that if he reported to Milgram what he found, all he would have gotten would have been a pat on the back."

"But if he sold the information to a competitor like Bauer, he would get a lot more," she says.

"He thought it would make him rich, but it made him dead."

"But how does that mean Bauer is alive?" she asks. "Maybe his partners in this killed him."

"Maybe, but I don't think so. Bauer has been lying to us all along, and in the process trying to find out what we know. Faking his death would make sense; after whatever this is goes down, no one would be looking for him."

It's incredibly frustrating sitting in New Jersey and wondering what is happening all those miles from here. For me the only thing worse than being far away when friends are in danger would be to be in danger myself.

As soon as I put the phone down it rings. I pick it up, assuming that it's Mulcahy, or Sam, or someone that's a part of the exploding events in Texas.

It isn't. It's Rita Gordon, the court clerk. "Andy, you need to be in court at ten A.M. tomorrow morning."

"Why?" I ask, though I know the answer.

"There's a verdict."

Mulcahy's first call was to the Houston bureau, the office closest to Galveston.

It was quickly put through to the bureau director, Ryan Van Pelt, who fortunately was in his office. The call was taken by Gary Summers, who served as Van Pelt's executive assistant.

Mulcahy explained the urgent nature of the call to Summers, who quickly grasped the situation and put the call straight through to his boss.

It look less than sixty additional seconds for Mulcahy to make the situation clear to Van Pelt, who promised to get every agent under his command into the field, and in this case the field meant the Galveston port.

There are emergency procedures in place at every bureau office, and the moment Van Pelt got off the phone he set them into action. Everything worked smoothly and according to plan, and within ten minutes every agent within range was on the way to Galveston.

Van Pelt then notified his contact at the Department of Defense that assistance might be needed, and that he would keep them apprised of developments. After that, he left the office to go down and personally supervise the operation in Galveston.

He issued instructions with Summers to patch all calls regarding this crisis to him in the field, which Summers promised to do.

Once Van Pelt was out the door, Summers took out his cell phone and dialed a number. When the connection was made, he simply said, "They know."

"I understand," said Alex Bauer.

The road narrowed into two lanes in each direction, causing traffic to slow down.

Marcus continued driving for another half mile, during which he got a look at what was up ahead. There were a series of exits, and different ways Bauer could go, all of which led to various areas of the port. They would have to be incredibly lucky to find him.

Instead, he made a U-turn and drove back to the place where the road narrowed.

"Where the hell are you going?" asked Sam.

Marcus didn't answer, which did not come as much of a surprise to Sam, since he had said maybe ten words in two days. When he reached the area where the road narrowed, he made another U-turn and pulled over, waiting along the side of the road in the direction heading to the port.

"You know Bauer?" Marcus asked.

"I don't know him; I mean, I've never met the guy. But I've seen his picture; I'd recognize him."

Marcus nodded and pulled back on to the road, in the right-hand lane. He then slowed to a stop and shut the car off. Before Sam could waste his time by asking what was happening, Marcus got out of the car, went to the front, and lifted the hood. He then propped the hood so that it would stay open, and got back in the car. To anyone coming along, it would look like the car broke down with mechanical trouble.

Marcus touched the rearview mirror, and said, "Watch."

This time Sam caught on. Their "stalled" car in the right-hand lane would cause the traffic to significantly slow down. Sam could adjust his mirror to see the drivers of oncoming trucks, rather than turning around and possibly tipping Bauer off.

They waited for almost fifteen minutes, and a few times Sam thought he saw Bauer, only to change his mind. "I can't be positive which one is him, you know? I'm afraid we could be letting him go by."

"Watch," Marcus said.

Finally Sam saw a man that he was positive was Bauer driving a large truck. "That's him," Sam said. "I'm sure of it."

Marcus nodded, waited for the truck to clear them and drive forward, then got out and closed the hood. He then proceeded to drive quickly, making up the ground between themselves and Bauer's truck.

They followed from a safe distance, watching as Bauer turned left, a surprise since it seemed away from the port area. And then, up ahead, they saw why.

"Andy, he's going to an airfield!" Sam yelled. "He's not going to the port!"

"Where are you?" I ask. I'm already sick from the realization that I've sent the FBI to the wrong place.

"We're about ten miles north of Galveston. There's what looks like a private airfield up ahead, and we're following Bauer toward it. I'm sure that's where he's going."

"Do you know the name of the airfield?"

"No, we haven't seen one yet."

"Can you tell me more about the location?"

"We got off the road at Deerfield. We just passed a Denny's . . . I'm sorry, I just don't know where we are." The panic in his voice is evident.

My guess is that somehow Bauer found out the FBI was waiting for him. Otherwise he would not have driven all the way to Galveston; he would have had a plane waiting much closer to the mine. His initial plan was to leave by boat, but the FBI's actions caused him to switch.

"Okay, here's what we need to do," I say. "I'm going to call the FBI and tell them what you've told me. You keep watching Bauer. Be careful, Sam, but I have to tell you, whatever Bauer is hauling cannot be allowed to get on a plane."

"Got it."

"Sam, let Marcus take the lead on this."

I get off and call Mulcahy. "He's not going to the Galveston port," I say.

"Don't shit me, Carpenter. I've got twenty agents there now, with two choppers on the way."

"The choppers you can use," I say, and tell him what Sam told me.

He's not satisfied. "An airfield near a Denny's? I've been looking at maps; you know how many airfields there are in south Texas? You've got interns working for those big oil companies that make enough to fly their own planes. There are almost as many airfields as there are Denny's."

"So get fighter jets up in the air; shoot the planes down once you identify them."

"Carpenter, with what he'll have on board, we can't afford to shoot it down."

The automatic private gate to the airfield opened as the truck pulled up.

Sam and Marcus could see that it was prearranged; they were waiting for Bauer to arrive. The gate then closed behind the truck, leaving them outside.

Up ahead on the tarmac were two medium-sized jets. Sam knew absolutely nothing about aircraft, but to him they looked like they could carry maybe seventy-five passengers each. If they were hollowed out, they could handle a lot of cargo.

The backs of the planes seemed to be open, an indication that they were specially designed to haul large items. Next to the jets were large machines that looked like cranes. There was no doubt in Sam's mind that they were there to transfer the cargo on to the plane.

Bauer pulled up next to the planes, and two men ran up to help him. There was no way to tell whether they were also the pilots, but no one else seemed to be around. Bauer opened the back of the truck and climbed on, while the other two men quickly started moving the machines into position.

"Marcus, we can't let them transfer that stuff on to the plane. I'm going to see if I can open the gate."

Sam got out of the car and started running toward the gate, but as he did he sensed motion behind him. He turned to see that Marcus was driving the car toward the gate at high speed.

Marcus hit the gate at seventy miles an hour, and it was no contest. The gate was obliterated, and Marcus continued driving out to the airplanes. The two men looked up, shocked at the noise of the gate getting smashed, and the car barreling down on them.

Marcus pulled the car to a screeching halt, crashing into the machines in the process. He was out of the car and on the men in an instant. If there were twelve of them it would not have been a fair fight; two of them was a total mismatch.

It took Marcus a total of two punches to end it, leaving the men unconscious on the asphalt. He then climbed up into the relative darkness of the truck to go after Bauer.

But in the process of disposing of the two men, Marcus did not realize that Bauer had exited the truck from the front, and had come up behind him.

He heard the click of the gun being cocked, and whirled. It was too late to do anything before the shot was fired, but just in time to watch Bauer blown sideways by the blast, into the wheel of the plane.

And there was Sam, about twenty feet away, unable to take his eyes off of Bauer. "I shot him," he said, as if he couldn't believe it himself. "I really shot him."

"Yuh," said Marcus.

I learn what happened from a variety of sources.

First is Sam, but all I can really get him to say is, "I shot him, Andy. He's dead. I shot him, and he's dead." After a few rounds of that I'm so desperate for information that I ask him to put Marcus on the phone. That doesn't work out so well.

Then Laurie calls. She had arrived on the scene well after it happened, but had gotten the lay of the land rather well. She describes what happened, and how the FBI and Homeland Security agents are now all over the airfield. There are also decontamination experts on hand, but no one seems terribly worried about that, as the canisters seem secure.

By the time she calls, Sam and Marcus are being questioned and debriefed by agents. Good luck with that.

I also get some information from the cable

506

news networks, though they don't really add much to the picture. They know that there was a shootout at the airfield, and that Homeland Security was called in.

No mention is made of any dangerous cargo, and more ominously, no mention is made of any possible connection to the Galloway case.

I have spent the three hours since I found out that Sam and Marcus were okay and Bauer was dead thinking about how I can make this impact Noah's situation. My only possible way to do that is through Mulcahy, to have him again go to De Luca, this time armed with the weight of the night's events.

I try him a bunch of times, but he doesn't answer the call, probably because he knows it's me. He finally calls me back at one-thirty in the morning, though he doesn't wake me. He could call at any hour tonight and not wake me.

"I've been trying to reach you," I say. "I want to know what happened."

"You already know what happened," he says.

"What was the cargo?"

"That's pretty much the only thing I'll tell you, because you were right. But I need your word you won't repeat it."

"You've got it," I say. "Uranium?"

"Uranium. But not the normal kind. Not the kind seen anywhere before."

"What kind is it?"

"More than ninety-nine percent of uranium taken out of the ground is called uranium 238. It has within it a tiny amount, less than half of one percent, of uranium 235, and that's the part that's needed to make a nuclear weapon, at least a basic kind. If you have enough 235, the enrichment process is easy."

"And this uranium contained a high level of 235?"

"The current estimate is twenty-two percent. It's never been seen before, and I hope it's never seen again. Whoever got their hands on this would in effect be getting their hands on the bomb."

"Who was trying to get it?"

"That's on a need-to-know, and you are not close to having that need. But I do want to thank you. You were right about an awful lot, and you saved a lot of lives today."

"Great," I say, "now all you need to save is one. Noah Galloway's."

"What do you want?"

"I want you to talk to De Luca."

"I've seen that movie," he says.

"Then see it again. Or have someone above you see it. But get De Luca to order

508

a directed verdict of acquittal before the jury convicts him tomorrow morning."

"Everything about this incident is classified, Andy. There is nothing I can do."

"I'll talk to the media."

"And people might or might not believe you. Or they might think you're a lawyer trying to protect a client with information that already didn't work at trial."

"He's going to go to jail for the rest of his life."

"You're worried about him, and I'm worried about everyone else. I can't help you."

I can see the strain on Noah's face as he is led into the courtroom.

It's the look on every defendant's face as they prepare to hear the verdict that will decide their fate. The problem for me in this case is that I put that strain there.

If not for me, there would have been no trial. Noah would have taken his punishment well, even willingly, and would never have hoped or expected freedom. I raised his hopes, and now the jury is going to wipe them away.

Becky sits directly behind him, wearing a similar expression. When I nod to her she mouths, "Thank you." I don't know if Noah's likely conviction will make her feel the guilt that I feel, because without her I never would have had the chance to take Noah down this path.

Noah sits down next to me. He smiles and says, softly, "The day of reckoning."

Across the way, Dylan and his team are assembled. They do not seem under any particular stress; either way they are going home tonight. If I had to guess, it's more important for Dylan to beat me than to convict Noah. Unfortunately, doing one means doing the other.

Mulcahy is also in the gallery. I would rather he were with the judge, but I saw him come in through the rear door and take his seat. He nods to me, but I don't nod back. That'll teach him.

De Luca is fifteen minutes late, which is not terribly unusual. For some reason I find that judges are often late on verdict day. I consider it a form of cruel and unusual punishment, at least for the defendant and his lawyer.

De Luca finally comes in, and gives a brief speech about how important it is for the courtroom to remain calm and quiet after the verdict. It's a packed house, and De Luca, realizing that, emphasizes the importance of postverdict silence even more than usual.

I see Laurie and Hike enter the courtroom through the back door, having come straight here from the airport. Coming down to the defense table would be disruptive, so they stand in the back and watch.

De Luca calls in the jury, and they come in looking properly solemn. I have no ability to read faces, so I don't try. If they convict Noah, I'll want to track them down and rip off those faces, so rather than read them, I should try to remember them.

De Luca asks the foreman if they have reached a verdict, and the woman says that they have. "Please give the form to the clerk," he instructs, and she does so. He then asks Noah to stand, and I join him in doing so.

I put my hand on Noah's shoulder, as a gesture of support but really because in the past I've put my hands on other defendants' shoulders, and they've been acquitted. My verdict superstitions continue until the verdict is read.

The bailiff then brings the form to De Luca. He opens it and takes what seems like a month to read it. He then hands it to the clerk, and asks him to read it aloud.

"In the matter of *New Jersey v. Noah Galloway,* as relating to count one, we the jury find the defendant, Noah Galloway, guilty of murder in the first degree."

I keep my hand on Noah's shoulder as the clerk reads the guilty verdicts for the other three counts as well. The hand-on-the-shoulder thing obviously does not work.

Becky moves forward and hugs Noah, and the bailiffs respectfully allow her a few seconds to do so. I lean in to both of them and say, "This will not stand," but I doubt they believe me.

The gallery is fairly loud, and De Luca slams his gavel repeatedly to achieve quiet. It takes a minute or so, but he finally gets it.

"First of all, I would like to thank the members of the jury for your service. You have worked hard, heard the evidence, and made your decision. Based on the facts presented to you, it is the correct decision.

"But I have just been given additional facts, some classified, that you did not have and therefore were not able to consider in your deliberations. It is for that reason that I am exercising my right to set aside your verdict and order a directed verdict of acquittal."

The gallery is quiet for a few moments, as if trying to digest what they have heard. I'm having a bit of a digestion problem myself. Then they explode in noise, and I barely hear De Luca tell Noah that he is no longer subject to the jurisdiction of this court.

"I'm free?" Noah asks me, understandably bewildered.

"You're not just free. You're innocent."

"I'll talk to lead counsel in chambers," De Luca says.

As I stand to obey the order, I spot Mulcahy out of the corner of my eye. He's smiling.

"I spent the past twenty minutes on the phone with the White House chief of staff and the attorney general. They told me in no uncertain terms that Noah Galloway was innocent of this crime, and that the events in Texas last night confirmed it beyond any doubt."

Dylan has looked stunned since the verdict was announced, but the shock seems to be slowly giving way to anger. "What specific information did they give you?"

"Not much, and what they did provide was classified. They relied on my security clearance from my days in Army Intelligence."

"So you took their word for it?" Dylan asks. "And disregarded the will of the jury?"

De Luca's eyes flash some anger, but he controls himself. Dylan has put a lot of hard work into this case, and won, and then lost. I think De Luca is giving him some leeway because of it.

"That's exactly what happened."

"Thank you, Your Honor," I say, smiling sweetly for Dylan. "What you did was courageous."

When I leave, the gallery is empty, except for Laurie, Hike, Noah, Becky, and Mulcahy, who is sitting alone near the back. I walk over to him first.

"You've got some pull," I say.

"When I want to, and when it's necessary."

"I thought you didn't consider it necessary."

"I changed my mind," he says.

"I'm glad you did."

He looks over at Noah and Becky. "Me too." Then he turns and walks out of the courtroom.

Whenever a jury rules in our favor, we have a victory party at Charlie's.

Tonight's is a particularly festive one, and we all get drunk toasting Becky and Noah.

Willie Miller is here. He's drinking club sodas, because he is a recovering alcoholic. He's leaving next month on a book tour, and the book has already gotten a rave advance review.

Pete and Vince are here as well. Pete is particularly grateful to me for getting this one right; as much as he wanted the case solved, he wanted justice to prevail. So this was pretty much a perfect resolution for him.

Things happened so fast at the end that Noah was out of the loop, and he has some questions for me. "How did you know that Bauer was alive?" he asks.

"I wasn't positive, but it seemed like a safe bet. Lockman flew to Philadelphia after

Texas, and the only reason I could think of for that was to talk to Bauer. He had discovered the uranium, and rather than just tell his bosses at Milgram about it, he saw a way to make a fortune by letting Bauer go after it. Also, when I heard the car was incinerated by napalm, I thought that it was an attempt to hide who the victim really was."

"And that was Fowler?"

"That's my best guess. Bauer was getting rid of everybody who knew what was happening."

"Where did Ricci fit in?"

"Just provided the muscle, and was paid well for it. I think once he saw the publicity and the danger it represented, and he found out that Petrone was pissed off, he stepped aside."

"But why me, Andy? Why did they set me up?"

"You were a backup plan. My guess is they scouted customers for the drug dealers in that house, and made you as a possible person to pin it on. Maybe you were unconscious from drugs, or maybe they injected you, but they were able to burn your arms, and get your DNA on that can. When the police started investigating the baby angle, they trotted you out to stop them."

Laurie comes over to join in the conversation. "I can't figure out why Bauer came to us," she says.

"To make himself look like one of the blackmail victims, so that when he faked his death, no one would be looking for him. With what he was doing, if people thought he was alive, there would be no place in the world that he could hide. He wasn't the type to live in Pakistani caves."

When I get a chance to talk to Becky alone, I take out a check that I had in my pocket and give it to her. She looks at it and sees that it is for forty-one hundred dollars. "What is this for?"

"It's the money that was in the box with Danny Butler's head," I say. "I figured you'd rather have it this way than the cash."

"Andy, you should keep it. We owe you this and a hundred times more."

"Noah gave me Tara," I say. "I'm still ahead of the game."

She kisses me and says, "I'm afraid to ask, but where's the head?"

"Marcus hasn't told me, and I don't want to ask."

Later, as the night is coming to an end, Noah comes over and says, "You know there is no way I can ever thank you. You gave me back my wife, and my son, and my life."

519

"Any chance we could give you back your dog?" I ask.

He laughs. "You don't like Bailey?"

"Actually, we love her. She's a gentle giant, and sweet as hell. We just can't afford to feed her."

"Can we come by tomorrow and get her? I'm also dying to see Tara. She saved my life; I want to thank her."

"Words won't do the trick," I say. "Better bring some biscuits."

The employees of Thorndike Press hope you have enjoyed this Large Print book. All our Thorndike, Wheeler, and Kennebec Large Print titles are designed for easy reading, and all our books are made to last. Other Thorndike Press Large Print books are available at your library, through selected bookstores, or directly from us.

For information about titles, please call:
(800) 223-1244

or visit our Web site at:
http://www.thomsongale.com/thorndike

To share your comments, please write:
Publisher
Thorndike Press
10 Water St., Suite 310
Waterville, ME 04901